KAR

M000014946

The

BEACHSIDE

Sweet Shop

The BEACHSIDE Sweet Shop

bookouture

Published by Bookouture
An imprint of StoryFire Ltd.
23 Sussex Road, Ickenham, UB10 8PN
United Kingdom
www.bookouture.com

ISBN: 978-1-78681-037-3
eBook ISBN: 978-1-78681-036-6

For Tim, Amy, Martin and Liam with all my love

Chapter 1

'I've got a new product I think you'll be interested in.'

'Go on,' I said, swapping a jar of mint humbugs with a jar of strawberry sherbets.

'They're made of liquorice,' said Rob Hancock, my long-time supplier, fanning out a selection on the counter.

I already stocked liquorice allsorts, laces, wheels, and toffees with liquorice in the centre. I didn't even like the stuff. 'What are they?'

Rob shifted some phlegm in his throat. 'Willies,' he announced, as proudly as if he'd invented the word.

Oh god.

Out of the corner of my eye I could see his excited face was redder than ever. As long as I'd known Rob, he'd looked on the verge of a heart attack. Whenever he dropped off a delivery I tried to look away from his straining shirt buttons and sausage fingers, and to not say anything he could interpret as a come-on. He was old enough to be my father. And married with five children.

'Liquorice-shaped willies?' I added, for clarification, still switching jars around so I didn't have to look.

'That's right.' He warmed to his theme, and I heard him rubbing his hands together. 'They'll go down a treat for hen parties, you mark my words. The ladies will go mad for them.'

I closed my eyes and rubbed my brow.

'It's good to appeal to a broader market,' he went on, perhaps misinterpreting my silence.

'And . . .' he did a drum roll sound with his tongue. 'We've got some sticks of rock with rude words in the middle.' He chortled. 'Teenage lads will *love* them.'

I'm sure their parents will too.

I often had conversations with Rob that didn't make it out of my head.

'Not *too* rude,' he added, preparing to be offended at the very suggestion. 'Nothing that would make your grandmother's eyes water.'

Nothing made my grandmother's eyes water, so that wasn't saying much. I resisted asking him which rude words he deemed suitable, but he was clearly keen to enlighten me.

'Just your regular bollocks, motherf—'

'I get the picture,' I cut in, turning to face him at last, hating how at home he'd made himself, leaning on the counter as if he owned it.

'And to keep the kiddies happy, we've developed a new sweet.' Never let it be said that Rob wasn't innovative.

'Surprise me,' I said.

'It's a chew with a fizzy centre that lasts all day.' He paused for dramatic effect. 'I've called it The Fizzer.'

Original.

'I see,' were the politest two words I could muster.

The sun that had slanted through the window when I opened up, making the sea in the distance glitter and dance, had vanished behind thick clouds, and the stretch of pavement outside reflected the grey sky. For the millionth time, I wished I was somewhere else.

New York for instance, with Alex. Why hadn't I gone with him while I'd had the chance? Whatever he was doing now, I doubted it involved liquorice willies.

'I thought they were usually chocolate,' I said, wondering why I was bothering. 'Willies, I mean.'

'But that's our USP.' Rob pounced on my words like a rabid dog. 'Chocolate's what people expect, so why not ring the changes?'

'Because people expect confectionery willies to be chocolate?' I repeated.

'Ah, but they haven't tried my liquorice ones.'

Dear god.

'So, what do you reckon, Mar . . . nie?' He always stumbled over my name, as though it had twenty-four syllables.

He'd asked me what it meant once, dislodging a gingery strand of hair as he scratched his scalp. 'I've often wondered, but didn't like to ask Leonard.'

No, because it might have alerted Gramps to his lecherous tendencies.

'It means rejoice in Hebrew, and in Latin it's a variant of Marina, meaning "of the sea",' I'd explained automatically.

'What, your mum thought you were a mermaid or something?'

'It's from an Alfred Hitchcock film, actually. My mother was a fan,' I'd said, stepping away from his garlic-and-beer breath.

'Which film?'

'Er, *Marnie*.'

His face had flushed magenta as though I'd tricked him.

'I don't want any liquorice willies,' I told him now, before he could launch into another sales pitch. 'I know what my customers like, and so do they.'

'But . . .'

'We mostly appeal to young children and old people,' I said, keen to get rid of him. 'I don't want to upset the locals.'

'I don't think it's fair that you won't even give them a chance.' His voice held a veiled threat. 'I bet Sweetums will snap them up,' he said, referring to a large chain sweet shop in Weymouth. 'They're not scared to take a risk.'

Fury sizzled up. 'You can supply Sweetums with liquorice bosoms, bums, and fingernails for all I care, Rob. I don't want them.'

'Just have a look,' he wheedled.

On an exasperated sigh, I moved behind the counter, narrowing my eyes so I wouldn't be able to see his products clearly, and as I drew closer Rob's arm shot out and snaked around my waist. He yanked me to his side, his hot breath gusting into my ear. 'Come on love,' he muttered. 'Make an old man happy.'

I didn't know whether he was referring to me placing an order, or something else, but my heart misfired as I wrenched myself from his grasp, bumping my hip on the edge of the counter.

'For god's sake, Rob.' I tried to calm my breathing. 'I think you should leave.'

He stared for a moment, eyes bulging. 'It was only a bit of fun,' he said peevishly, swiping his samples back into his box. 'Where's your sense of humour?'

'I'm saving it for something funny,' I said, injecting my voice with steel. 'Now go, and don't come back.'

'What?' As he turned, one of his willies fell on the floor. He picked it up and stuffed it in his pocket. 'Not ever?'

I shook my head. 'You're fired,' I said.

When he'd gone, muttering under his breath, I stood for a moment, blood pumping through my veins. OK, so 'You're fired' wasn't quite the right phrase – I wasn't Sir Alan Sugar – but hopefully he'd got the message.

I fist-pumped the air. *Finally*, I'd got rid of horrid, leery sex-pest, Rob Hancock.

Then panic rose.

As I paced the office out the back, I mouthed sorry to the photo of Gramps above the desk. Everyone used to comment on his resemblance to Uncle Albert from *Only Fools and Horses*, once his hair and beard turned white, but to me he was just Gramps.

Would he have been disappointed I'd mugged off Rob?

The phone rang and I snatched it up.

'Does that mean you *won't* be placing your usual order?'

Certainty flooded through me. 'Never again,' I said, and hung up.

It was the most animated I'd been in weeks.

I'd been running The Beachside Sweet Shop for nearly two years, since my grandfather passed away. I hadn't planned on staying so long, but it meant I could keep an eye on my grandmother, Celia, and carry on saving up for my grand escape.

The one I'd planned with Alex.

We'd managed to get away for a while – we were in Peru when I got the call to say that Gramps was dying – but now Alex was in New York, and I was still in Shipley.

Not that I needed a man to escape with. My mother went to India on her own when she was eighteen, so there was no reason I couldn't travel solo at the age of twenty-nine.

'You look odd,' said Beth, bounding through the door on a blast of damp air. Rain was bouncing energetically off the pavement. 'Are you constipated?'

'Ha ha.' It wasn't the sort of thing a member of staff should say to her boss, but as my best and oldest friend she could get away with it.

'I've just fired Hancock.'

'About time.' Beth shrugged off her coat, revealing her sizeable baby bump. 'You should have done it ages ago.'

'But he's cheap,' I said. 'And Hancock's have been around so long they're practically an institution. At least, that's what Gramps used to say.'

'Rob Hancock should be *in* an institution,' Beth said. 'And your granddad only ever saw the best in people. If he'd known Rob was a perv he'd have sacked him off years ago.' She patted my arm. 'Anyway, I heard on the grapevine his business isn't doing so well.'

It was typical Beth knew more than I did about what was going down in the confectionery world, despite only working at the shop part-time while she studied for a history PhD and waited for her baby to arrive.

'Where will I find another supplier?' Doubts were setting in again. 'I don't think I can be bothered with all this.'

Beth shuffled past to hang up her coat, looking remarkably un-bookish for a history student with her irrepressibly curly blonde hair, button nose, and shining grey eyes. She had a penchant for vintage dresses – when she wasn't pregnant – and looked more like a primary school teacher, or a PA to a fashion designer.

Next to her I was all ungainly angles, constantly knocking things over with my pointy elbows. My eyes were big and brown, but my nose was more toggle than button, and I'd had the same mid-length brown hair since school. I occasionally wore it in a top-knot that invariably fell down at some point, and not in a sexy way, and I was constantly growing out my fringe and cutting it back in again.

'I don't think you'll have any problems in the supplier depart-ment,' she said, pushing back a lock of her own hair. Pregnancy hor-mones had lent her curls a luxurious sheen I was deeply envious of.

'What are you talking about?' I noticed an aura of suppressed excitement about her that had nothing to do with the approaching birth of Bunty, as she insisted on calling her unborn child.

Beth winked. 'All I'm saying is, have you checked your emails?'

'That's all you're saying, is it?'

Beth always had plenty to say, and I doubted she'd be able to resist elaborating, but to my surprise she waddled through the office into the kitchen, and didn't say another word.

This was unprecedented.

Outside, the rain stopped as quickly as it had started, and the clouds parted to reveal a glimmer of sunshine. It felt like an omen.

I turned to the shelf behind the counter – where I'd moved the office computer so I could look on Google Earth when the shop was quiet – and fired it up.

Chapter 2

The screen had frozen. 'Come on, you bugger.' I slapped it in the time-honoured fashion, but it wouldn't budge.

Of the two of us, Alex had been the technology expert and would no doubt have suggested something clever to get it working, other than turning it off and on again – which is what I was doing when Doris Day came in.

Not *the* Doris Day, obviously. I was fairly certain the once-famous actress wouldn't have chosen to move to an old-fashioned seaside town on the Dorset coast, however picturesque Shipley was to the thousands of tourists who flocked there every year.

Doris – for whom the novelty of being named after a Hollywood icon had never worn thin – clutched her chest as though she'd been shot, as she always did when the chimes jangled over the door.

'That thing will give me a heart attack one of these days,' she huffed, smoothing her short, ash-coloured bob. Evidently, her heart was stronger than she gave it credit for as she'd been saying it for years.

She transferred her canvas shopping bag – in use long before it was the norm to reject plastic carrier bags – from the crook of one elbow to the other, her shrewd blue eyes scanning the shelves of jars.

I knew she'd ask for a bag of pineapple cubes, and felt a bit weary at the thought of going through the pretence.

I wondered what would happen if I forced a bag of bonbons upon her, then immediately felt guilty. Gramps used to say that what people were buying when they came into the shop was nostalgia. They liked the sweets they'd enjoyed as children; sweets that reminded them of happy, innocent times.

Most of my customers these days were pensioners, harking after the olden days, unworried about tooth decay now they all had dentures. I sometimes wondered what would happen when that generation had gone, especially with Jamie Oliver urging everyone to give up sugar.

'How's your grandmother, dear?' asked Doris, though she probably knew perfectly well. Not only did she live on the same street as us, she seemed to know everything.

'She's OK,' I said, glancing around for Beth.

I could hear her singing an aria from *Madam Butterfly* as she made some camomile tea. She was convinced singing opera and reading history books to her belly would ensure Bunty's future as a cultured intellectual.

God help the child if it turned out like its father, who was a builder by trade, and never missed an episode of *EastEnders*. Beth adored Harry, and accepted they were polar opposites, but had aspirations for their offspring that extended beyond fish and chip suppers, and darts in the pub on a Sunday lunchtime.

'Just, OK?' persisted Doris.

'Celia's fine,' I said, forcing a smile.

My grandmother was well-known locally as 'the dog-training lady' and her fall a year ago, after being pulled over by an unnaturally strong Jack Russell, had elicited a lot of sympathy. 'She's got a bit of a limp, but otherwise making good progress.'

Celia preferred not to talk about her accident – just as she preferred 'Celia' to 'Grandma' – but I appreciated people's thoughtfulness.

It had been lonely caring for her after Alex left, and though Beth had been a rock, working extra hours at the shop, I'd gratefully accepted all offers of help.

'I thought your mother might have come home to lend a hand,' said Doris, and I froze in the act of clicking random keys on the computer keyboard. 'I suppose she's still gadding around the world with her toyboy,' she added, cocking an eyebrow.

'A quarter of pineapple cubes, is it?' I said, whipping the jar down and shaking the contents onto brass weighing scales my grandfather used to polish reverentially. 'Maybe you'd like half a pound to see you through to the weekend?' None of my elderly customers had gone metric.

'What's his name again?' Doris said, swinging her eyes upwards. 'Pablo, Geronimo, Diablo . . .?'

'Mario,' I butted in, before she could run the gamut of Italian-sounding names. 'And he's thirty-eight, so hardly a toyboy.' I mentally kicked myself for rising to the bait, batting away an image of Mario's bristling moustache. 'And they've lived in Italy for five years, so she's hardly gadding about.' *Shut up.* 'And she did come back to visit, but Celia didn't want her there.'

'I'm surprised she made it back for your granddad's funeral.'

'Of course she did,' I shot back, moved to defend my mother. 'He was her father.'

'She doesn't take after either of them, does she?' Doris persisted, as though we were in the habit of having a gossip about my mum.

'Morning, Doris, how's tricks?' Beth appeared, smiling broadly. 'I bet you know a thing or two about giving birth.'

Doris immediately launched into a sickening tale of a three-day labour, and how her son Eric was so big his head got stuck in the birth canal and he had to be vacuumed out. 'He looked like a little alien for the first two weeks of his life,' she said. 'I was cut from here to here.' She held her hands apart, in what I hoped was a massively exaggerated demonstration. 'I could barely sit down for a month,' she concluded with grim satisfaction. 'Put paid to the idea of having any more children.'

Beth's face had paled, and I quickly bagged up Doris's pineapple cubes and changed a twenty-pound note.

'I've still got some of his baby clothes in the attic,' Doris went on, tucking her sweets away. 'I was saving them for when I had grand-children, but I don't suppose I'll be having any now Eric's come out as a gay.'

Beth nearly choked on her drink, and I didn't dare catch her eye. We'd known for years that Eric Day preferred boys, but Doris had been in denial until he introduced her to his partner.

'I'll let you ladies get on then,' she said, fluttering her fingers as she headed for the door. 'Ooh!' She turned, as if she'd just remembered something. 'Have you heard about—?'

'Bye, Doris,' Beth interrupted.

I shot her a look and caught her signalling something to Doris with her eyebrows.

Doris, seeming to catch on, gave a stuttering laugh.

'Silly me!' she yelped, and clapped a hand to her mouth as she hurried off to do whatever it was she did on blustery Wednesday mornings in mid-May. Head to Main Street probably, to buy a lottery ticket at the newsagent's and pump Mr Flannery for gossip.

'What was all that about?' I asked Beth, replacing the half-empty jar of pineapple cubes, noting the shelf was dusty. The thought of cleaning it made me feel as if someone was pressing on my chest.

'Did you check your emails?' Beth put down her mug and nudged past me to the computer. She barely fitted behind the counter and we had to do a little dance to accommodate her bulk.

'It's not working,' I said glumly. I supposed I would have to find someone to repair it, or replace it.

Beth jabbed a few keys with the concentration of a Bletchley Park code-breaker.

'I've tried everything,' I said, just as the screen sprang to life.

'Looks like I've got the magic touch.' She expertly logged into my email account.

'How do you know my password?'

'It's your date of birth,' she said. 'A hacker's dream.'

'I keep meaning to change it,' I grumbled. 'I just haven't got round to it yet.'

'No.' Beth lifted her gaze and gave me a steady look. We'd known each other since primary school and could usually read each other's thoughts, but for once I couldn't tell what she was thinking.

She returned her attention to the screen.

'Oh,' she said, after scrolling up and down the contents of my in-box. 'I thought it was today.' She strummed her lips with her fingers.

'What was?'

'Oh, nothing,' she said lightly.

I wondered if she was planning something for my birthday in November. I was approaching the big 3-0 and she'd mooted the idea of us going away somewhere – though how she'd manage it with a baby I had no idea.

She opened the till and plucked out some twenty-pound notes. 'I'll pop to the bank and get some change,' she said, 'before it starts raining again.'

'Can you bring me back a sandwich?'

'Cheese and pickle on wholemeal?'

As she left, without her coat, a teenage girl paused outside the shop to check her reflection, flicking her hair extensions and baring her braces, oblivious to my presence.

I sighed, a bell sound alerting me to a new email.

Beth had left my inbox open.

Blowing my fringe from my eyes I read the subject header, written in bold capitals.

CONGRATULATIONS!

'Ooh, I've probably won a trillion pounds, as long as I provide my bank details,' I said crossly.

Preparing to delete the message, I noticed it was from News South-West, the TV station where Alex had worked for a while.

I opened it warily, hoping I wasn't downloading a virus, and read,

Congratulations, Miss Appleton!

I'm delighted to inform you that viewers of News South-West have overwhelmingly voted The Beachside Sweet Shop the winner of our local, independent business competition! Our roving reporter will be along to interview you on Friday morning at 10 a.m. and present you with £10,000 prize money. In the meantime, if you have any queries please call, or email, Sandi Brent.

WHAT? I read the email three times, trying to work out if it was an elaborate scam.

'What does this mean?' I asked Beth when she returned with what looked like half the bakery in a damp bag. It was pouring again, and her hair looked like spaniels' ears.

She plonked down the bag on the counter and hurried to the computer, dripping raindrops on the floorboards.

As she read it, her face broke into a grin.

'There's something I haven't told you,' she said.

Chapter 3

'You entered me into a competition?'

'Yep,' said Beth, squeezing rain out of her hair. 'I thought winning might give you a boost.'

'But . . . how . . . when?' I groped for a fully formed sentence. 'Why didn't I *know*?'

'*Because*,' she was still grinning, 'it was a secret,' she said. 'And a secret is something you keep from someone else.'

'I know what a secret is,' I huffed. 'How did you know I would win?'

She shrugged, eyes sparkling. 'I just knew.' Her smile dimmed. 'Aren't you pleased?'

I thought about it, as her expression slid into worry.

'Of *course* I am, it's amazing!' Something flickered in the pit of my stomach. It *was* amazing, now I thought about it. 'I've never won anything, apart from the three-legged race at school,' I said, breaking into a grin.

Beth's eyes narrowed. She knew I only won because everyone else, including her, fell over after a shoving incident. 'You're going to be on the telly!' she said, letting it go, reaching for my hands.

'I can't believe the public voted for me,' I said. 'It's not as if I've been that busy lately.'

'People like that the sweet shop has a history,' said Beth. 'And social media helped.' Her grin was back. 'I've been tweeting and Facebooking like mad.'

I'd come off Facebook when Alex left, because the temptation to stalk him had been too strong.

'So, who was I up against?'

'Everyone.' Beth's bounced my hands up and down. 'The competition was mentioned on News South-West a couple of times, but I know you don't watch much television since . . .' I knew she was about to say since Alex left, but stopped herself.

It was true. Alex was a sound engineer, and was in New York working on a series of documentaries that a friend recommended him for. If Celia hadn't broken her leg I'd have been with him.

As it was, I rarely turned the television on, as if it was the whole of broadcasting's fault that Alex had gone without me.

'The closing date was last week, and I knew they were announcing the winner today.' Beth's smiling enthusiasm was infectious. 'I just *knew* you'd win.'

My cheeks were aching from smiling. 'The prize money will be useful,' I said. 'I'll be able to replace the computer, for a start.'

Beth made a mournful face. She had no more respect for technology than I did. 'Why not tart the place up? It would be nice to get rid of the brown.'

'True.' As a child I'd loved the cave-like interior of the shop, with the concealed lighting that lit up the rows of jars and the pick and mix sweets, but it all looked rather dingy now, like being inside a mud hut.

'And you know the "e" is still missing from Beachside?' Beth went on.

'Yes, I know.' A gaggle of schoolboys had pointed it out just last week.

'We're in The Bachside Sweet Shop,' the ringleader sniggered. 'Backside, yeah?'

His mate had fallen about laughing.

'Can I have a kilo of arses please?'

Even I'd struggled to contain a childish giggle.

'There's some gold spray-paint in the drawer, left over from that Christmas display,' Beth said. 'You could spray it back in, just for the television interview.'

'Good thinking, Batman.' I should have thought of that myself. 'What would I do without you?'

'God knows,' she said. 'Harry could help out,' she added, letting go of my hands. 'Sort out a new shelving unit, and sand the floor-boards.'

'Sounds great!' I wasn't sure he would. Beth's husband, though lovely, wasn't my biggest fan, for reasons that had never been made clear.

While Beth nipped out the back to retrieve some champagne she'd hidden 'just in case', I hurried to serve an elderly couple buying sweets for their grandchildren, and found myself telling them I was going to be on the telly.

'We voted for you,' the man said.

His wife nodded, her crest of dyed red hair bobbing vigorously. 'I remember when your granddad used to work here with his dad,' she said. 'Their pride and joy it was.'

'Thank you,' I said, but the warm feeling in my stomach curdled as they left.

'What's wrong?' said Beth, glugging champagne into a mug.

'Oh, nothing,' I said. 'It's just that the shop's my grandfather's achievement, not mine. All I did was take over when he died.'

'It's a family affair,' Beth said, generously. 'You've been running it on your own for nearly two years, and you've worked here on and off since your teens. You've earned it.'

She was right, I supposed. And winning competitions didn't happen to me – ever. I picked up my mug and downed my drink in one, then had a sneezing fit. 'Bubbles,' I gasped, eyes streaming.

'You'll need to do something about this.' Beth tugged at my clothes while I dried my eyes with a tissue. 'What is it?'

'It's a poncho. One of Celia's.' I glanced at the dung-brown garment. 'It's nice and warm and it matches my hair and eyes, and the shop.'

'I think that's the problem,' Beth concluded. 'You do blend in a bit.'

'Obviously, I won't wear it on Friday.'

'What about your hair?' She gave my limp tresses a critical once-over, clearly picking up that I hadn't so much let myself go, as dropped into bag-lady territory.

It wasn't that I needed a man to have a reason to make an effort – more that I hadn't the energy to choose a nice outfit every day. Last week, Celia had asked if I was housing a nest of starlings in my hair.

'You always look lovely,' Beth said loyally, 'but maybe make an effort for the TV. You know, to give the shop a boost.'

I could feel the alcohol whooshing to my head. 'I'll have a boob job, get some Botox, and have surgery on my fringe.' I did a twirl and curtsied.

Beth giggled. 'No more of this,' she said, lifting the bottle of champagne. 'You shouldn't be drinking at work.'

Overcome by a swell of affection, I splayed my hands over her belly and rubbed it gently. It felt so taut it scared me – ready to split like a melon.

'Not long to go now,' I said. I'd felt the baby move a few times and, once, Beth had pulled up her dress to show me the outline of a knee, or elbow, jutting under the skin. It had completely freaked me out.

'Leave Bunty alone,' she laughed now, slapping my hands away. 'She's having a sleep.'

We spent the rest of the day in high spirits, and by locking-up time we'd mentally redecorated the shop to look like something from the Wild West – Beth's idea – and I'd sourced a new sweet supplier in Poole and placed an order.

'Things will pick up now, you'll see,' said Beth as she dropped me off at the bottom of Maple Hill, which led to my grandmother's house. 'Ooh, I won't be in tomorrow, remember, I've got that online tutorial about policing prostitution in Tudor England.'

'Brilliant.'

It baffled me why Beth was so fascinated by the past, but history had been her favourite topic at school, and she was hoping to teach it herself one day.

I watched her zingy red Fiat zip towards Wareham, where she and Harry were living with his parents until the barn conversion Harry seemed to have been working on forever was ready to move into.

Hitching my bag over my shoulder I walked past the row of grey-stone cottages on the steeply sloping street.

Doris lived in the bottom house, and was polishing the ornaments on her windowsill as I passed, keeping an eye out for 'goings-on' as if she was Sherlock Holmes.

'Say hello to Celia,' she called through the open window, flapping her duster.

'Will do!'

My grandmother's house was at the top of the hill, with a sweeping view of Shipley from the upstairs windows.

It was the oldest property in the village and had lots of 'character' – which meant weathered stone on the outside, rattling windows on the inside, and plumbing straight from the dark ages. Inside was a lot of dark-wood panelling, offset by colourful rugs and cushions, and the jugs of sweet peas and dahlias scattered about added a delicate scent I associated with 'home'.

I let myself in and went straight to the farmhouse-style kitchen, where Celia's old Labrador, Chester, was snoring in an armchair by the Aga.

I'd spent a lot of time at my grandparents' house growing up while my mother continued the nomadic lifestyle she'd embarked upon before having me, aged nineteen.

It had caused a scandal at the time, because she'd gone to India as a beautiful, dreamy-eyed heartbreaker (from photos I'd seen she looked like Angelina Jolie and, according to Celia, most of the men in Shipley were in love with her) and returned heavily pregnant with me.

My father, it turned out, was a fellow traveller she'd hooked up with and, after a night of wild passion on a deserted beach, she'd never clapped eyes on him again.

'He was called Juan something or other and he was from Spain. Or was it Mexico? Somewhere like that,' she'd explained when I asked who my daddy was, as if it was so inconsequential it was barely worth recalling. 'You don't look anything like him.'

Her wanderlust, or quest for true love and spiritual meaning as she sometimes called it, had never left her and she'd often take off, leaving me with my grandparents, only to reappear and attempt to settle down for a while – usually with a new boyfriend.

In truth, it hadn't mattered as much as it might have. My adoration for my grandparents had been returned in spades, while Mum's older brother, Uncle Cliff, had been like a surrogate dad, and my cousins Phoebe, Ben and Oliver like siblings. And, although unconventional, I'd never doubted that Mum had loved me, and used to look forward to her visits with the excitement most children reserved for Santa Claus.

'Dinner won't be long,' said Celia.

Her normally upright figure was hunched over a cookery book at the scrubbed pine table that had seen us through years of dinners, homework, reading, and occasional baking sessions.

'What are you planning?' I said, knowing better than to tell her she should put her feet up. Celia hadn't been the easiest of patients, and wanted to carry on as normal now her leg was on the mend.

'I thought I'd cook up some steak for Chester,' she said, squinting at the page in front of her through her reading glasses. 'I was looking for ways to make it tastier.'

'Guess what?' I said.

She raised her eyes. They were an alert, bright blue, set in a softly dimpled face, with gentle features that belied a steely nature. 'You're pregnant?'

'For god's sake,' I said. 'How would that even be possible?'

Her eyes inflated. 'The usual way, I imagine.'

'I'm not seeing anyone,' I reminded her. 'I'm still getting over Alex.'

'Oh, him.' She shrugged, though I knew for a fact she'd thought the world of him. 'You don't need a man,' she added, going from one extreme to the other.

'I do, if I'm going to get pregnant.'

'Not these days.' She slammed the cookbook shut. 'You can use a donor, or squirt yourself with a syringe.'

For a seventy-something, generally more interested in dogs than humans, she was remarkably well informed. 'I've just written up a training programme for Paddy's new dog,' she said, referring to the friend and neighbour who'd whittled her a wooden stick out of briar when she rejected the one the hospital gave her. 'He's been impregnating bitches in the area.'

I assumed she wasn't talking about Paddy, who at around sixty-five was probably too old to be spreading his seed around.

She moved to the Aga, leaning on her stick, clearly frustrated by her body's frailty.

'I don't know why we're talking about pregnancy,' I said, getting the meat out of the fridge. 'The sweet shop has won an award.'

'What?' Her reaction was gratifying. It wasn't easy to surprise Celia Appleton, and I'd long ago given up trying. 'An award for what?'

'Best local independent business.'

'Well, that's not difficult,' she said, slamming a pan down and turning on the hob. 'And it's about bloody time.'

'Thanks. I think,' I said.

'You know what I mean.'

I did. She wasn't one for sentimentality, but I could tell by the tilt of her chin and little smile that passed her lips that she was pleased.

I left her to it, and made my way up to the back bedroom that was mine whenever I stayed. It had made sense to move back once Alex left. I couldn't afford to stay in his house on my own, and had suggested he rent it out. Anyway, it had been easier to be at Celia's, to care for her when she came out of hospital.

I crossed to the window, drawn by the view. Past a sweep of brightly coloured beach huts I could see the parade of white-washed buildings where the sweet shop nestled, between a guesthouse and what used to be the old post office. It was the only single-storey building, and looked inviting from a distance, with its steeply pitched roof and shuttered windows.

Opposite, the ancient pier jutted into the sea, which was sequinned with sunlight, and bordered by a stretch of beach. In the distance, the ruins of Corfe Castle stood sentry, its battlements etched against the pale blue sky.

For a moment, I could fool myself into believing that I didn't need to be anywhere else, but I knew deep down, I was lying.

Like my mother, I longed to leave Shipley and explore the world beyond.

I just didn't know how to make it happen.

Chapter 4

By Friday morning I'd whipped myself into a frenzy of nerves. Having been in a rut for so long, my impending TV appearance had taken on the magnitude of winning the Nobel Peace Prize.

I had no clue what to wear, and had tried on and discarded everything in my wardrobe. I was currently dressed in a neon-pink hoodie and a pair of ripped jeans – an outfit I last wore as a teenager with style issues.

While ferreting through my drawers, I'd uncovered all manner of mismatching socks and tiny crop tops I couldn't believe I'd once been brave enough to wear.

I tore off the jeans, looking forlornly at the mess of items scattered around the room. It looked like a landfill site.

My gaze landed on a photo on my bedside table, of Alex and me, and I subconsciously rubbed the space on my finger where the ring he'd bought me had been. Not an engagement ring exactly. *A promise ring*, Alex had called it, slipping the simple gold band, which bore my birthstone, onto my ring finger. *I promise I'll love you forever.*

I couldn't believe I'd given it back to him before he left, and told him to forget me.

Beth had suggested I smash the photo, symbolically, but I couldn't bring myself to do it.

In it, he was wearing his old baseball hat, and I was grinning so hard my eyes had disappeared. A tourist had taken the photo the day he gave me the ring in Machu Picchu, and the Inca Trail we'd been trekking was visible in the background.

My memory flashed back further, to the day we'd first met; an unusually mild one for the time of year, when I'd nipped out to eat my lunch on the beach, leaving Gramps in charge of the shop.

A man had emerged from the sea in a pair of white swimming shorts, like Daniel Craig as James Bond. Seeing me watching he'd played up to the image, as though he'd read my mind, running a hand through his short brown hair, lip curled in a moody smile as he approached with an exaggerated swagger.

'Can I breathe out now?' he'd said when he was standing in front of me, broad shoulders eclipsing the sun. 'I haven't got the six-pack to carry off this look.'

'I prefer a four-pack, anyway,' I'd said, blood rushing to my face at the unexpectedness of the exchange.

'I have to warn you, I don't normally dress like this.'

He'd grabbed a towel from a rucksack nearby and rubbed his hair. 'In fact, these aren't even mine.' He'd gestured to his snug-fitting swimwear with a hint of embarrassment, while I made a valiant effort to tear my gaze from his thighs. 'They belong to a mate.'

'That's not weird at all,' I'd said, brushing sand off my skirt, glad I'd finished eating my egg sandwich. Locking eyes with him, I'd felt a powerful attraction that took me by surprise.

'Bond. James Bond,' he'd said, sticking his hand out, burning right through the resistance I'd built up to good-looking men, after seeing so many of them pass through my mother's life. 'Actually, it's Alex Steadman.'

'Marnie Appleton,' I'd said, allowing his hand to engulf mine.

'I just fancied a swim.' He cast his gaze to the stretch of postcard-blue sky, and by the time he'd pulled on a pair of battered jeans and a T-shirt, we'd fallen into easy conversation.

He lived in Wareham, about half an hour away, and was working as a sound engineer for News South-West. On his days off he loved swimming in the sea – even in winter. He normally carried his swimming shorts, but had come to Shipley without them.

'Are you local?' he'd asked, with what seemed like genuine interest, and I had ended up giving him the low-down on my life, encompassing grandparents, business degree, and sweet shop – which I was helping to run until I had enough money to leave – and bypassing all the messy bits involving my mother.

I'd told him I longed to travel, having never been further than France on a school trip. 'I didn't even leave home after school,' I'd said, embarrassed. 'I did business studies at Bournemouth University.'

'Well I studied sound engineering at Plymouth.' He'd grinned. 'Not exactly a metropolis.' He'd told me he fancied travelling too; that he regretted not taking a gap year like some of his friends had after university.

Like me, he'd been focused on work for the past few years, and had just bought a house in Wareham.

'You know how some people inherit a reckless or daredevil streak?' He'd given a small, enigmatic smile. 'Well, I've inherited a sensible gene. Grandparents, parents, my sister – all teachers, all excellent with money.'

Crucially, he didn't have a girlfriend, and despite my problem fringe and bony knees, and the fact that when he met my mother she stroked his cheek and declared him 'edible', he apparently found me as funny, fascinating, and loveable as I did him.

Before I knew it I was spending more nights at his than at Celia's and within a year had sold my car, persuaded Gramps's Saturday assistant to take on more hours at the shop, and Alex and I were in Peru.

We'd been making plans to extend our trip when I got a call to say my grandfather was dying, and two days later I was back in Shipley.

'What's taking you so long?'

I blinked back to the present. Celia's head was poking round the door, eyebrows stretched at the sight of me in hoodie and knickers.

'I've got a two-piece you can borrow,' she said, hoicking the ripped jeans off the floor with her stick and flicking them onto the bed. 'It's come back into fashion.'

She ducked out, returning moments later with a custard-yellow jacket I was certain had *never* been in fashion, and a pair of black pleather trousers. Celia's lack of dress sense had been a constant source of embarrassment to my mother.

'She once turned up to a parents' evening in a *cowboy* hat,' she'd told me once, with an exaggerated shudder of horror at the memory.

'I'm not sure they'll fit,' I said diplomatically. It was obvious to anyone with eyes we were totally different heights and body shapes.

'Just try,' she urged, in the quiet but no-nonsense tone that brought even the most disobedient dog to heel.

I did as I was told, though I knew it was hopeless. The trousers were far too short and squeaked and strained over my hips, while the yellow jacket wouldn't do up properly, leaving glimpses of bra through the zip. An image of a banana poking out of a bin liner sprang to mind.

'It's not too bad from a distance.' Celia's head was cocked, like a fashion reporter at a red-carpet event.

'Actually, I think I'll just wear these,' I said, grabbing a pair of navy jeans, and a floaty top I'd discarded as mumsy.

I peeled off the trousers, which had made my thighs look flushed. 'Are you sure you want to come?'

Celia had brushed her cap of white hair until it shone, and was wearing the blue cashmere jumper she brought out for special occasions, overlaid with a string of pearls.

'Of course I'm coming,' she bristled. 'I wouldn't miss it for the world.'

'We'll have to get a taxi,' I said, knowing the short walk would be too much in her current condition – knowing too she'd hate being reminded.

'I'll go and ask Paddy,' she said. 'He owes me a lift for sorting out Muttley.'

I deciphered Muttley must be Paddy's new dog – the one with the out-of-control libido. 'Great,' I said, starting to shiver with nerves.

My teeth were still chattering with fright when we alighted on the pavement twenty minutes later. I'd stayed late the night before to clean the shop inside and out, and although it was too late to do anything about the shabby exterior, it looked presentable.

I'd even dragged the stepladder out of the stockroom and spray-painted a rather wonky 'e' back into Beachside.

Inside, soft sunshine picked out sherbet colours in the jars, and glinted off some gold-foil-wrapped chocolates I'd placed in bowls on the deep window ledges. Lollipops and striped candy canes were strategically positioned for effect, and a jar of gobstoppers on the counter added a pop of brightness.

'I hadn't realised it was so drab,' Celia concluded, looking round with an air of surprise. She hadn't set foot in the place since my grandfather died, and not very often before. The sweet shop had been his pride and joy, and although she supported him fully she'd shown no more inclination to work there than he had to help her train dogs.

'Ooh, I used to love these,' she said, drawn to a jar of pear drops, as I'd known she would be. It was my theory that all people over the age of sixty-five were hardwired to eat pear drops; it was probably in their DNA.

'You can have one, if you like,' I said, through clattering teeth. I couldn't stop fiddling with my fringe, and glancing at my watch.

'No thanks.' Celia moved behind the counter and eased herself onto the stool I kept there for quiet moments.

'What time are they coming?' she asked, even though I'd already told her.

'In about half an hour.' I couldn't move. It felt like my feet were welded to the floorboards, and I wondered why I was so scared. At university I'd been so confident – driven even. I'd soaked up ideas, and contributed to discussions with the fervour of a presidential hopeful.

It was as if my brain had calcified since then, and winning the award was reminding me just how much.

Beth bowled in, looking majestic in an olive, scoop-necked dress that complemented her mass of curls and skimmed her baby bump.

'There's a television van pulling up,' she said, dumping her bag and grazing the side of Celia's mouth with her lips. She loved my grandmother almost as much as I did. 'I suppose they've come early to set up.'

'Oh god,' I said, heart leaping like a cannon-ball. 'I need a wee.'

'You'll be fine.' She came over to hug me as best she could. 'The shop looks great, and so do you.'

She gave my newly washed and straightened hair an approving look.

'Glad you got rid of the poncho.'

'What if I throw up, or say something random?'

'You won't,' said Beth.

'And if you do, it's not the end of the world,' Celia chipped in. 'Even dogs get giddy when they're stressed.'

Brilliant.

Before I could escape to the loo, there was a commotion at the door and the camera crew descended.

After a flurry of introductions, air-kissing, and effusive congratulations, it transpired that Celia once helped the cameraman's mother with a rescue dog that kept snapping at visitors, which was a good ice-breaker.

By the time Beth had made some coffee for everyone, and face powder was dabbed on my cheeks and forehead – 'It's to cut the shine,' explained a bubbly make-up girl – and the lighting was deemed suitable, my nerves had subsided a little.

As I was handed my certificate of excellence, and a comedy-sized cheque for £10,000, I couldn't help wishing Alex was there to see it. He'd have been thrilled.

When we first talked about going away, he'd asked if I really wanted to give up my job. He was touchingly proud of what I did, and loved telling people his girlfriend ran a sweet shop.

'Sooooo! Congratulations!' cried Sandi Brent, with a dazzling smile, interrupting my thoughts. She was probably my age, with dark, almond-shaped eyes, and caramel hair that swished when she moved her head. Her pale skirt-suit and candy-striped shirt were simple but stylish, and I felt lumpen in comparison.

'Thank you!' I said, creatively.

'So, how does it feel to win?'

Unbelievable, considering I've been coasting along, and didn't expect to still be working in a sweet shop at the age of almost thirty.

'Wonderful!' I said, copying her tendency to speak in exclamation marks, wondering how she maintained her perfect eyeliner flick. Whenever I tried, it looked like a child had attacked my face with a marker pen.

'I still can't believe it!' I added, thinking I ought to elaborate. Knowing there was a lens trained on me made my face want to twitch. 'I'm so pleased that people voted for me!' Sandi kept nodding encouragingly. She had a tiny lipstick smear on one of her pearly white teeth. 'My grandfather would have been proud!'

Unexpectedly, a lump swelled in my throat. He would have been *very* proud. He was the one who should have won an award, not me.

I glanced at Celia, and saw her passing a tissue over her nose. I sometimes forgot how much she must still miss him.

'You should be proud too!' Sandi said, her hair swishing in earnest. 'You were up against some stiff competition from Brian's Pet Emporium among others, but The Beachside Sweet Shop was by far the most popular choice!'

I suddenly wished she'd tone it down. I didn't want rival business owners taking umbrage, and setting the shop on fire in the dead of night.

'Well, we're situated right by the beach which probably helps, especially on a day like this!' I gestured outside. The tide was in, and the sea was a perfect swirl of turquoise beneath a duck-egg sky. 'Location, location, location!'

'Kirstie Allsopp eat your heart out!' Sandi gave a throat-splitting cackle. 'You do have a *glorious* outlook!'

Filming had drawn quite a crowd, and the shop was swarming with people – most of whom I'd never seen – pretending to browse the sweets while covertly asking what was happening. At the edge of my vision, I could see a pair of teenage boys making rabbit ears over my head.

Spotting them, Sandi's neat eyebrows puckered. 'Can you two piss off?' she hissed, shattering her girl-next-door illusion.

'Why should we?' One of the boys gave her the finger.

'Because time is money, you little shits.'

I turned and met Beth's eye, and could tell she was as overwhelmed with a choking urge to giggle as I was.

'So, Marnie – gorgeous name, by the way . . .' subduing her inner bitch, Sandi pasted her smile back on, 'where do you see yourself five years from now?'

In the foothills of the Himalayas, I was tempted to say, but with so many ears listening avidly, including Celia's, I couldn't.

'Hopefully, still here!' I trilled, brandishing an arm to encompass the entire shop. 'Selling our wonderful sweets to tourists and locals . . .'

'Rotting the nation's teeth,' someone piped up.

A ripple of laughter went round.

I opened my mouth, hoping for a witty riposte, but nothing came out. My arm dropped to my side.

I could feel a spot trying to break the barrier of my make-up, and in the sudden silence, I gulped.

'What do you say to that?' Sandi's voice was soft, but her posture had altered. Her shoulders were pulled back and her eyes had sharpened. She reminded me of Chester when he caught a whiff of fox poo.

Doris arrived, parting the crowd. 'Well, I was brought up on dolly mixtures and I've still got my own teeth,' she said, stepping into the breach; which was just as well as every sensible thought had fled my brain.

She bared her molars as proof. 'And I couldn't get by without my pineapple cubes,' she added. She was sporting two stripes of electric blue eyeshadow, in honour of the TV cameras, and positioned herself at Sandi's elbow. 'Sweets are part of our heritage,' she went on. 'My cubes were the only thing I could stomach when Roger died.'

The silence had an air of respect for her dead husband.

'I think that says it all!' I said, bright and breezy, and murmurs of agreement grew to a swell of competing voices, culminating in a spontaneous round of applause.

'Hurray, for The Beachside Sweet Shop!'

'Long may she live!'

'God bless all who sail in her!'

As the mood turned hysterical, Sandi's smile wavered.

'Let's wrap things up!' she said, with a bounce on her spiky-heeled shoes. 'Do you see what I did there?' she chirped. 'Wrap things up? Sweets? Wrapping up sweets . . .?' Silence descended. Two mottled patches of red appeared on her cheekbones.

'Chris!' Turning, she gestured with a click of her fingers, and a reporter sporting a wispy brown goatee and a top-knot stepped forward.

He introduced himself as Chris Weatherby a reporter for *The Shipley Examiner*, and sister newspaper *The South-West Recorder*. He clumsily assembled Celia, Beth and me in front of the counter, each of us holding a confectionery product, and by the time he'd fired off several shots, I was almost starting to enjoy myself. Shame I could feel my fringe frizzing up.

'One more for luck,' Chris said, dropping into a serious-photographer crouch. 'Say chocolate éclair!'

As we mouthed the words self-consciously, a question zipped into my head.

How could I possibly leave Shipley, when I'd just become an award-winning businesswoman?

Chapter 5

'Have you seen this?' Beth slammed a newspaper on the counter the following Monday.

It was *The Shipley Examiner* and the sweet shop, along with our faces, had made the front page.

Beth looked luminous, Celia was unusually coy as she fingered her pearls, and I was cradling a jar of bonbons like a lion cub. My fringe didn't look too bad all things considered. Shame my eyes were shut.

'Hang on.' I quickly served a middle-aged woman who'd been trying to describe a sweet from her childhood she couldn't remember the name of, settling for a quarter of mint humbugs instead.

Business had picked up since I'd appeared on the news, though the piece had been edited down to just me receiving my cheque and thanking the public for voting, in between lingering close-ups of Sandi's face. The cameraman was obviously in love with her.

'Ooh, is that you?' said the customer, peering at the upside-down newspaper. 'I voted for the sweet shop, because I remember your granddad,' she added with a treacly smile. 'He was lovely to me and my friends when we were little, and would give us a bag of free sweets if we were his last customers of the day.'

'Typical Gramps,' I said, a swelling feeling in my chest. Most of my regulars had similar happy memories of my grandfather.

She looked at me a second longer than was comfortable.

'That'll be two ninety-nine, please.'

'Fine,' she said, handing over the money in a way that suggested she now regretted voting. *You're clearly not your grandfather*, her back seemed to say, as she flounced out of the shop.

'She can afford to pay for her sweets,' I said to Beth, as the door smacked shut. 'She had a wad of notes in her purse.'

'Well you might be giving them away after this,' she said, bringing my attention back to the newspaper.

I scanned the headline.

Rotting the Nation's Teeth!
Has the Humble Sweet Shop Had its Day?

'*What?*' I returned Beth's horrified gaze, then read the paragraph beneath.

With the soaring obesity crisis and a generation of pre-schoolers suffering tooth decay, should we be celebrating a business that basically peddles sugar?

'Peddles?' I burst out. 'They make it sound like cocaine.'

'It gets worse,' Beth said. 'Apparently, The Beachside Sweet Shop is responsible for an increase in visits to the dentist last year.'

I stared at her. 'How on earth can they prove that?'

'They probably can't.' Beth shook her curls. 'But it makes for a sensational story, and that's clearly the angle . . .' she leaned over to read the writer's by-line, 'Chris Weatherby was going for.'

'Wasn't he the guy who took the pictures?'

Beth nodded. 'Clearly not just a photographer.'

I felt oddly shaken, imagining how Gramps would have felt. 'Do you think anyone will read this?'

'Well, they haven't yet,' said Beth, as the door opened to admit a clutch of children in uniform, who looked like they were on a school trip.

'We saw you on TV, and thought we'd stop off and see what the fuss was about,' said a short, round woman who appeared to be in charge. 'It really reminds me of the sweet shop near where I lived as a child.'

'It's lovely,' agreed a larger woman, in half-moon glasses. 'And what a lovely view.'

Everyone turned to look through the window. It was another brightly lit day, sunshine spilling across the sand to the sea, where a couple of yachts were bobbing in the distance, sails billowing in the breeze.

'You're so lucky,' said the first woman, 'having a job like this.'

I felt a prickle of guilt. I rarely bothered to look at the view when I was at work.

'What would you like?' I said briskly, wondering whether Chris Weatherby had a point. Should I really be selling sugar to pre-schoolers – or anyone else, for that matter? Was I on a par with the Child Catcher from *Chitty Chitty Bang Bang*?

But if I was, it meant my grandfather had been too, and the thought of Leonard Appleton intending anyone harm was completely ludicrous.

'Are you OK?' asked one of the women, and I realised I was gripping the edge of the counter as if about to vault over it.

'I'm fine,' I said, trying to relax my face.

'Go and make some tea,' Beth hissed, then made the children giggle by pretending to drop a jar of sweets, but catching it at the last minute.

'Are you famous?' asked a little boy, before I could make a quick exit. He was pink-cheeked beneath a windswept mop of dark hair, and his cheeks dimpled when he smiled.

'Not really.' I smoothed a self-conscious hand across my hair. 'Not in the sense of someone who's won an Oscar or . . .'

'Yes she is,' said Beth.

'Can I have a selfie, please?' He produced a smart-phone from his blazer pocket, and one of the teachers sucked in air through her teeth.

'No phones, Christopher,' she said, snatching it from him and popping it in her bag. 'You can have it back at the end of the day.'

'What's up?' Beth asked, when the group had finally left, the teachers wishing me all the best and thanking for me for an 'authentic' experience.

'That.' I pointed to the newspaper. 'People will turn against us because of him, and it's not fair. Not after everything Gramps worked for.'

'Oh, don't be silly,' Beth scoffed, grabbing the paper and stuffing it in the recycling bin. 'I doubt anyone even reads it and, even if they do, you're hardly responsible for people's choices. If they don't want to buy sweets, they don't have to.'

'I suppose so,' I said, but Chris Weatherby's words had lodged in my brain, and I felt unusually rattled.

'Don't let it spoil everything.' Beth rubbed my arm. 'You've looked happy since Friday. You've even done your hair again.'

'I *was* feeling good,' I allowed. 'I was going to ask you to ask Harry if he'd give me a quote for doing the shop up a bit.'

'Brilliant!' Beth's smile was replaced by a grimace.

'What's wrong?'

'I keep getting these twinges,' she said, cradling her belly with both hands. 'They've been happening on and off over the weekend.'

'Have you told your midwife?'

'They're probably Braxton Hicks,' Beth said, moving her hands to her lower back and moving them in small circles. 'Practise contractions.'

It hit me that Beth could actually give birth any minute, and I still hadn't found anyone to replace her. My Saturday girl, Agnieszka, had several jobs already, and although I'd put a notice in the window, the few applicants I'd had weren't happy that I couldn't give an exact start date. Plus, I wasn't keen on the thought of bringing in a stranger.

'You should go home and put your feet up,' I told her, realising how heavily I'd come to rely on her help. Harry complained I saw more of her than he did, though I know it suited her to work at the sweet shop until she got her degree.

'I'll sit out the back for five minutes,' she said, wincing again. She did look rather pale, and there was a sheen of perspiration on her upper lip.

'Go on,' I instructed. 'I'll make some weak tea.'

'Who are you, my gran?'

But she did as she was told, which was worrying. From the start, she'd refused to be pampered, insisting pregnancy wasn't an illness, and she wanted to carry on as normal.

'I think you should call Harry,' I said, spooning two sugars into her tea, as though she was in shock. The chimes above the door kept jangling as customers entered the shop, but I didn't want to leave her.

'Don't be silly, I'll be fine.' Beth picked up her mug, a defiant spark in her eyes, and I doubted Bunty would dare put in an appearance before her due date.

'OK,' I said. 'Just take it easy.'

When I emerged a man was leaning on the counter.

'Please could I have some sherbet lemons, miss?' he said, his face lighting up when he saw me.

Despite a Northern accent, there was something of the surfer about him; wavy, blond-streaked hair, green eyes, and golden forearms dusted with fine hairs.

'I, er, sure, yes,' I stuttered. He wasn't wearing a shirt, revealing a tanned and muscled chest, and my pulse started racing in a peculiar fashion.

I fumbled the jar off the shelf behind me, not realising the lid wasn't on properly. Half the sherbet lemons spilled across the floor.

'Oh, god, I'm sorry,' I said, dropping on all fours and scooping up a handful.

'Five second rule,' the man said. He was leaning over the counter, a teasing look on his face.

'Sorry?'

'If food's on the floor for five seconds, it's fine to eat. Longer than that . . .' He gave an eloquent shrug. From this angle he looked naked and my face inflamed with heat.

'It's been longer than that now,' I said primly. Flustered, I began chucking sweets in the bin. 'I'd better wash my hands,' I said, moving too quickly and smacking my head on the underside of the counter. 'OW!' I cried, rubbing my scalp.

'Are you OK?' the man said.

Tears of pain pricked my eyes. 'No, I'm bloody not.'

'When you're ready, love, I haven't got all day,' someone snapped from the other side of the counter.

'I thought this place had just won an award.'

'It can't have been for good service.'

The man's head disappeared. 'Give her a break, she's here on her own, and she's just bumped her head,' he said.

'Where's the rest of the staff?'

'I don't know, I've never been in here before.'

'It wasn't like this in her granddad's day, he was always very professional.'

Oh for heaven's sake. I stood up, ready to give them a piece of my mind, but before I could speak, the man stuck out a hand and said, 'I'm Josh. Nice to meet you . . .'

'Marnie,' I said automatically, pumping his hand as though we were at a business meeting. 'Look, I'm sorry about that.' I took a breath. 'Let me start again.'

'No worries.' His grin made my heart skip a beat. I dusted my hands on my skirt, then picked up the metal scoop and decanted the few sherbet lemons that were left onto the scales, aware of everyone watching with eagle eyes.

'Enough?' I met Josh's amused glance and looked away, cheeks burning. What was wrong with me?

'I'll have the rest,' he said. 'You can't have too many sherbet lemons.' He'd folded his arms, as if settling in for a long wait, while behind him customers fidgeted and muttered.

'Beth!' I called, aiming for a light-hearted tone that came out strangled. 'Need a bit of help here!'

'Jesus wept,' said the man behind Josh. He was holding the hand of a little girl with Goldilocks curls, who was sobbing as though her heart was broken. 'How much longer is this going to take?'

'My hair's grown an inch while I've been waiting,' said some bright spark behind them.

'BETH!' I called. Was she OK?

Josh stiffened, unfolding his arms. 'Listen,' he said. 'I've had a bit of experience working in a shop. Why don't I give you a hand?'

I stared at him. 'What?'

'Let me help.'

In a fluid movement, he unfastened a shirt from around his waist and pulled it over his surfer shorts, before joining me behind the counter.

'What can I get you, sir?' he said politely to the man with the sobbing child, and within seconds she was smiling through her tears as he handed over a handful of lollipops.

'Yes?' I said to the next customer, simultaneously grateful and bemused by the presence of a man by my side – one who looked as if he'd been born to work in a sweet shop.

We worked our way steadily through the queue, choreographing our movements to avoid bumping into each other. I kept casting him covert looks, but he seemed to know how to work the till and find what people wanted without asking where things were.

I'd begun to fret about Beth, when I became aware of a high keening noise rising from somewhere behind us.

'What the hell's that?' asked Josh, poised with a bag of jelly babies in one hand, and a ten-pound note in the other.

'MARNIE! Heeeeeeeeeeeeelp!'

Dropping a bag of rhubarb-flavoured chews, I shot through to the kitchen to find Beth on her back on the floor, knees drawn up, her face frozen in a grimace.

'I think I'm having a baby,' she whispered.

Chapter 6

'So, it was a false alarm?' I perched on the side of Beth's hospital bed and smoothed a stray curl off her forehead.

She looked sheepish. 'I'm really sorry, Marnie.'

'Don't be ridiculous,' I said, leaning over and plumping her pillows. She was being kept in for a few hours, for monitoring. 'It looked completely real from where I was standing.'

'It felt real too,' she said, eyes shining with tears. I'd never seen Beth so thoroughly unsettled. Going into early labour hadn't been part of her plan and, false alarm or not, the episode had thrown her.

'I've got to take it easy for the next few weeks, put my feet up, that kind of thing,' she said crossly, as if she'd been quarantined. 'I won't be able to work.'

'I was going to fire you anyway,' I joked, in an attempt to bring back her smile.

'Ha ha,' she managed. 'I don't understand how it could hurt so much and then come to nothing.'

'Well, the doctor explained the baby could have been lying on a nerve,' I reminded her. She'd seemed too shocked to take in what he was saying, unable to comprehend why the agony had stopped almost as soon as she was examined. 'Plus, you have a really low pain threshold.' I was thinking of the time she twisted her ankle on the way to school, and wailed loudly enough to raise the dead in the graveyard we were passing.

'Oh god,' she said, looking panicked. 'Do you think I might need knocking out when it happens for real?'

To date, Beth's birthing plan had optimistically involved being in bed at home, doing some light chanting intended to induce a trance-like state that would block her pain receptors.

'We'll see,' I said, handing her a beaker of tepid water. 'It might not be as bad as you think.'

Straightening up gingerly she shook her head, looking uncon-vinced. 'I still can't believe you left a stranger in charge of the shop.'

'I didn't have much choice,' I said. After seeing Beth writhing on the floor I'd immediately tried to call Harry, but when I got his voice-mail rang for an ambulance instead.

'Don't worry,' Josh had said, when I shot out to explain what was happening. 'I'll keep an eye on the place if you want to go with your friend.'

His stance was casual but confident, but though his level-head-edness had calmed me down, I was reluctant to leave him alone. 'I don't even know your surname,' I said, hunting around for my keys. 'I should close the shop. People will understand.'

'It's Radley, and it seems a pity to close when you're so busy.' He nodded at the steady trickle of customers. 'Honestly, I'll be fine.'

I hadn't taken much persuading; mostly because Beth was making such a terrible noise by that point, people were giving me suspicious looks. I'd had to explain that it wasn't someone being tortured, but that Beth was having a baby – which amounted to much the same thing.

'I'll keep an eye on him,' Doris had said, sticking her hand in the air like a schoolgirl. It was unlike her to make three visits to the shop in a week, but I guessed now my profile had been raised she was keen to capitalise on our connection. 'You go, sweetheart. Beth needs you.'

It was almost as if they couldn't wait to be rid of me, but while I wasn't exactly relaxed about it, I figured not much could go wrong with beady-eyed Doris in charge.

'What if they've robbed the place, and divvied up the takings?' Beth said, a flush of colour returning to her cheeks. 'They might run off together.'

'Unlikely,' I said. 'You know what a stickler Doris is for obeying the letter of the law.' Her husband, Roger, had been a policeman before his retirement, and she was a member of our local Neighbourhood Watch.

'Well, wotsischops might knock her out and take off with the money.'

'You're talking like I've thousands of pounds stashed away,' I said with a laugh. 'Takings have only gone up since Friday, I'm hardly rolling in cash.'

'He might be desperate,' Beth insisted, her forehead creasing. 'You sound as if you don't care.'

'Of course I care,' I said, feeling as if something had shifted and brought the sweet shop more sharply into focus. Maybe it was winning the competition. I could hardly let down all the people who'd voted by letting the place go to wrack and ruin.

Which brought me back to Josh.

'I wonder if he'd be interested in a job,' I said to Beth. 'Now you're out of action for the foreseeable.'

'Talking about work again?'

Harry came through the double doors with three cups of coffee in a cardboard holder, and a bag that smelt of meat underneath his arm.

'I've bought refreshments,' he said, putting the items on the locker by Beth's bed and stooping to kiss her hair.

He was still in his paint-splattered overalls, his copper-wire coloured hair sticking up in tufts. Despite being the boss, he wasn't afraid to muck in and do the dirty work.

Harry was the boy-next-door that Beth had known since the age of six, and married three years ago on her twenty-seventh birthday.

'When you know, you know,' she'd say matter-of-factly, when people expressed their astonishment that he was the only man she'd ever been in a relationship with. 'There's nothing I need from anyone else that I haven't got with Harry.'

'I knew you were working her too hard,' he said now, his hazel eyes marble hard as they met mine across the bed.

'Harry,' Beth warned.

'It's OK,' I said quickly. 'I think he's right actually. I should have sent you home as soon as you said you were having twinges.'

'She tried,' Beth said, grabbing Harry's hand and kissing his fingers. 'You know what I'm like.'

His gaze softened. 'Will you let me look after you now?'

'Ugh.' She laid her head back and rolled her eyes. 'I don't like being looked after.'

'Well, you'll have to get used to it,' I said firmly, and the look Harry gave me this time was less hostile.

'Drink your coffee, it's decaf,' he instructed her, clearly relishing being in charge as he handed her one of the cardboard cups. 'And I don't want you sitting up studying until all hours, either. You need more sleep.'

'I'll sleep when I'm dead,' she grumbled, letting him crumble up a sausage roll and pop some into her mouth. 'I suppose I've got to do what's best for Bunty.'

'Don't you mean Herbert?' said Harry, who was equally convinced their baby was a boy.

'I'll leave you to it,' I said, sliding off the bed. My stomach growled with hunger, but it was clear Harry hadn't thought to get me anything to eat. I picked up one of the coffees and kissed Beth goodbye, with a promise to ring her later to see how she was.

I returned to the shop in a taxi to find it empty, and no sign of Josh or Doris. My heart missed a beat. Had Beth been right, and Josh had absconded with the takings? Was he a drifter passing through, conning people on the way, or had I read too many thrillers?

I opened the till, relieved to see it was packed with notes and coins. Though we had a machine for customers to pay by card, the sweet shop was one of those places where people preferred to use cash.

'Josh?' The sun dipped behind a cloud, and the shop plunged into gloom. Was he hiding somewhere, waiting to cosh me over the head?

Had he murdered Doris and hidden her body?

'Out here,' came a distant voice. 'I've just checked in a delivery.'

I crossed behind the counter, through the office and into the stockroom, where Josh was tearing open a cardboard box.

'Hope you don't mind,' he said, a grin crinkling his eyes. 'I thought it would save you a job.' His hair was amber under the glow of the overhead light, and he looked like the stranger he was – albeit a friendly and incredibly handsome one. 'How's your friend?'

'It was a false alarm,' I said absently, seeing the room through someone else's eyes. It was long overdue a clear out. There were stacks of empty boxes, some half-open, spilling contents that were probably out of date. Rob Hancock had tended to deliver the way he had when my grandfather was alive, taking little or no notice of my orders. Often,

I hadn't required any stock at all, but he'd still turn up with something 'new and exciting' that didn't make it onto the shelves.

'Looks like this place could do with a tidy,' Josh said, echoing my thoughts. 'I can help, if you like.'

'Where's Doris?' I peered around as if he might have stashed her on a shelf.

'She wanted to get to the butcher's before it closed and buy some sausages for her dinner.'

'Of course she did,' I said. 'Doris loves her sausages.'

We looked at each other and laughed.

'Do you want a job?' The words burst out before I had time to dress them up. 'I mean, you don't have to answer right now, and you've probably already got a job, but Beth – that's my pregnant friend by the way – won't be back, probably ever, and unless I can find someone to help out I'm stuck—'

'I'd love to work here,' he butted in. 'It's funny, because I was going to apply for the job advertised in the window.'

'You were?'

His eyes appraised me in a way that made me wonder if a few buttons on my shirt were undone. 'The thing is, I'm only passing through,' he added. 'But it should give you enough time to find somebody else.'

'Perfect,' I said, letting a smile unfurl. I stuck my hand out, and he wrapped mine in both of his. 'Welcome to The Beachside Sweet Shop.'

Chapter 7

'You look cheerful.' Celia stopped me by the front door, her face suspicious.

'There's no need to say it like that,' I said, failing to repress a grin. 'Anyone would think I went around with a face like thunder.'

She was right, though, I did feel cheerful. Not only had I found someone to help at the shop, but Beth was back at her in-laws', determined to finish her thesis before the baby arrived. She'd also asked Harry about giving the shop a facelift, and he'd agreed to give me a quote.

On top of that, I'd received an email from my cousin Phoebe, who lived in London, congratulating me on my award, and suggesting we meet for a drink the following week, as she was coming to visit Uncle Cliff.

The only thing that had threatened to burst my bubble of good humour was a text from Sandi Brent while I was eating my porridge. She wanted to know if I'd be willing to give a follow-up interview, addressing some of the 'issues' raised in Chris Weatherby's newspaper article.

I'd ignored it. I didn't want to address any issues; I wanted anyone who'd read the article to forget it.

'I *am* feeling good,' I said to Celia, who appeared to be waiting for an answer she could believe in. Chester, sitting patiently beside her, cocked his ears at my tone. 'Are you sure you'll be OK today?'

I asked her the same thing every morning, and the answer never varied. 'Stop fussing, I'll be fine,' she said.

I'd initially organised a rotation of neighbours to keep an eye on her until she was back on her feet, but she'd made it clear she could cope now, as long as Paddy-next-door was on hand to help if required.

'So who's this young man you've taken on?' She never showed much interest in the shop until something out of the ordinary happened, then behaved as though she'd built the place herself.

'I explained last night,' I said, patiently. She'd listened, but hadn't said much, and I knew from the glassy look in her eyes she was wrestling a dog-training problem in her head.

'I hope you've checked out his references,' she said, now.

'I don't need to.' I popped a kiss on her cheek, which smelt faintly of Pond's cold cream. 'It's obvious he knows what he's doing, and I trust my instincts.'

'Instincts,' she snorted, as though it was a made-up word. 'People can tell you anything, it doesn't mean it's true.'

'But it's what they do that counts,' I said, quoting her own, oft-repeated words. 'Actions speak louder than words.'

Tutting, she waved her stick. She was wearing a violently patterned jumper that Sarah Lund would have rejected. 'Get away with you,' she said, a smile appearing at her lips. 'You've always got an answer.'

Just like your mother. She didn't say it, but the words seemed to shimmer between us.

We rarely talked about Mum. Celia hadn't forgiven her for 'neglecting' me as a child, but while I appreciated her loyalty it felt wrong for them to still be at odds – especially since Celia's fall.

'Have a good day,' I said, shrugging my bag over my shoulder and setting off for work.

It had rained overnight, but the sky was clear, and a balmy breeze billowed through my fringe and curled up my bare legs. I'd picked out a khaki shirt-dress, and teamed it with a pair of cream Converses that made my legs look tanned. I'd even painted my toenails coral – not that anyone could see them.

I felt unusually sprightly, like a car that had been given a reviving injection of engine oil, and was gently humming a Dolly Parton song when a woman stepped through the gate of Seaview Cottage and blocked my way.

She'd moved in a month or so ago, with her husband and baby boy, but had so far rebuffed all friendly overtures, leading Doris to refer to her as 'hoity-toity'.

Up close, she was stunning; slim, with clear pale skin, choppy blonde hair, and slanted sea-green eyes. Even her fudge-coloured tan looked natural.

'Hi,' I stuttered, like a schoolgirl with a crush. 'Marnie Appleton.'

'Isabel Sinclair.' The intonation implied I should know the name, and I suddenly recalled seeing the removal men carting a blown-up copy of a magazine cover, under glass, featuring a half-nude model draped on a chaise longue.

Clearly, the model was her.

As her rather imperious gaze swept over me, I felt like a troll.

'Are you the dog-training woman?' she said, in a cut-glass voice.

'Ah, you need to speak to my grandmother, Celia.' I turned to point up the hill. 'She lives in the top house.'

'It's my Pollywollydoodle,' she said, the breeze catching the hem of her chambray tunic. She was wearing cuffed denim shorts, revealing long toned legs and shapely knees.

'Your . . .?'

'She's a Cavapoo.'

'Beg your pardon?'

A frown touched her brow. 'My *dog*,' she said, folding her slender arms. 'She's not settling in very well.'

No need to be rude. 'Well, I'm sure my gran can help,' I said, damping down a sneeze as her overpowering perfume attacked my nostrils.

'You're the one who won the competition.' It wasn't a question. 'You run the sweet shop.' Neither was that.

I brushed a strand of hair from my eyes. 'That's right.'

Her gaze wasn't warming up. 'You'll be quite the topic of conversation at mothers and toddlers this morning.'

'That's . . . good?' She must mean the group that met twice a week at the community centre, not far from the shop. Beth and I called them The Perfect Mums.

'I doubt it,' she said, with a smile that didn't reach her eyes. 'I'll be seeing you.'

She strutted back through her gate and up the garden path without saying goodbye. Definitely a model. And clearly not a people person.

I hurried on, past the beach huts and along the parade, past the souvenir shop with its colourful buckets and spades outside, feeling as if some of the brightness had leached out of the day.

The stretch of sand opposite the shop was almost deserted, apart from a few dog-walkers, who wouldn't be allowed on the beach once the holiday season was underway.

Improbably, Josh was standing atop a skateboard outside the sweet shop, shuffling a deck of playing cards, a sporty head band holding back his tousled hair.

'How old are you?' I asked, taking in his frayed laces and calf-length shorts as I pulled my keys from my bag.

He gave me a quizzical look. 'Twenty-five.'

Phew. I'd suddenly worried he might be seventeen, despite his self-assured attitude.

'You?' He raised an eyebrow.

'Mind your own beeswax.'

'Charming.'

'Where do you live?' I said, eyeing his skateboard.

'I'm staying with friends.' He swung his arm in the direction of the pier, presumably meaning the other side of the bay. 'I do have transport, but a skateboard's a good way to travel around here.'

'I'll take your word for it.' I watched him execute a complicated manoeuvre. 'Isn't it a bit nineties?'

He leapt off and picked it up. 'Keeps me trim.'

'And the playing cards?'

'I was practising,' he said, stuffing the deck in his shorts pocket. 'I do a bit of magic.'

'Is there no end to your talents?' It wasn't meant to sound flirty.

'I guess that's for you to find out.' He widened his eyes suggestively, and I jammed the key in the lock to hide my confusion.

'Who's that dude?' he said once we were inside and I'd turned off the alarm and stowed my bag in the office.

'That's my grandfather, Leonard Appleton,' I said, following his gaze to the photo above the desk. 'This was his shop. He inherited it from his dad.'

'Cool.' He studied the picture closely. 'Nice to keep it in the family,' he said, almost to himself.

Keeping it in the family. It had a lovely ring to it, and I warmed to Josh even more. 'Did you read that article in the paper?'

Turning away, he propped his skateboard against the wall. 'What article?'

'The shop won an award last week.' I tried to sound modest. 'I was on the news . . .'

'Hey, that's great.' His face split into a smile. 'But I don't really read newspapers.'

'Well, it's turned a bit negative,' I said. 'Apparently, I'm rotting the nation's teeth and ruining their health.' I felt another stab of indignation, recalling Chris Weatherby's words. 'Just putting you in the picture in case anyone mentions it,' I added, fetching the float for the till.

'It'll be old news by now.' Josh dug his hands in his pockets. 'You're not taking it seriously, are you?'

I shrugged. 'I don't want my grandfather's name dragged through the mud, that's all. This was his livelihood, and it's down to me to protect his good name.'

'Is it?' Josh looked at me for a second, then in a dramatic voice said, 'You shall win over any doubters with your beauty and natural charm. They will be hypnotised by your salesmanship, and your dashing new assistant.'

I couldn't help a burst of laughter. 'Maybe you should lose that hairband,' I suggested.

'Hey, if it's good enough for David Beckham!'

All the same he pulled it out, and ruffled his hair into place with his hands.

'Now go and wash them,' I said. 'Health and hygiene.'

'Yes, Mum.' He tugged an imaginary forelock. 'Shall I make a drink while I'm out there?'

'Coffee, white with two sugars.' It was almost like having Beth back. A younger, ridiculously good-looking, male version.

I realised I'd started humming Dolly Parton again, as I turned the old-fashioned sign on the door to 'OPEN' and checked that the pick and mix was full.

Finding a duster, I nudged it over the edges of the shelves, though they didn't really need it, and then stuck my certificate to the window with Blu-tack in a fit of optimism. Why not show it off?

There was a steady stream of customers all morning, all friendly, and interested in my award, and when there was a lull, Josh showed me a trick which involved me picking a card, which he pushed into the middle of the deck, yet somehow made appear at the top every time.

'You're good at this,' I said.

'I know.' He bowed.

'Now go and put the kettle on.'

At lunchtime, after I'd eaten a cheese sandwich out the back, I peeped round the door to see him charming a pretty, thirty-something woman. She was saucer-eyed and attentive, fake-protesting as Josh flourished his arm back and forth, trying to persuade her to try something different, before caving in and buying more than she came in for.

'Nice work,' I said as she left, casting Josh a last, lingering look. 'We'll be doubling our takings at this rate.'

'Happy to help,' he said. 'A satisfied customer will be back. Hopefully with friends.' He accepted the mug of coffee I was holding out. 'I noticed your delivery yesterday was from Kandy Kings.'

Thrown by the change of subject, it took me a second to respond. 'Do you know them?'

'I know *of* them,' he said, lifting his shoulder. I noticed the way his grey T-shirt clung to his chest. 'Have you used them for a long time?'

'Actually no,' I said, tearing my gaze from his biceps. 'That was my first order, why?'

He grimaced.

'I know. Kandy with a K's a bit naff.'

'True,' he said. 'But it's not that. I heard they were in trouble recently. Something to do with health and safety. Rats on the premises, I think.'

'Oh.' Taken aback, I wondered if I should have checked them out, but they were well-established wholesalers as far as I knew, with a good reputation. 'I didn't know.'

'Who did you use before?'

'Oh, a family business called Hancock's,' I said. 'They used to supply my grandfather back in the day, and carried on when I took over.'

'So why the change?'

I imagined explaining about Rob Hancock's wandering eyes and fleshy face; his threatening tone when I turned down his liquorice willies, and how I'd resisted buying elsewhere out of a sense of loyalty to my grandfather. Instead I said, 'Oh, he was getting a bit unreliable, why?'

A wave of colour swept over his face and his gaze edged away from mine. 'Just being nosy, I guess.'

With a sinking feeling, I sensed he wasn't telling the truth, and remembered Celia asking if I'd checked him out.

'Where did you work before?' I asked, adjusting the weighing scales. They desperately needed a polish. 'I should call them for a reference.'

Josh put down his mug of steaming builder's tea, and scratched the side of his head.

'Look, Marnie.' My name sounded oddly exotic in a Northern accent. 'I don't have a lot of work experience,' he confessed. 'I've been trying to decide what I want to do with my life since finishing uni. Doing a bit of this and that, travelling around the country, staying with family and friends.'

'O-*kay*.' I could relate to that. 'But you seem experienced.'

'That's because I worked in a sweet shop during the summer holidays, years ago,' he said, dipping his head and rubbing the back of his neck. 'It was up in Yorkshire, where my family are.' He paused. 'I'm not sure whether it's still there, but I can find out if you like. The owner will probably remember me.'

'And no other jobs since then?'

'Some bar work here and there, and I worked in an office for a bit for a friend of a friend, but didn't enjoy it much. I had to wear a suit.'

'Hmmm,' I said. 'I can imagine that might have been a problem.'

We exchanged conspiratorial grins as the door burst open and a woman approached the counter, carrying a baby boy who'd got his fingers tangled in her hair.

'Hello,' I said, recognising Isabel Sinclair, the neighbour I'd bumped into on my way to work.

Josh's eyes were out on springs, and I could hardly blame them. She was almost unnaturally beautiful, even if her eyes were less than friendly.

'How can I help?' I said, giving her my warmest smile.

Outside were a clutch of The Perfect Mums, fresh from their mother and toddler session. They sometimes popped in to buy sweets for themselves, but today were gathered with their buggies, talking amongst themselves.

'A shop like this shouldn't be allowed to win an award in this day and age,' said Isabel, in a hostile voice. 'I'm going to start a campaign to get you closed down.'

I looked at Josh, and saw my bemusement reflected back at me.

Before either of us could respond she stalked out, trying to disentangle her son's chubby fingers from her tresses, and joined her friends, who greeted her with sickening effusiveness.

The door pushed open again. 'Sugar monster!' shouted one of the women, then suddenly they'd all gone, leaving a clear view of a pair of fighting seagulls.

'What the hell?' Josh's eyes swivelled to mine. 'Did that just happen?'

'It did,' I said grimly. 'Are you sure you still want to work here?'

Chapter 8

'It can't be a coincidence that there were hardly any customers for the rest of the day,' I said to Beth later, pacing up and down to work off my anger. 'The newspaper article was bad enough, without that woman and her friends spreading the word.'

'Why would she be so vindictive?' Beth said, perching on the stool behind the counter while Harry got busy with his tape measure.

It was after six, but the only time Harry could get away, and Beth had insisted on accompanying him. She said she needed to get out from under her mother-in-law Jacky's feet, but I knew it was because she didn't want to leave me alone with Harry, when things were awkward between us.

'Probably because she's got nothing better to do,' I fumed. 'How dare she when she's only lived around here five minutes? She has no idea how much people loved my granddad's sweet shop.'

'Still do,' Beth said, with a sympathetic pout. 'Take no notice.'

'Anyway, it's everything in moderation,' said Harry, squatting to scribble down a measurement. 'It's not like people eat sweets instead of meals.'

Beth and I raised our eyebrows at each other. It wasn't like Harry to be supportive where I was concerned.

'Some might,' I said, coming to a standstill. 'I remember trying to persuade Celia once that strawberry-flavoured laces were practically a vegetable so I didn't have to eat my cabbage.'

'You could always start selling something else,' he added, spoiling the moment. 'There hasn't been a decent ice-cream place on the parade since Vincent's closed last year.'

'I heard rumours it's going to be a dance school,' Beth butted in. 'I'd go, wouldn't you, Marnie?'

'Why is ice-cream any better than sweets?' I said to Harry, refusing to be swerved. 'And anyway, ice-cream's more seasonal, which is why he went out of business. People want sweets all year round, and if it was good enough for my granddad—'

'Can't have it both ways,' he butted in. 'Maybe you should sell fruit and veg instead.'

'Harry!' Beth gave me an apologetic look, and for the hundredth time, I wished I could get to the bottom of Harry's ambivalence. Beth and I had discussed it once and she agreed to talk to him, but apparently he'd said I 'wasn't his cup of tea'.

'He's one of those people who doesn't like someone knowing her as well as he does,' Alex had concluded, when he first met Harry – at a fancy-dress party Beth had arranged for one of her history buddies; dress code, medieval (obviously). Beth and I went as wenches, Harry was in a codpiece and tights, and Alex was dressed as an ermine-cloaked aristocrat. Despite Harry's efforts to bond, Alex had been guarded on my behalf and conversation had stalled. We hadn't met up as a foursome again.

'People buy their fruit and veg at supermarkets,' I said to Harry, unwilling to give him the upper hand. 'And all I know about is sweets.'

'Maybe you need to think about a change of career.'

'Hey, whose side are you on?' said Beth, throwing a lollipop at him. He caught it deftly and threw me a grin that relaxed his face.

'You're the one who was complaining,' he said. 'Now, where do you want the new shelving unit?'

I showed him and stood back while he measured up, half-wishing Josh had stayed. He'd left at five, explaining he'd arranged to meet friends. I could hardly complain, especially as he'd reorganised the stockroom while the shop was quiet, and brought me several cups of coffee, reassuring me the woman who'd threatened me was just making empty threats.

'Watch this,' he'd said at one point, popping a jelly baby beneath each of our empty mugs, and somehow making one vanish.

'How do you *do* that?' I'd made him turn out his pockets to show they were empty.

'A magician never reveals his tricks,' he said, lifting the mug to reveal the jelly baby I'd thought had gone.

'You should do that for a living.'

'I'd love to,' he confessed. 'I quite fancy working on cruise ships, that way I'd see a bit of the world too.'

'So, why don't you?'

He looked bashful. 'I don't think I'm good enough yet. Plus the parents don't approve.'

'They should be proud.'

He'd given me a warm, appreciative look that had sent me scuttling to prop open the door to let some fresh air in.

A warm salty breeze was flowing through now, and the last of the day's sunshine had turned the beach a rich gold.

It really was the perfect spot to work, I reflected. My great-grand-father had known what he was doing when he bought the place back in the twenties. For a moment I felt the weight of history pressing down, and the importance of hanging onto it.

Avoiding Beth's speculative stare, I politely thanked Harry as he finished measuring up.

'I'll pop the quote in tomorrow,' he said, his gaze not quite meeting mine as he keyed some figures into his tablet computer.

I squashed down a flare of irritation at his off-hand tone, sensing Beth tensing up.

'Thanks,' I said coolly, locking up as we left the shop.

A gang of youths had congregated on the beach, laughing and shoulder-barging each other. Although I knew they were simply bored teenagers with nothing better to do, I didn't protest when Beth said pointedly that Harry would drop me home.

'Laura called,' Celia greeted me, placing a bowl of steamed chick-en with vegetables on the table as I entered the kitchen. Chester hovered, nose twitching, and she dished up another portion on his special china plate.

'Ooh, goody,' I said. My mother rarely called the house phone, in case she had to endure a tortured exchange with Celia, about the weather – if Celia was in the mood for talking. She'd recently discovered Skype, but hadn't quite got to grips with it, and for the first five minutes after calling, only her back-combed hive of hair had been visible on-screen, then she pressed the wrong key and cut us off. 'What did she want?'

'She wants you to call her back,' said Celia, lips pursed. I guessed they hadn't managed a cordial exchange, and wondered if they ever would.

As a child, I'd sometimes hear them arguing when I sneaked out onto the landing at Celia's. Peering through the banisters I'd see Mum's earrings swinging, her freckled shoulders bare in whichever dress she was wearing; usually something long and brightly patterned.

'It wouldn't hurt you to read her a story, before you go,' Celia said once in a tired sort of way. 'It's about time you started behaving like a mother.'

'Marnie's fine,' Mum had said, reaching for her tapestry-woven bag. I knew inside, among other things, was a tube of apricot lipstick called Hippie Chic, a powder compact, some spearmint chewing gum, and a bottle of scent she called patchouli, which smelt of nuts and spice. She'd talked me through each item once, scattering them across the kitchen table, and I'd wanted to snatch them up, like a magpie, and keep them.

'I don't know why you need to go out every night,' my grandmother said one evening, her hand pressing the front door. 'I suppose you're still looking for a man to make everything right.'

'I'm open to options from the universe, Ma,' Mum had said with a shrug. She never lost her temper, but although she took Celia's disapproval in her stride, she never acted as though she deserved it either. She was a 'free spirit' she'd say, blowing wherever the wind took her, and I'd imagine her as a leaf, fluttering away from me.

My grandfather always calmed things down with a careful word and a smile, while my mother shot into the night like a bird from a cage, and I'd feel her absence like a draught.

I sometimes wondered if it troubled Celia, that she could train a dog with simple commands, but couldn't control her daughter.

'Did she say anything else?' I asked now, as I tucked into my dinner. I'd decided not to tell her about Isabel Sinclair's visit to the shop, knowing it would only worry her.

'Nope.' Celia's grip tightened on her knife and fork, and I knew she wouldn't be drawn into further comment.

'Do you want me to let Chester out?' I said after we'd eaten and I'd washed the dishes – the one job she was happy to relinquish.

'I'll do it.' She rose from the table, more easily than she had in a while. 'I could do with a breath of fresh air.'

I watched her go out of the back door and into the garden, then snatched up the phone and ran to my bedroom to call Mum.

I flicked on my bedside light and sat on my unmade bed, and was about to dial her number when my mobile burst into life, on the dressing table where I'd left it charging.

Alex. My heart gave a thud. For a while we'd tried to keep in touch, but knowing he was so far away, having experiences we couldn't share, had proved too hard – it was like Mum, all over again. And as I was the one who'd insisted he go, I could hardly complain if he was trying to make the best of it.

Still, I felt a flare of longing as the phone screen flashed up his name.

No. I wouldn't be drawn in to talking to him.

There was no point.

I reached over and pressed the 'end call' button, then used the house phone to ring Mum.

'Marnie, sweetheart, how are you?' she cried, her raspy voice oozing warmth down the line. She always sounded delighted to hear from me, and a smile spread over my face.

'Celia said you'd called.'

Her voice became confidential. 'I hear you won an award!'

My smile broadened. 'How?'

'I was looking online for news back home, and came across the little television clip of your interview.'

'You were looking for news about Shipley?' This was unprecedented. Mum had spent so long wanting to escape it was hard to imagine her scouring websites for snippets about the town she once referred to as 'the seventh circle of hell'.

'I sometimes miss it,' she said, with a hint of defiance. I pictured her, lolling by a sparkling pool in her oversized shades and a kaftan, a sun-drenched olive grove in the background. Mario's family were wealthy wine-exporters, and Mum and Mario lived in a villa on the estate his father owned. Mum kept inviting me over, but as much as I was desperate to visit, I hadn't yet had the chance.

'You're living in Italian splendour, but you're missing Shipley?' I said, wondering if I'd got the right number.

'Look, I just wanted to say congratulations, that's all.' The words came out on a gusty sigh, and some deep-rooted instinct told me that all was not well in Mario-land. Their relationship had lasted longer than any she'd had before, and I'd let her convince me she'd found true love at last, but now I wasn't so sure.

'Well, thanks,' I said, knowing better than to ask. 'I didn't know anything about the competition, Beth entered on my behalf.'

'Good for her,' Mum approved. 'You deserve it, Marnie.'

There was something in her voice I couldn't remember hearing before . . . nostalgia? *Regret?* Surely she wasn't genuinely hankering for home?

'I'm still saving up to go travelling,' I told her, fidgeting up the bed and making myself comfortable. Downstairs, I could hear the *Coronation Street* music. It was the only thing Celia watched, apart from the news, and reruns of *The Dog Whisperer* featuring her hero, Cesar Millan. 'I thought I might start with Thailand.'

'Oh, Thailand.' I'd been hoping to prompt her favourite story, about the steamy summer she'd spent hiking through the jungle with her old friend, Dee, but she sounded as if I'd reminded her of a trip to the dentist's. 'Do you remember when we used to make sweets together?' she said, out of the blue.

'Of course I do.' A memory of pink and white coconut ice popped into my head. Batches and batches of it, laid out in foil trays that Mum brought home from the supermarket in Weymouth where she'd worked briefly, when I was eight or nine. 'I ate so much of it, I was sick.'

'Me too,' said Mum, with her throaty laugh. I imagined her head thrown back, revealing her long, slender neck. 'And the fudge! Do you remember the fudge?'

'Oh god, yes.' A smile tugged at my mouth. 'You wanted to invent a new flavour, and kept adding different ingredients . . .'

'Chilli powder, Marmite, pecans!' Mum took the baton and ran with it. 'The pecans worked really well actually. The strawberry jam, less so.'

She sounded animated. I'd forgotten how much she'd liked cooking, when she was in the mood. Sometimes I helped, but I'd loved to sit and watch her, the tip of her tongue poking out in concentration, and sometimes we sang along to one of her country and western CDs. We'd sample the results together, laughing and exclaiming with excitement when one of her 'experiments' worked.

'You were ahead of your time,' I said, admiring my coral toenails. 'Everyone's adding chilli and salt to chocolate now.'

'Those were the days,' she said, and hearing the smile in her voice I felt close to her, as if we'd been transported back to that tiny, steamy kitchen in the cluttered flat above the supermarket where we'd lived when she was seeing the manager, Derek; a kind man who'd tried to be fatherly.

'Good times,' I said. *If you ignored the bit where she dumped him and we had to move out.*

There was the sound of ice-cubes in glasses clinking in the background, followed by the low rumble of a man's voice.

'I'm so jealous of you, being over there,' I said.

She gave a heartfelt sigh. 'My dinner's ready, sweetheart,' she said, still with a trace of wistfulness. 'Got to go.'

Abruptly, the dialling tone sounded in my ear.

'Bye,' I murmured, unsettled by her tone.

For a long moment I stared at my bathrobe, hanging on the back of my bedroom door, while outside the window the sunset streaked the sky crimson.

An idea was taking shape for the sweet shop.

I got off the bed, pulse pattering, and paced the rug by my bed.

'What if I make my own sweets?' I said, aloud.

'Great idea,' replied a tinny voice.

I spun around, clutching my throat.

'Sorry, but I couldn't help overhearing.'

What the hell? It sounded like Alex.

Pulse bouncing I snatched up my phone, realisation dawning.

I hadn't ended his call earlier.

I'd answered it.

Chapter 9

'Why did you stay on the line?'

'I know I shouldn't have,' said Alex, an apology in his warm-caramel voice. 'I shouted your name a couple of times and I was going to hang up, then I realised you were talking to your mum and couldn't resist listening in.' He'd always been honest to a fault.

'You heard everything?' Heat shot to my face at the thought that I could have been talking about him.

'Well, only your side of things.'

'*Ob*viously.'

'I was going to stop, but I really wanted to talk to you.'

'Alex . . .'

'I know, I know,' he said, and I pictured him threading his fingers through his hair, the way he used to. He'd grown it longer since leaving, and it suited him. Beth had showed me a photo on his Twitter feed, and I'd stared at it for ages, torturing myself that he looked happier without me.

'So, what's with the homemade sweets?' he said, his familiar Dorset lilt – no hint of an American twang – shredding my resolve to be firm.

I ended up back on the bed, telling him about my award, and the newspaper article, and the woman who'd called me a sugar monster.

'She's clearly the monster,' he said, with gratifying outrage. 'How bloody rude.'

'I'm trying not to take it seriously,' I said, thinking of Josh's reaction. 'But Mum just reminded me that we used to make sweets when I was little, and it gave me the idea of making some for the shop. If I could adapt them and use less sugar.'

He seemed to consider for a moment. 'That could work,' he said. 'At least you'll have some control.'

I was glad he got it, rather than trying to talk me out of it, and decided not to remind him I was a terrible cook. I couldn't even toast bread without burning it.

'Do you remember when you tried to make caramel and it turned into lava?' So, he hadn't forgotten. 'I can't even remember *why* you were making it.' He sounded like he was trying not to laugh.

'I was concocting a sticky toffee pudding,' I said, wincing at the memory. 'But I didn't have the right ingredients.'

'You should get a recipe book, do it all by the letter.'

'I think my mum had one.' I could see it suddenly – bright red cover, well-thumbed pages. 'I'm sure it belonged to Celia.'

'You should see if she's still got it.'

Silence fell as if he'd suddenly remembered we weren't a couple any more.

'What time is it there?' I said, hearing the music downstairs that signalled the end of *Coronation Street*. 'Shouldn't you be working?'

'Half-three,' he said, and I could tell he'd flicked his wrist up to look at the gold watch his dad had given him for his twenty-first birthday. 'I've got the day off,' he said.

'It must be so great over there,' I said, trying to picture it, as I had so many times.

'Well, it's just work.' His voice sounded a bit flat. 'I mean, I love the job, but I could be anywhere now the novelty's worn off.'

'Isn't your contract nearly up?'

'Yeah,' he said. 'There's another job coming up in Canada . . .'

'Canada, that's amazing!' I felt like crying. Though whether it was the thought of him travelling without me, or because it meant he might never come back, I couldn't tell.

'It's a job, Marnie.' He sounded the teensiest bit exasperated now. 'You always think something amazing is happening on the other side of the world, but it's just people working and doing normal stuff.'

'Yes, but in fantastic surroundings!'

'Anyway, I'm not taking the job.'

'You're not?'

In the pause that followed I guessed what was coming, and my body grew as taut as a violin string. It was the thing I'd been dreading since he left.

'I'm coming home for a few days next Friday,' he said, and I silently breathed out my relief. 'It's my parents' thirtieth anniversary and they're having a party.'

'I know,' I said brightly. I'd got on well with Max and Helen and they were upset when Alex and I broke up. 'I got my invite last month.' I didn't add that I'd hoped he might turn up. He'd probably guessed.

My heart lifted as I imagined falling into his arms to a string accompaniment, and kissing that tender spot on his neck that made him groan.

'The thing is, Marnie, I've . . . I've met someone.' He stumbled over the words and cleared his throat. 'She'll be coming with me.' My spirits slammed down again. 'And that's why I've decided to stay in New York.'

'That's . . . that's lovely,' I managed. My heart was kick-boxing my ribs. 'What's her name?'

He hesitated. 'Bobbi-Jo. With an i not a y.'

'Wow.'

'I know,' he said, a little bashful. 'But she didn't choose her name.'

'It just sounds so . . .' I was going to say American, but didn't want to sound bitchy. 'Wholesome.' It still sounded bitchy. 'Do you work together?'

I didn't know why I was asking. The reality of him doing things with Bobbi-Jo – things he'd once done with me – was worse than I'd imagined. There was an actual ache in my chest, as though someone was squeezing my heart.

'Definitely not,' he said, as though the idea amused him. 'She's my housemate's sister, actually. We met at a barbecue. She's a nurse.'

Brilliant. She might have a silly name, but she saved people's lives for a living. No poisoning children with sugar for the saintly Bobbi-Jo. 'Lovely!' I chirruped. 'What an amazing job!' *Ugh.* I was talking in exclamation marks again. 'So, how old is she?'

As if it mattered. Bobbi-Jo would get to hear Alex's jokes, see the way his eyes crinkled when he laughed. She'd watch him topple over trying to put his socks on in the mornings, and smile when he brought her a cup of coffee in bed. She'd discover he drank hot water with a tot of whiskey when he had a cold, because he swore it made him feel better, and that he once ran naked down Wareham High Street for a bet, and got cautioned by the police. She'd get to cuddle into him in the mornings, and feel his strong arms close around her last thing at night.

'She's thirty-five, divorced, and has a five-year-old son.'

'Oh.' Emotions clumped in my chest. I desperately wanted to say something positive, but could only manage a half-hearted, 'Well, it'll be good to meet her.'

It wouldn't. In fact, I probably wouldn't go to his parents' anniversary party after all. I wasn't ready to see Alex playing happy families.

'Marnie, I . . .'

'Sorry, Alex, I've got to go. Celia's calling me,' I lied, blinking back hot tears. I didn't want to cry any more over Alex and, besides, crying made my face swell up.

'OK then.' He sounded disappointed. I probably hadn't responded enthusiastically enough to him finding his future wife. 'How is she?'

You don't get to ask me things like that any more. 'Fine,' I said shortly. 'Thanks for calling, have a nice day.'

I rang off, and opened a photo file on my phone called Marlex – a mashup of our names that had seemed hilarious at the time.

The first picture was of Alex, looking serious in headphones in the studio News South-West. He'd invited me to watch him at work and I'd sneakily snapped a photo, proud of how popular and clever he was, and how seriously he took his job. In the next picture we were on a boat on the Amazon, tanned and smiling, our heads close together. Alex looked sexy with a half-grown beard, and I was having a good fringe day despite the humidity.

The third picture was taken the winter it had snowed. Alex had made a snowman in his back garden, and put the carrot somewhere suggestive. He was wearing a woolly scarf and hat, and his eyes were bright with laughter.

I closed the file and chucked my phone on the floor.

'Everything OK?' Celia was on the sofa when I entered the living room, her feet up on a pouffe, flicking through *Dog Monthly*. Chester gave me a cursory glance from the rug, his tail thumping a greeting.

'I'm fine,' I said, plumping a couple of cushions with unnecessary force. Mum had made the chintzy covers during a 'nesting' phase, and although the stitching was wonky with stuffing poking through, it spoke volumes to me that Celia had kept them.

She looked at me over her reading glasses. 'You look flustered.'

'Alex has met someone,' I blurted out, turning the television volume down. 'I'm just letting it sink in.'

'Oh dear.' She put her magazine down, and pulled her glasses to the end of her nose. 'Well, it had to happen sooner or later,' she said. 'At least you can move on now.'

'I don't want to move on,' I said, feeling a childish urge to throw myself at her and let her cuddle everything better. 'I thought he loved me.'

'He does,' she said matter-of-factly, patting the seat beside her. 'But you made it clear you didn't want him, so what could he do?'

'What?' I dropped down and stared at her. 'Of course I wanted him!'

'Then why didn't you go to America with him?'

Was she being serious? 'I had to look after you.'

'But you didn't *have* to, Marnie.' She adopted the low, soothing tone she used to calm excitable terriers. 'I told you I'd be fine, but you chose to stay.'

I dropped my eyes from her probing gaze. How could I tell her that going, after everything she and Gramps had done for me, was unthinkable? She'd broken her leg, she lived alone now, and I wouldn't have enjoyed a second of being in America, knowing I'd left her like that.

'You could have gone once I was better,' she said, with her uncanny ability to read my thoughts.

'There was the shop,' I said, crossly. 'I could hardly leave it to run itself.'

'Ah, yes.' Her eyes grew round. 'The shop.'

'What's that supposed to mean?'

She looked as if she was weighing up her words. 'Maybe you used it as an excuse, because you didn't want to be with Alex any more.'

I blinked a couple of times. 'That's just not true.'

'But you don't really like working there.'

My mouth dropped open. Was this some weird side effect of the painkillers she'd been taking? 'It doesn't matter whether I like it or not,' I said. 'Mum was never going to take it on, Uncle Cliff and my cousins weren't interested, so that left me.'

'So you feel a sense of duty?'

'Well yes, I suppose so, but not in a bad way.' I felt suddenly close to tears, my memory stretching back to me and Gramps behind the counter, his comforting smell of barley sugar and soap as he taught me to weigh out sweets, and his shiny-eyed pride whenever a customer complimented him on his 'little helper'.

'*That young lady will be running rings round you one day, Len.*'

That had been Doris's husband, Roger, in his police uniform, come to buy a pound of Army & Navy sweets for his cough.

'You never *look* very happy,' Celia persisted.

'That's just my face,' I said, blinking away the past. 'I always look miserable when I'm not smiling. It's called "resting bitch face".' I'd read it on the *Mail Online*.

'What absolute nonsense,' Celia scoffed, examining my features more closely. 'Your face is lovely.'

'*You* didn't want to work at the shop.'

'No,' she said simply. 'It was Leonard's passion, not mine, and that was fine.'

'Do you think selling sweets is immoral?'

Her eyebrows drew together. 'Immoral?' She pulled her chin in. 'That's the second silliest thing I've ever heard,' she said, dusting dog hairs off her trousers. 'I love sweets as much as the next person. I just didn't want to be stuck indoors all day.'

'Well, now I've won that award, I'm thinking of doing something new there,' I said, determined to steer her away from the subject of Alex and whether or not I was happy. Romantic love must seem like an ancient concept to her now; she was probably too old to remember how it worked.

'What sort of new?' she said. 'Don't let a prize go to your head, Marnie. Things have worked perfectly well at the shop all these years.'

'I know, but I was thinking of selling some homemade sweets.'

'Homemade . . .?'

I cut her off before she could launch into why it was a bad idea. 'You had some recipes, do you remember? Mum used them, and I helped her sometimes.'

'She did?' Her eyebrows did a disbelieving wriggle. 'They'll be in the kitchen, I expect.'

Feeling better I shot through, and found it crammed on a shelf with the others that Celia had collected over the years. Not a proper cookery book, as I'd suspected – more of a notebook, filled with handwritten scribbles.

'Oh that one,' said Celia, coming through and frowning at the pile of books I'd scattered on the kitchen table. 'That one belonged to *my* mother.'

'Coconut ice,' I murmured, flipping through pages of scrawled ink in various colours. It was a shame there were no pictures, but I could see the coconut ice vividly in my mind.

'Here it is! Look!' I flapped the page at Celia, who pulled her glasses back on.

'Oh yes.' She grimaced. 'I ate so much of the stuff when I was little it put me off for life. Probably why I've never made it myself.'

'So, what do you think?' I said. She looked at me as if I was talking Mandarin. 'About making it for the sweet shop?'

'There'll be regulations about that sort of thing.'

'I know that,' I said. 'It shouldn't be a problem.'

I carried on flicking through the book. *Nut brittle, brownie-bites, caramel thins, strawberry fudge* . . . hang on. They weren't any healthier than the sweets we already sold. I would have to replace the sugar with something else. What, I wasn't sure. Kale was the latest super-food, but I was fairly positive you couldn't make sweets with it.

'But what's wrong with the sweets you already sell?' Celia's gaze grew suspicious. 'It's not like there isn't enough choice already, and you've just won a competition. You don't *need* to do anything different.'

I feigned fascination in the recipe, not wanting to tell her about Chris Weatherby's article in *The Shipley Examiner*, or Isabel Sinclair's visit. 'It's the best time to try new things,' I improvised, 'when we've got new customers checking out the shop.'

Celia was studying me forensically and my cheeks began to throb with colour. I was hopeless at lying, but I couldn't tell her the real reason. I wouldn't put it past her to call the newspaper editor, to put her own point of view across, which was bound to make things worse, and the stress might set back her recovery.

'I'm not ill, I broke my leg,' she said, as if my thoughts had flashed in lights across my face. 'I can handle you making some changes, if you really want to.'

Phew. 'Harry's going to give the shop a facelift,' I confided, keen to move the conversation along.

To my surprise, a shadow passed over her face.

'He'll do it cheaper than anyone else,' I added, knowing it would appeal to her sense of frugality.

'I'm sure he will,' she said stiffly.

I suddenly remembered she'd had a run-in with Harry's father, Steven, a couple of years ago, over payment for several sessions with a nervous Alsatian he'd bought. Celia had got really tough with him then, but even before that, she'd never seemed to like him very much; I was surprised he'd even asked her to train his dog.

'I don't know what you've got against Steven Fairfax, he's lovely,' I said. In fact, Harry's dad had always been far nicer to me than Harry was. If he'd spotted me next door, at Beth's house, he always used to ask after my family. She'd said he probably felt sorry for me, because I didn't have a dad. When I was a bridesmaid at Beth and Harry's wedding, he'd become emotional after a few drinks at the reception, and said if I wanted someone to walk me down the aisle one day, he'd be honoured.

'Hmm,' said Celia. Her face had settled into wrinkles of tiredness. 'It's up to you what you do, Marnie. I'll support you, you know that.'

I did, but as I watched her limp towards the dining room, which we'd fashioned into a makeshift bedroom until she could manage the stairs again, I had the strangest feeling she was hiding something from me.

Chapter 10

'Make your own sweets?' Josh's expression suggested I was deranged. 'Why bother?'

'They'll be healthier,' I said, my sudden rush of euphoria fizzling into flatness. Based on nothing tangible, I'd expected him to be as enthusiastic about the idea as I was. 'I can use sugar alternatives, like maple syrup, and stevia, and other sugar-free . . . well, sugars.'

I'd looked it up online the night before, then lain awake for hours, fixated on images of ribbon-wrapped cellophane bags, stuffed with handmade delicacies, a queue of customers snaking out of the shop, and Sandi Brent falling over herself to interview me again.

At least it had stopped me dwelling on Alex's bombshell. If my mind switched from sweets for a nano-second, I started creating images of Alex and Bobbi-Jo, wafting down the aisle in their wedding finery, a cute little page-boy with a bowl-cut trailing behind.

At one point, I got out of bed and stood at the window, watching the moonlight cast a silvery light across the landscape.

Celia was wrong, I'd thought, pressing my forehead against the cool glass. I *had* wanted to go to America with Alex; it was just that the timing had been all wrong.

'I need to show I'm taking the public's concerns seriously,' I said to Josh, shaking off thoughts of Alex. 'You heard that woman yesterday.'

'It was just one woman, and she was bluffing,' he said easily, filling up a jar with chocolate limes. They were a line that Hancock's hadn't stocked, and I'd been thinking of putting them on promotion.

'I still think you should go back to your previous supplier,' he said, plucking out one of the sweets and rolling it under his nose, as if testing a cigar for quality. 'These don't smell fresh to me.'

How could he tell? 'I'm not going back to Hancock's,' I grumped. He'd been at the shop less than forty-eight hours and was already telling me what to do.

'Sorry,' he said with a penitent smile. How hadn't I registered those dimples in his cheeks? The sight of them melted my irritation. 'Will you make the sweets here?'

'There's no oven,' I pointed out. 'I thought I could make them at home and bring them in.' My enthusiasm levels were already starting to dip. It would be a lot of hassle, and I had no real idea what the process entailed.

As a child, I'd taken a trip with Gramps to see how sweets were made, but it had been a factory, with everything on an industrial scale: men in aprons and hats and gloves, stirring sugar and water in massive vats, and pouring it onto metal tables to cool.

'You'll have to contact the environmental health department,' Josh said, killing my domestic goddess vibe stone dead with his common sense.

'Whatever,' I said, heading for the office to fetch the float. 'I didn't say I was definitely going to do it, just that I'd had an idea.'

His hand shot out as I passed and closed gently around my arm. 'It was a good one,' he said, eyes penetrating and sincere. He smelt deliciously of the sea, and sunshine and lemons . . . *for god's sake, Marnie, get a grip.*

One minute, I was tearful over Alex, the next I was swooning over a man young enough to be my . . . younger brother. Only four years younger. And he seemed mature for his age. Apart from the skateboard, and his candy-pink T-shirt which bore the words *I'd like mornings better if they started later*, above a silhouette of a snoozing cat.

But age was only a number. And if Alex could move on, maybe it was time I did too. Not with Josh, obviously. Apart from anything he was my employee, and I knew better than to mix business with pleasure, and I didn't want anything long-term if I was planning on leaving soon . . .

'Are you OK?' Josh's face had folded into concern and I realised I was staring, as if he was a toffee I wanted to sink my teeth into.

'I'm fine,' I said, pulling my arm free and fleeing to the relative safety of the office.

'Oh, someone pushed this through the letterbox,' he said, holding out an envelope when I returned. I'd taken an extra minute to switch on the kettle in the kitchen and check my appearance, annoyed at my face's tendency to flush at the slightest provocation.

'It's a quote,' I said, recognising Harry's handwriting. Once I'd placed the float in the till I ripped the envelope open. He could have emailed, but Harry preferred to put things in writing. Beth once confessed he'd written her love letters when they were dating, but wouldn't let me read them no matter how much I begged.

'Quote?' Josh was eyeing another box of sweets with deep suspicion, as if it contained live snakes, instead of toffee éclairs.

'I'm giving the place a bit of a makeover,' I said, scanning the neatly written breakdown of work and materials, and total cost. It seemed pretty reasonable. I would have plenty of prize money left to reinvest in stock, and perhaps a new computer and website.

Looking up, I watched Josh's gaze sweep over the tired paintwork. 'Not much point if you're going to go out of business.'

It took me a moment to realise he was joking. 'Less of your lip, sir,' I said, making a mental note to call Harry and set a date to have the work done. 'Get those jars filled up and I might even pay you.'

'Pay me, how?' He quirked an eyebrow and my heart flipped over.

'In penny chews, of course.' Was he flirting? Was I? I was so out of practice, I couldn't tell.

'You spoil me,' he said, clutching his chest. 'I simply adore penny chews.'

I tried to stay on target. 'Actually, I'd better take your bank details later and get you on the system.'

'Say that again,' he said, leaning on the counter and making his eyes smoulder. 'I love the way you say, system.'

Shaking my head with mock indignation – definitely flirting – I flipped the door sign to open, then returned to the office to phone Harry.

Beth picked up. 'He's working, but I'll let him know you want to go ahead.' She sounded pleased. 'How's it going to happen?' she said. 'You'll have to close the shop.'

'Hmm, I'd rather not,' I said. 'Customers are fickle. They might go elsewhere.'

'Well you're shut on Sundays, I could see if he can do it then. He can get the team in, work fast.'

'That would be great.'

'You sound chirpy.' Beth's voice was loaded with curiosity. 'It's going well with my replacement, I take it?'

'He's called Josh,' I reminded her. 'And he's got nothing to do with how I'm feeling.'

'Really?'

'Really.' I paused. 'Alex has met someone.'

I heard Beth's intake of breath. 'Oh Marnie, I'm so sorry.'

Tears flew to my eyes. 'I didn't actually think he ever would,' I admitted, lowering my voice in case Josh could overhear. 'He's bringing her over to his parents' thirtieth anniversary.'

'Meeting the parents,' Beth said grimly. 'Must be serious.'

'Thanks for reminding me.'

'Sorry.' She sighed. 'So, will you go?' Beth knew I'd been hoping to see Alex, and that maybe he would tell me he was moving back. 'You could weigh up whether or not it's *really* serious between them.'

'No,' I said. 'I don't want to see them together, ever.' I sniffed, and dashed a hand over my face. 'It's time I moved on, anyway.'

'Well now you're an award-winning businesswoman you'll be fighting them off.' Her voice became brisk. 'You need to get back in the saddle, start dating again.'

'I never was any good at that,' I said, but my tears had dried. I prodded around my feelings a bit more, and found myself wondering whether Josh needed me out front. 'Listen, I'd better go,' I added.

'Great,' said Beth. 'I'll just hang around here, feeling like I'm going to burst any minute, while my mother-in-law tries to force me to eat cake.'

'So what's new?' I said.

'I could come and hang out there.'

'I thought you were studying.'

'I am, but not all day.'

'Well, what about baby stuff?'

'Not much more we can do. Harry's mum's transformed the back bedroom into a nursery, and is knitting up a storm.'

'Don't you mind not being in your own place yet?'

'Harry's doing his best,' she said, a little reproving. 'It wasn't his fault that planning permission took longer to come through than we thought.'

'So, daytime telly it is then.'

'Ooh, I could watch *The Tudors* on iPlayer.'

'Or you could watch Jeremy Kyle.'

She gasped. 'Not even if there was nothing else on television.'

I returned to the shop as two pimple-faced teenage boys entered, shouldering rucksacks, clearly late for school and not caring one bit. They were the same pair who'd annoyed Sandi Brent while she was interviewing me.

One of them already had the build and demeanour of a future cage-fighter, the other the skinny shoulders and arms of someone who hadn't grown into himself.

'Watch them,' I murmured to Josh, joining him behind the counter. When he didn't respond, I noticed a set of wires emerging from his ears. He caught my eye and did some body-popping, arms and legs contorting in a way destined to lead to arthritis.

'Pharrell,' he shouted, singing a bit of whatever he was listening to, badly out of tune.

Catching sight of him, the teenagers elbowed each other.

'What a knob,' said the big one, who had the most pimples. His whole face looked sore.

'He's pretty good, Biff,' his mate said, radiating envy. 'Wish I could do that.'

Biff snorted. 'Looks like he needs a doctor.'

While the pair of them cracked up, I snapped on a latex glove and pretended to be busy with a bowl of dolly mixtures on the counter, dipping my hand in and swirling it around.

'Not very hygienic, is it, miss?' said Biff, pushing his knuckles into his trouser pockets. They were school uniform trousers, but worn low, and his shirt had come untucked. 'I mean, wearing a glove's the same as using your hand, when you think about it.'

'She *is* using her hand,' his mate said, looking delighted by his own brilliance. 'I mean, she ain't got the glove on her foot.'

'Shut up, Daz, you retard.' Biff glowered at him. 'You know what I mean.' Daz looked crushed. 'I'm just saying, if she picks her nose, yeah, or, like, messes wiv 'er 'air, like, or scratches her arse wiv the glove on,' he stuck his bottom out and raked at it with his fingers, ''ow's that any different to using her bare 'and, like?' His grammar worsened as he warmed to his theme. 'I mean, what's the point of it, yeah?'

He feigned bewilderment, looking from Daz, to me, to Josh, who'd clearly reached some sort of musical climax as his eyes were screwed shut, hands beating a frantic tattoo on the counter with imaginary drumsticks.

'I think he's just wet 'imself,' said Daz, cracking a grateful grin when Biff roared with appreciative laughter.

'Nice one, mate!' he bellowed, slapping Daz's puny back. Daz winced, and staggered forward.

'Shouldn't you two be at school?' I asked, aiming for light and matey, and settling on frosty matron.

'Ooh, get her!' Biff clapped a grubby palm to his mouth, his sleep-encrusted eyes inviting Daz to join the joke. 'Been on telly once, and thinks she's that bird off *The Apprentice*,' he said through his fingers.

'But not as fit,' said Daz, eyes darting nervously, as if scared he'd gone too far.

'Oh, I don't know. She's got a nice pair of—'

'What's going on?' Finally emerging from his music-induced trance, Josh yanked out his earphones. 'Why are these two goons still here?'

'Good question,' I said, peeling off my glove. 'I think they're going to buy something on their way to school.' I gave Biff a hard stare, emboldened by the sight of my award certificate in the window. And maybe by Josh's presence. 'What will you have, boys?'

'It's sixth-form, actually, not school,' muttered Daz, seeming to shrink a little so his blazer looked too big. It occurred to me he might be a nice boy, away from the influence of Biff. 'I'll have some chocolate mice, please.'

'Loser,' said Biff into his fist, in the guise of a cough.

'Do you want anything?' Josh directed an icy gaze at Biff. His voice was calm, but I could easily imagine him vaulting over the counter and grabbing Biff in a headlock. Or maybe it was wishful thinking on my part.

'No thanks.' Biff's voice dripped scorn. 'My mum says sugar's bad for me.'

'It's probably the least of your problems,' Josh observed, placing a hand on his heart. 'You're in dire need of a personality implant.'

Biff's acne flushed an ugly crimson. 'You're not supposed to talk to customers like that,' he said. 'I hope this place does close down.' He backed away, almost toppling Daz in the process.

'Ow, that was my foot,' Daz protested, grabbing his bag of chocolate mice and throwing down a grubby two-pound coin, before stuffing the sweets in his rucksack.

Out on the pavement they flicked V-signs through the window, and as they drifted away the sound of their raucous laughter blended with the cry of a particularly cross-sounding seagull.

'Pair of idiots.' Josh shook his head. 'Fancy a coffee?'

'Go on then.' I kept my voice bright, but could feel my forehead sinking into a frown. Why had Biff left with that particular parting shot – as if he knew it would hurt? 'I'll have three sugars in mine, please.'

Chapter 11

'What's going on?' Celia entered the kitchen, giving a series of explosive coughs. 'Smells like the house is on fire.'

Smoke was seeping from the edges of the Aga. Eyes watering I opened the door, fumbling blindly inside.

'OW!' I spluttered, a string of expletives springing from my mouth as I flung the tray onto the worktop. I'd forgotten to put oven gloves on.

'Language,' said Celia, her cough miraculously easing.

I'd risen early to experiment with some sweet-making, and had nipped upstairs for a quick shower while the results were in the oven. I'd clearly overestimated the cooking time.

'What is it supposed to be?' said Celia, wiping her watering eyes with a sheet of kitchen roll.

'It was my version of coconut ice,' I said, thrusting my hand under the tap and jigging up and down on the spot. 'God, that stings.'

Celia flung open the window and huddled deeper into her dressing gown. 'The burnt version?' she said, eyeing the mess of charred cubes spilling across the worktop.

'I don't know what went wrong.' I couldn't believe I was still living up to my terrible-cook reputation. 'I had the right ingredients, and followed every step of the recipe.'

Celia fixed me with a stare. 'You don't *cook* coconut ice, Marnie,' she said. 'You do the opposite. You put it in the fridge.'

'*What?*' I grabbed a tea-towel and roughly bandaged my hand. 'But I did what the recipe said.'

Celia's face, puffy with sleep, was a picture of fond despair. 'Where is it?'

'Where's what?'

'The recipe.'

I nodded miserably at the table. 'On my laptop.'

Bending down, she read the screen. 'There are two recipes here,' she pointed out. 'One for coconut ice, and one for chocolate brownies. You must have got them confused.'

I let out a groan. 'I should have remembered,' I said. 'Mum never used to put it in the oven.'

Celia folded her arms. 'I thought you were going to use my mother's recipe book.'

'I wanted to update things,' I said, a sulky note creeping in. It was as if I was a teenager again, experimenting with my appearance and getting it wrong.

Celia turned back to the recipes. 'Organic?' She sounded vaguely disappointed, as if I'd been looking at porn. 'Why?'

'It's healthier,' I said, quickly tacking on, 'and probably better for the environment,' in an attempt to distract her.

She was reading the recipe out loud in a posh voice. 'Himalayan sea salt? Bee nectar? Beetroot, or raspberries, for colouring?'

'I thought you believed in natural ingredients,' I said, leaning over and slamming my laptop shut. 'Better than artificial food colouring.'

'Insects *are* natural,' she said, giving me a no-nonsense look. 'Ground-up bugs, that's all. Never did us any harm.'

'Actually, it explains a lot.'

'Cheeky.' She unwound the tea-towel and studied the pink patches of skin on the tips of my fingers. 'You'll live,' she said, giving my hand a squeeze. I tried not to scream.

'I haven't got time to make another batch,' I said.

Her eyes thinned. 'How much do these fancy ingredients cost?'

'Not much,' I said quickly. 'The big Tesco's has them all.' I'd caught the bus there after work the evening before, more certain than ever after Biff and Daz's departure that I wanted to try something different, despite Josh's reservations.

'Have you got enough to make some more?'

I looked at the packets and containers scattered around the kitchen. 'Probably,' I said, wondering how much profit I was going to make when the bee nectar alone had set me back almost eight pounds for a miniscule pouch.

'I could make it for you,' Celia offered, glancing at her elaborate wall planner, where the days were shaded in with different coloured pens. She'd never had any trouble filling her time before she'd broken her leg, and it looked like her schedule was piling up again. 'I'm seeing a Cavapoo at eleven, but otherwise I'm free.'

'What the heck *is* a Cavapoo?'

'A cross between a poodle and a King Charles Cavalier Spaniel,' she said, as though it was blindingly obvious.

'Does it belong to the woman who moved into Seaview Cottage recently?' I affected a casual tone as I scooped the burnt coconut and bee nectar (or honey, to us mortals) in the bin.

'That's her.'

Chester scratched the back door open, and Celia decanted some brisket into his bowl and anointed it with *jus* left over from last night's dinner. 'Her Cavapoo – Pollywollydoodle, would you believe? – isn't settling in, apparently.' She looked at me over her shoulder. 'Have you met her?'

'Not really,' I said, quickly. I didn't want to prejudice her against a potential client.

'She popped round after you'd gone to work.'

'Did she seem nice?'

'Oh, I don't know about that.' Her gaze swung to the ceiling, thinking. 'Actually, she was a bit snooty,' she said. 'Acted like she knew more than me, which begged the question, why did she want my help?'

'Did you ask her?'

'Of course I did.'

'And?'

'She apologised and said I'd been highly recommended.' She handed me a mug of tea, and I almost screamed again as my injured fingers closed around the scalding china. 'Why are you so interested in her, anyway?'

Transferring the mug to my other hand, I took a quick gulp. 'No reason,' I said, one eye on the clock.

'Doesn't look like she's done a day's work in her life.' Celia sniffed. 'She said she feeds the dog at the dining table.' Her eyes grew big. 'Is there any wonder they're having problems?'

'I heard she used to be a model.' I'd looked her up, but hadn't found any information online about her.

'Well, she's skinny enough,' said Celia. 'How's your hand?'

'It's OK,' I said. 'I'd better get to work. Sure you'll be . . .?'

'I'll be fine,' she said crisply, knowing what I was going to ask. 'My stick's in the hall, just in case.'

'Good.'

'I'll make some coconut ice then, shall I?'

'Actually, forget it.' I didn't want her doing too much too soon. 'I'll do it another time.'

Josh wasn't at the shop when I opened up but arrived ten minutes later, pink-faced and panting.

'Sorry I'm late,' he said, leaning over to rest his hands on his knees, hair flopping forward. 'A wheel fell off my skateboard so I had to run here.'

'That's a first,' I said, buoyed up by the sight of him. It occurred to me I hadn't told him what hours he should work. The truth was, I'd got used to opening the shop on my own and often working alone. Sometimes, Beth had turned up early, but mostly fitted work around her studying, which suited us both. Agnieszka often asked for more hours, so she could give up her other jobs, but I didn't feel there was enough to do to warrant taking on someone full-time.

But I already liked Josh being around. He brought something vital with him to the shop; a shot of energy I hadn't realised was missing. With our long-established friendship, Beth and I had been set in our ways and routines, and spent a lot of time chatting and drinking tea and coffee. Once, we had a Pilates session behind the counter while it was quiet.

'Hey, I was thinking we could wear these,' he said, pulling me out of my reverie. He was standing behind the counter, pulling on an apron. 'What do you think?'

'Where did you find that?' I said, staring. It looked identical to the one Gramps used to wear; yellow and white striped, like the awning we pulled down outside the shop, when the sun was so bright it hurt our eyes.

'It was in the stockroom, in one of the boxes,' he said, smoothing his hands down the front. 'I thought it might be a nice touch if we both wore them.'

Gramps had suggested the same thing, once. He'd had some made especially but I'd refused to wear mine. I couldn't tell him, but had felt that by putting it on I was accepting I was going to be at the sweet shop forever, part of the fixtures and fittings, and I couldn't bear it – not when I'd already told Mum I was planning to follow in her foot-steps, and visit all the countries she'd been to when she was younger.

Gramps had hid his disappointment well, but thinking about it now, tears prickled my eyes. Why couldn't I have worn the damn thing?

'Have I said something wrong?' Josh's hands paused in the act of stroking his chest.

'No, no, it's fine.' I blinked to clear my vision. 'It's a good idea, actually,' I said, making a split-second decision to wear the apron in memory of my grandfather. 'I think there's more out the back.'

'It also means we can wear what we like underneath,' Josh said, looking at my cornflower blue top and white skinny jeans. 'It'll save thinking what to put on in the mornings.'

'Is that something you struggle with then?' I said, moving away from the twin beams of his eyes. 'You don't strike me as having an extensive wardrobe.'

'That's the point,' he said, unruffled. 'I can wear the same thing every day, if I'm putting an apron on top.'

'That's fine, as long as you remember to shower.' My cheeks pulsed with colour. Why was I talking about him showering?

'I could even be naked underneath.' He unleashed a grin. 'The naked sweet shop assistant,' he said. 'Has quite a ring to it, don't you think?'

'Only the ring of someone calling the police, which is what will happen if Doris clocks your bare backside.' *No!* Why had I mentioned his bare backside?

As if wondering if he'd overstepped a line Josh held up his palms. 'How about I get the float, while you put the kettle on?' he suggested.

I smoothed my fringe and took a few steadying breaths, before switching my mind into business-mode.

The shop was unusually quiet all morning, so I busied myself looking over my website with a view to updating it, wincing every time my sore fingertips came into contact with the keyboard.

It would make sense to pay for it to be redesigned, as befitted an award-winning sweet shop, and could perhaps include a section for customers to leave feedback. Although, thinking of Isabel Sinclair, that might not be such a good idea.

Everything seemed to come back to either Chris Weatherby and his horrible article, or Isabel bloody Sinclair. I was starting to despise the pair of them, and was overcome with a fierce determination not to let them win.

'Why don't you get out for an hour while I keep an eye on things?' Josh suggested around lunchtime. 'You never seem to take proper breaks.'

'Beth used to pop up to Bob's Bakery for us,' I said, removing my apron. 'What about your lunch?'

'I can always nip out when you get back,' he suggested. It sounded so sensible I couldn't think of a reason to say no. I hadn't any qualms about leaving him in charge; especially after watching him earlier, charming twin toddlers with a magic trick, effortlessly making a chocolate bar disappear and reappear to their open-mouthed delight.

'He sounds too good to be true,' Beth said, rather grudgingly, when I phoned her on my way to buy a sandwich, which I intended to eat on the beach. The sun was streaming down from a cloudless sky, and there was a hint of summer in the air. It felt good to be outside.

'You're just jealous because he's more hard-working, better-looking, and less pregnant than you are,' I said.

'True.' She sighed. 'I'm struggling with Thesis,' she confessed. We'd started referring to it as a person; a demanding one that sucked up a lot of her time as she struggled with the topic: Katherine Parr, and the degree of her influence on politics and religion in the last years of Henry VIII's reign.

'I'm making Katherine sound boring as hell, and I've somehow drifted over to Anne Boleyn,' she said. 'Did you know, in a love letter, Henry referred to her breasts as "pretty duckies"?'

'Yuk.'

'Exactly,' she said. 'Nobody wants their boobs called that.'

'It was probably the "jugs" of its day.'

Beth snorted back a giggle. '*Nobody* calls them jugs.'

'Funbags?'

'Stop right now.' She released a sigh. 'I managed better when I had my little breaks at the sweet shop to look forward to.'

'My original point exactly,' I said. 'You regarded your *job* as a little break from studying.'

'You know you'd have gone mad without me.'

'True,' I conceded. 'You kept me in line. And in sandwiches.'

'But now you're award winning it's time to get serious?'

I thought for a moment. 'Something like that,' I said.

'Well good for you.' Beth sounded intrigued. 'It's about time.'

After choosing a chicken baguette at the bakery, I paused to admire the colourful buckets of flowers at the stall in the square, before wandering over to the beach. I was looking for somewhere to sit that didn't remind me of Alex, when I spotted a cluster of people on the pavement outside the sweet shop.

Straightening, I darted across the road, and narrowly missed being hit by a woman on a mobility scooter.

I couldn't leave Josh on his own. Not with that many customers queuing up.

But as I grew closer I realised they weren't customers. They were protestors, all women, some with toddlers, holding placards plastered with painted-on slogans – **Ban the Beachside Sweet Shop, Sugar is Poison** – and they were chanting the words out loud, fists punching the air for emphasis.

'There she is,' cried Isabel Sinclair as she saw me approaching, a malicious smile curving her perfectly proportioned lips.

Battling an urge to run in the opposite direction, I folded my arms around myself as I drew closer. 'What do you think you're doing?'

'What does it look like?' she said, sweeping towards me in tight, cream jeans and a fine-knit jumper, almost buckling under the weight of her placard. It looked professional; as if she'd sat up all night making it. 'I'm getting you closed down.'

Chapter 12

'I'll call the police and have them moved on,' said Josh. He looked older when he wasn't smiling. Still handsome, but stern, with brackets around his mouth.

'I've a feeling she'd love that,' I said, watching Isabel sashay about like one of those ladies at boxing matches, holding aloft a card announcing the next round. 'She'll flutter her eyelashes and they'll be eating non-sugary products out of her hand.'

'But isn't there a law against protesting?' Josh persisted, arms folded across his chest.

'I don't think so, as long as they're not violent.' I was touched by his concern.

'I'm sure there must be.'

'You're probably thinking of begging,' I said, plucking a couple of sweet wrappers off the floor and dropping them in the bin, to show Isabel I wasn't remotely bothered by her presence. 'You can only beg if you play a musical instrument, because then it's called busking.' I'd picked up that morsel from *Police Interceptors*, the only programme I could bear to watch after Alex left. I'd become horribly addicted for a while. 'That's why homeless people carry mouth organs, to blow into if they see a police officer approaching.'

'They also make more money if they have a dog,' Josh said, momentarily diverted. 'Have you noticed, the dogs always look incredibly well fed?'

'Even the homeless put their dogs first,' I said, thinking of Celia's tendency to put Chester's needs ahead of everyone else's. 'It's because they don't have a choice, I suppose.'

'So you're going to let them carry on?'

'Begging?' I was momentarily confused.

'Protesting.' Josh returned his gaze to the window, where one of the women – a tanned brunette in animal print leggings – caught his eye and winked. She was old enough to be his mother.

'They'll get fed up if we ignore them,' I said, with more conviction than I felt. Surely Isabel had better things to do. Who was looking after her toddler? And Pollywollydoodle? Unless, this morning, Celia had trained the dog to babysit.

'What do you want me to do?' asked Josh, a frown hovering over his brow. I had the sense he was holding back – that he'd like to storm outside and scatter the women like birds.

I held up the bag containing my uneaten baguette. 'You could go out the back and eat this.'

His face brightened. 'Don't you want it?'

'I ate mine on the way back,' I lied, not wanting to admit I'd lost my appetite, thanks to Isabel Sinclair. 'I got this one for you.'

'Cool,' he said, taking the bag and peering inside. He inhaled, eyes shut. 'How did you know chicken was my favourite?'

'Lucky guess,' I said, envious his mood could be so easily restored. 'Go on,' I said as he hesitated. 'I'll be fine.'

'You sure?' He backed away, narrowing his eyes at the window. 'Yell if you need me.'

'I will.'

As he disappeared, the shop door opened to admit a middle-aged man, wearing too-short shorts in honour of the sunny weather. They were made of flimsy nylon, in emerald green with white piping, at odds with the chunky sports socks hugging his ankles. At least he wasn't wearing sandals.

'What's all that about?' he said, nodding to the women outside. They were drawing attention and a crowd had gathered. One of the women was handing out flyers, while another talked animatedly to a passer-by with a toddler balanced on her hip, sucking a carrot. She pointed at me through the window, her round face scrunched with disgust.

Panic rolled in my stomach. What was she saying? Was I really so terrible that she had to make a face like a bulldog chewing a wasp?

'They're protesting about me selling sweets,' I said stiffly. There was no point lying. Unless he couldn't read, it was glaringly obvious from the placards. 'Because of the sugar.'

'They wouldn't be sweets without it,' he said benignly. I wanted to lean over and hug him, in spite of the damp patches spreading from the armpits of his shirt. 'I'll take a pound of toffee whirls please.' His bottom lip popped out as he turned to look out of the window. 'Actually, make that two,' he said. 'I'm not going to be dictated to by a bunch of bored housewives.'

'Bravo!' I said – the first time I'd ever uttered the word – and added some extra toffees to show my gratitude.

Hope welled inside me. Maybe Isabel's plan would backfire. People didn't like being preached to, or told what to do.

'What's the flyer for?' I asked, noticing he had one scrunched in his hand as he wrenched a five-pound note from his bum-bag.

'Haven't a clue, love,' he said, handing it over with his money. 'Unless it involves golf, Morris dancing, or chess, I wouldn't be interested.'

'Shouldn't you check?' I joked, counting out his change.

His face grew hostile. 'That's right,' he said. 'Always make fun of the Morris dancer.'

'Oh no, I wasn't . . . I mean . . .' But he'd stomped out, leaving behind a scent of sweat and fury.

'For god's sake,' I muttered. 'Get a sense of humour.'

I smoothed out the flyer on the counter and read:

For more information about keeping your loved ones healthy and SUGAR-FREE, as well as my witty observations about life as a busy mum in a small seaside town, read my blog at www.izzywizzymummysbusy.co.uk Book deal coming soon . . .

The bitch.

'Josh!' I called.

He hurtled through, creating a draught that blew his hair off his face. 'What is it?' His eyes darted around as if seeking the armed intruder I must have apprehended.

'This.' I stabbed the flyer with my finger and almost screamed in agony. 'She's promoting her blog,' I said in outraged tones. 'I reckon that's why she's doing this.'

'Who?' Josh was still looking around for marauders.

'Isabel bloody Sinclair.' Blood was hurtling round my body, unsure where to settle. 'It looks like she's hoping to get some sort of book deal and I'm her "theme".' I scraped quote marks in the air.

'Who's Isabel Sinclair?' Josh's bemusement would have been comical if I hadn't been so wound up.

'She is!' I pointed to the window to see some of the mums had lost momentum and were chatting, placards propped on the ground. One was fighting a seagull, swooping to steal her toddler's rusk, while another flicked through pictures on her phone. Only Isabel looked truly committed, waving her flyers and waggling her placard to grab the attention of passers-by.

'Isabel Sinclair,' I enlightened Josh. 'She lives near me, has problems with her Cavapoo.'

'Sounds painful.'

'It's a *dog*.'

'Really?'

'A cross between a spaniel and a cockatoo.'

Josh scratched the top of his head. 'I think I'm missing something.'

I let out a puff of distress. 'She's using me as publicity.'

Comprehension swept over his face. 'Ah,' he said. 'I get it.'

Propelled by a desire to wipe the supercilious look off Isabel's face, I dived for the door.

'Can I have your attention?' I yelled, feeling like I'd stepped onstage at the O2. What felt like a thousand pairs of eyes swivelled towards me and in their midst I recognised those of Chris Weatherby, the reporter from *The Shipley Examiner*.

Had Isabel invited him down?

'You're going to try and convince us your sweets are healthy?' she said, treating me to a hard, unblinking stare.

'My sweets are meant to be treats,' I said, trying to quell the wobble in my voice. 'They shouldn't be eaten every day.'

Chris Weatherby inched forward, smart-phone extended, presumably recording me. 'But by having sweets readily available on a popular route into town with schools nearby, how can you live with yourself?' he said, radiating a sickly earnestness.

Oh, for god's sake. I wasn't selling cigarettes and whiskey to toddlers.

My mind flailed for a solution and appeared to find one. 'I'd like to make an announcement,' I said, which was news to my own ears never mind anyone else's. Clammy-faced, I broadened my smile.

'You're closing down?' Chris Weatherby's deep-set eyes gleamed with malice. I stared at the wispy goatee, clinging for dear life to his chin, and longed to yank it off.

'Just the opposite,' I said hotly, as Josh came to stand beside me in a gesture of solidarity. 'After winning independent business, sweet shop . . . woman, I mean, owner of the year,' *was that right?* 'I've been inspired to make some changes. The shop, which has been an important part of Shipley life for several generations, is to have a makeover.' A buzz ran round the crowd. 'That will be happening on Sunday,' oh god, I hadn't even checked with Harry, 'and on Bank Holiday Monday I'm going to hold a taster session for my own range of low-sugar, handmade sweets, adapted from a family recipe book, with a view to selling them alongside our existing sweets.'

As I ran out of breath, I noticed a splodge of red had appeared on Isabel's creamy throat.

'What?' she barked. 'Do you have experience of making your own?'

'I know what I'm doing,' I lied, lifting my voice above the roar of questions being lobbed at me.

'Won't they be out of most people's price range?' She looked around for vindication.

'The taster session will be free,' I blurted. 'And anyway, I'm sure people don't mind paying for something that's homemade . . . with love.'

I could almost hear her grinding her perfect teeth as onlookers showed signs of interest.

'So what will you use instead of sugar?' one asked.

'Will you be making them on the premises?'

'Will they be replicas of the sweets you already sell?'

'Come down on Monday and try them,' I suggested, encompassing everyone in what I hoped was an encouraging gaze. 'You can write about it on your blog,' I added to Isabel, and immediately wished I hadn't. I didn't want to give her any more publicity.

'Oh I will,' she said silkily. 'You can be sure of that.'

'Why are you working for her?' This was to Josh from the slinky brunette, her gaze openly lustful. 'I could find you something to do at my house, if you're desperate for work.'

'Bloody sexist,' Josh muttered.

'I bet he looks like that actor from *Poldark* with his shirt off!'

Isabel scowled her annoyance at the woman. 'I think we're straying from the point here.'

'Marnie's a great boss,' said Josh, placing a protective hand on my shoulder and squeezing it gently. 'I've only been here a short while, but I'm looking forward to working with her over the summer.'

I glanced at him, just as a camera flash went off.

Bloody Chris Weatherby.

'So, a free taster session on Bank Holiday Monday?' he clarified, into his phone.

'That's right!' The clammy feeling had spread to my armpits. 'I'll expect to see you there.' *Unfortunately.*

'Are you sure about this?' Josh said out of the side of his mouth.

'It's too late now,' I muttered.

Sensing more questions coming, I ducked into the shop before my confidence collapsed like a soufflé.

As the protestors drifted away, Isabel threw a smug smile my way as she linked her arm through Chris Weatherby's, and whispered something that made him fondle his goatee in a thoughtful fashion.

'I don't think you should pander to them,' Josh said, following me in. 'None of these people care what she has to say.'

'She won't give up.' I recalled her dog-with-a-bone expression. 'She looks like someone used to getting her own way.'

'I think you'll find Shipley folk have more sense,' he said, exaggerating his Northern accent.

I wasn't so sure. 'I need to check out her blog,' I said. 'See what she's saying.'

Leaving Josh to serve the few stragglers who drifted in once the protestors had gone, I grabbed the crumpled flyer off the counter, switched on the computer and found the website.

It was all pastel shades and loopy fonts, with a photo at the top of a make-up-free Isabel in nerdy glasses, sucking a sludge-coloured smoothie through a straw.

There weren't that many posts and most were mummy-based, littered with exclamations marks, and thrillingly titled:

We love creamed spinach with rice!
Don't forget to carve out some me time!
How I got back in my size 6 skinnies!!

There were photos of baby Fitzgerald, looking cute in a series of Baby Gap outfits, and lots of random fashion tips: *Feminise your boyfriend blazer with a clutch! Florals are a girl's best friend!* Her mother had commented, *Never mind florals, darling, when are we going to see baby Fitz? Your father didn't mean it when he said he'd cut you out of the will, so stop being a silly girl.*

There was nothing to attract a book deal as far as I could tell, until the day of my appearance on News South-West, which was when she must have miraculously found her focus.

Under the heading 'SUGAR MONSTERS' she'd written, *Local sweet shop wins best business award? Really?? A friend of mine – also vegan by the way, try it, you won't look back! – agrees with Sir Jamie Oliver, that we should all be sugar-free, and I have to say I agree. We shouldn't be celebrating Marnie Appleton, folks, we should be warning people about her!*

So it wasn't even her idea. She'd stolen it from a friend – and Jamie Oliver. But it had attracted the attention of someone called Clive who'd commented, *That's more like it Izzy. Find an angle and we'll talk publication* ☺

After the article in *The Shipley Examiner*, she'd written, *Looks like I'm not the only one concerned for the health and wellbeing of our children – and our nation. This calls for action, folks. I can feel a healthy recipe book coming on!* Chris Weatherby had commented, *You go girl. Look forward to interviewing you when it comes out xx*

'Turncoat,' I muttered.

'That bad?' said Josh, screwing the lid on a jar of jelly snakes.

'She wasn't even a very successful model,' I said, clicking on a few links. 'Apart from a *Vogue* shoot in her twenties, she's better known for an ad campaign for yoghurt.'

Josh's eyes lit up. 'The one where she smears it all over herself, thinking it's sun-cream, and that chiselled bloke with the hair starts licking it off?' He grinned. 'I *thought* I recognised her.'

'Traitor.' I logged off before he could ogle the images. 'I think I'll take the morning off tomorrow and practise making some sweets.' I hadn't mentioned my already disastrous attempt.

'Oh.' Dismay clouded his face. 'Don't you think you should be here, showing your customers you don't give a damn about her?' he said. 'What will they think?'

'They'll think I'm at the dentist,' I said. 'Especially if you tell them.'

He looked at me from under his eyebrows. 'Do you think that's the best option under the circumstances?'

Fair point. 'Optician's then.'

He looked like he wanted to protest, but instead said, 'Well you'd better leave me the keys, and the code for the alarm so the police don't turn up and arrest me.'

Chapter 13

As I walked into the kitchen the following morning, Doris Day looked round from the Aga, where she was stirring something in a pan.

'Have you left that young man in charge of the shop again?'

'Yes I have,' I said, zipping my onesie up to my neck and shuffling my feet into Celia's sheepskin slippers. 'He knows what he's doing.'

'He's very handsome, isn't he?' She gave a little hip wiggle. 'Quite the stud.'

Ew. 'What are you doing here, Doris?'

Celia was in the garden, conducting a puppy-training session, a series of yaps and reprimands drifting through the back door.

'I came to see if your grandmother needed anything,' Doris said, looking at home as she rinsed a couple of mugs at the sink, and passed a cloth over the worktop. 'Just doing my bit.'

'That's kind of you,' I said. She did make a good cup of tea, and she'd constructed a pan of fluffy scrambled eggs.

'Have some,' Doris urged, spooning some onto a plate.

We stood side by side at the window while I ate, watching Celia instruct several owners to bring their puppies to heel, demonstrating her well-worn technique on a cute retriever.

'She's looking much better,' Doris observed.

Celia was using her walking stick as she moved up and down, seeming to rather enjoy flourishing it about.

'You'll soon be able to join that young man of yours in . . . where is it?' Doris cocked her head and looked at me sideways. 'China.'

She clearly knew where it was, though I was sure Celia hadn't told her. How Doris came by her information was a mystery.

'I won't be going to America,' I said bluntly, putting my plate down, appetite fleeing. 'He's met someone else.'

Damn. Still, it was hardly a secret.

'I'm sorry to hear that,' Doris said, continuing her bustle around the kitchen, putting away cups and plates as though she came round and did it every day. 'I thought you made a lovely couple.'

She removed a bunch of wilting dahlias from a vase and tenderly refilled it with some long-stemmed white flowers she'd brought with her.

'What do you think?' she said, fussing with the white arrangement. 'They're from my garden. I've been having a competition with my neighbour, Jane, to see who can grow the best ones.'

They looked a bit 'rest in peace' but I didn't like to say so. 'Lovely,' I said, marching to the corner of the kitchen where I'd left the carrier bag of sweet-making ingredients.

'So, this young man of yours.'

I swung round to look at her. She was holding the vase, her eyes like lasers over the top. 'You could try to win him back,' she went on. 'That's what my Eric did, after his Lance went off with a hairdresser chap from Torquay.' She paused. 'He said he would do whatever it took, because Lance was the love of his life; that he would even learn how to do highlights.' She looked a little misty-eyed. 'And it worked,' she said. 'I was telling Celia before you came down that they're planning a civil ceremony later this year, and a surrogate's having a baby for them.'

'That's wonderful,' I said, meaning it. 'But I really need to get on, Doris. I've a lot to do this morning.'

She snapped to attention. 'My bus isn't due just yet.' She plonked the vase down on the table. 'Can I help?'

'I think this is something I need to do on my own,' I said, regretting it when her eyes lit up.

'Ooh, that sounds mysterious.' She rubbed her hands together. 'Do tell.'

'I'm going to do some . . . baking.' Better not to mention sweets.

Doris's hand flew to her throat. 'But didn't you almost set the kitchen on fire yesterday morning?'

How did she *know*?

'Practise makes perfect!' I said, pushing my fringe back and praying she wouldn't ask to look in my bag. I couldn't face explaining.

To my relief, the thought of me cooking had her pulling her jacket over her neat, cream blouse, and reaching for her handbag. 'I suppose I'd better get myself to the bus stop,' she said, fluffing her hair with her fingers. 'Tell your grandmother I'll pop her shopping in later.'

'Will do.' I gave her a jaunty salute that made her frown.

'Sure you're alright, Marnie?'

'I'm fine.' *Please go.* I'd told Josh I'd be at the shop by lunchtime, and it was already approaching ten.

I still wasn't dressed, having decided there wasn't much point if I was going to get messy in the kitchen.

'Hmmm.' Doris didn't look convinced. 'Your grandmother was talking to Steven Fairfax when I got here,' she said, unexpectedly.

'Steven Fairfax?' I paused in the act of taking a jar of maple syrup from my Tesco's bag. 'Harry's dad?'

Doris nodded, tightening her jacket-belt. She was proud of her slim figure and liked to emphasise that she still had a waist. 'Looked like he was walking his dog and they'd got chatting by the gate. She seemed a bit cross with him, from what I could make out.'

Her eyes locked on mine, hopeful I'd reveal something.

I wondered why Beth's father-in-law was walking his dog in Shipley when they lived in Wareham now. 'I think there's some dispute about money,' I said, surprised Doris didn't already know.

She drew in a breath and blew it out again. 'That's still ongoing?' she said.

Was there any information she wasn't privy to? 'Do you know Isabel Sinclair?'

'Seaview Cottage?' Doris shook her head, mouth turning down. 'Not really,' she said, resting her hip against the edge of the table. 'Only that she moved in there with her husband, Gerry, a month or so ago, after the price had been dropped, and that they used to rent in a posh part of London, and have a baby boy called Fitzgerald and a dog called something ridiculous that I refuse to say out loud.' She took a pineapple cube from the supply in her pocket and popped it in her mouth. 'She used to do modelling, had quite the celebrity lifestyle before the baby, and he was a big shot in the publishing world. But he had an affair with a member of staff then lost his job and they had to downsize because she gave up modelling to be one of those yummy-mummies. They haven't got much cash now.' She clacked the sweet around her teeth. 'She's furious, because she never wanted to come here, but her parents wouldn't bail them out. They said she should have saved the money she made from modelling instead of blowing it on fancy holidays and silly shoes, and that they should have invested in property instead of renting. His folks coughed up the deposit for Seaview Cottage, it was all they could afford.' She paused for breath. 'They used to holiday in the Maldives, but haven't been away for ages. He watches a lot of Netflix, and she's into yoga, because it helps relieve tension, and she doesn't eat anything with a face. She wants to reinvent herself and be taken seriously, and is trying to write one of them lifestyle books, but it's not going very well.'

My mouth was hanging open.

Doris sniffed. 'Like I said though, I don't *know* them.'

'But how . . .?'

'My friend Ellen Partridge's daughter runs yoga classes in the church hall on Thursday evenings and got to know her quite well.'

'Ah.'

'And she has size nine feet.'

'Pardon?'

'Isabel. They take their shoes off at yoga, and Ellen's daughter was shocked, because Isabel is so skinny, but her feet are enormous.'

'Riiight.'

'Look at the time!' Doris gave a horrified glance at her watch. 'I can't stand here chatting all morning.'

I stood for a moment when she'd gone, head reeling as it absorbed all the new information she'd imparted. I had no idea what to do with any of it.

'Has she gone?' Celia poked her head round the back door, hair ruffled by the breeze.

'Just left.'

'Thank god.' She came inside, nudged out a chair with her stick and sat down. 'She's got a good heart, but she doesn't half go on.'

Tell me about it. 'Has your session finished?'

'Not yet,' she said, unzipping her navy puffa jacket. 'It's getting warm out there.' She pointed her stick at the Tupperware box of dog treats she kept for rewards. 'Could you pass me those, please?'

As I handed them over, a volley of growls and woofs outside, along with a delicate call for help, indicated the training session had gone awry. Tutting, Celia shot to her feet and went out, Chester at her heels.

I wondered about her dispute with Steven and resolved to ask her later, then turned my attention to the recipe book.

Peanut brittle, one of my favourites as a child, but using brown rice syrup instead of sugar.

As I stared at the words on the page, my mind zoomed back to a cruise down the Amazon with Alex in Peru. We'd stopped at a market on the outskirts of Iquitos, where the stall-holder cut open exotic fruits for us to try: a purplish *camu camu*, so sour it had made my mouth pucker, then a sugar-apple bursting with sweetness on my tastebuds. Even more delicious, a *caimito* – or star apple – that left our mouths covered with stickiness.

'Is called a love-fruit,' the vendor had explained, and Alex leaned forward and sank his mouth onto mine in front of everyone, flicking his tongue over my lips.

In the steamy surroundings, everything had taken on a seductive air and we couldn't wait to get back to our hostel and make love, whispering and laughing as we recalled the time Celia had walked in on us 'topless' (as she referred to it afterwards), hoping the people next door couldn't hear us.

My vision cleared, and the recipe swam back into view. Peanut brittle no longer had any appeal.

I looked at the clock. I should probably go to work.

'Why are you still here?' Celia's head appeared, as if it had only just struck her I should be at the shop.

'I was just wasting time before I go to the optician's,' I fibbed, closing the recipe book. 'I've an appointment for a check-up.'

She looked at my pony-patterned onesie. 'You'd better put some shoes on with that.'

Chapter 14

The next few days passed without incident, but I was constantly on edge, waiting for Isabel to reappear, or for customers to start haranguing me.

'Stop worrying,' Josh hissed on Thursday afternoon.

He was weighing out wine gums for a couple of French tourists while I peered out at the street, as if someone might sling a petrol bomb through the window. 'Even our European cousins love your sweets.'

'They remind me of 'olidays in England when I was a leetle girl,' said the younger woman, overhearing. 'You cannot buy these in Lille.'

'What sort of sweets would you buy over there?' I said, grabbing a pen from the drawer underneath the counter.

'Mmmm,' she pursed her lips and looked to her glamorous, older companion. 'Mama?'

'*Caramel au beurre salé*,' the woman said at once, with a toothy smile. 'Salted caramel.' She kissed her fingertips. 'Exquisite.'

Salted caramel. I scribbled it down on the back of a till receipt. Salted caramel did indeed sound delicious. I was sure I could make it with less sugar.

'I thought you'd given up that idea,' Josh said when they'd gone, leaning over my shoulder. 'You said you felt paralysed every time you looked at the oven.'

'How can I give up?' I said, discreetly inhaling the warm, outdoorsy scent of him. 'Apart from anything else, I've told everyone now.'

'Hardly everyone.'

'Well most of Shipley will know tomorrow, when *The Examiner* comes out.' I felt guilty for snapping. It was hardly his fault I'd announced my intentions to the public, but it was true that every time I opened the recipe book I was overcome with a feeling of ennui. Part of me was hoping the whole thing would go away, but a stronger part kept imagining how Gramps would feel if his business was under threat. I wasn't sure which part was going to win.

'Look on it as a challenge,' Beth said, when I nipped into the office to phone her. 'Why don't you come round here and make some sweets?'

'Or I could just stick to coconut ice, which apparently doesn't need cooking.'

Beth snorted lightly, having heard about my *faux pas*. 'You'll need to boil your low-sugar sugar with water, if you're going to make anything other than coconut ice, and that requires a state-of-the-art oven like the one my in-laws have.'

Steven Fairfax floated into my head and out again. 'I'm not sure they'd take too kindly to me experimenting in their house.' Harry definitely wouldn't like it.

'They're going away for a few days this afternoon,' Beth said. 'Visiting Harry's brother in Oxford. We'll have the place to ourselves.'

'In that case, you definitely won't want me interrupting.'

'Interrupting what?' She laughed. 'We won't be having sexy times, if that's what you're imagining.'

'I can promise you, I wasn't imagining *that*,' I said. 'Though maybe you should,' I added. 'Isn't it supposed to help pop the baby out?'

'Pop it out.' She sighed with longing. 'If only it were that simple.'

'Wouldn't it be brilliant if Bunty could shrink to the size of a lemon just before being born, and inflate into a baby-shape afterwards?'

'Even a lemon sounds too big.'

'An olive?'

'Might fall out unexpectedly.'

'A pomegranate.'

'That would be *so* brilliant.'

We were silent for a moment, picturing it.

'Anyway, she's not due for another week or so.'

'No more twinges?'

'Nothing serious.'

'How's Thesis?'

'I'm on a bit of a roll,' she said. 'I'm in bed, in my jammies, coffee and biccies to hand, typing away like a demon. At least I was until you phoned.'

'Sorry.'

'How's lover-boy?'

My gaze flicked through the doorway, but I couldn't see Josh from where I was standing. 'He's no Beth Fairfax, but he's popular with the ladies and young children and does a good magic trick.'

'Sounds like he's popular with you,' she teased.

'In a work capacity,' I replied, reverting to what Beth called my Karren-Brady-business-voice, to forestall further probing. 'I hardly know him, remember?'

'I can't believe I haven't seen him yet.' She'd been wheeled out of the back door and into the ambulance without clapping eyes on him.

'You could always pop down, if you fancy a breath of fresh air.'

'I don't think I can be bothered to get dressed. Ever again.'

I ended the call with Beth and went back through to the shop to find Josh studying his phone, a frown marring his face. A couple were browsing some ribbon-wrapped boxes of chocolates, fingers entwined, oblivious to anyone else.

'Won't be a sec,' Josh said without looking up, and vanished in the direction of the stockroom. Perhaps he needed to make an urgent call. I could hardly complain, having just spoken to Beth for fifteen minutes.

I doodled on another till receipt, drawing a salted caramel, but it just looked like a box with wonky edges. I'd never had a gift for art.

The couple bought two boxes of chocolates, their eyes barely leaving each other's. I had an unsettling vision of him feeding them to her on a four-poster bed, having blind-folded her first.

'Goodbye,' I said loudly as they left, but neither responded.

There was no sign of Josh.

I wondered idly whether he had a girlfriend. It was hard to imagine he didn't, though he hadn't mentioned one. He could probably pick and choose, unlike me, when I was younger. I'd been too gawky and awkward, and suspicious. It had been such a relief to finally meet Alex and know he was The One.

Or had been.

Trying not to think about him flying back with Bobbi-Jo the following day, I looked at my apron and decided I'd better take it home to wash. It was smudged with red, from handling some candy melts that had . . . well, melted, and looked as if I'd been chopping raw meat.

I could hear voices; faint but unmistakeably male. Cool air wrapped around my ankles, which meant the back door was open.

I was about to investigate when a woman came in with a smartly dressed boy with neat brown hair, parted in the middle.

'You can have two pounds' worth,' his mother said, pulling a purse from her bag while the boy looked around at the sweets with solemn interest. 'It's a special treat, as he just passed his Grade 8 violin exam,' she told me, pride written on her care-worn face.

'That's amazing,' I said. Wasn't five, or six (seven, nine?) a bit young for Grade 8?

'We saw you on the news, but it took ages to find you,' she said, as though the shop was deep in a forest, only accessible by helicopter. 'We don't live around here, you see.'

'What would you like?' I asked the boy, noticing my voice was more posh.

'I'm not sure,' he said, in a tone that made the royal family sound common. 'What would you recommend?'

'Erm . . .' I looked at the array of sweets, then back at his serious face. 'Flying saucers?' I offered. 'Rhubarb and custard?' Pity we hadn't any caviar or oyster-flavoured sweets. Rob Hancock had missed a trick there – catering for the discerning, upper-class customer. 'Or I could do you a selection if you can't decide?'

'What do you think, Sebastian?' His mum seemed anxious to please. 'He's gifted,' she whispered, round the side of her hand, as Sebastian walked ponderously round the shop, hands laced behind his back like a visiting diplomat. 'He likes to take his time.'

'He doesn't have a favourite sweet?'

'He used to like Turkish delight,' she said, throwing him a look of wonder. 'But since he tried the real thing in Istanbul, when he played the violin at the French ambassador's residence, he won't touch the stuff you sell. No offence,' she said, watching her son peer closely at the fizzy cola bottles in the pick and mix section. If he wouldn't touch mass-produced Turkish delight, there was no way he would eat those bad boys.

'Take your time,' I said, discreetly pulling my till receipt forward and writing *Turkish delight?* under *salted caramel*. Maybe I could find an original recipe and adapt it. On impulse I added *ginger balls*. Lots of my customers liked the wholesale ginger cubes, but I doubted there was much ginger in them.

'Sometimes I wish he'd make do with a Twix, but that's me,' she said in an undertone.

Sebastian returned to the counter and fixed me with intelligent grey eyes. 'I'll take one fruit salad, one black jack, one shrimp, and one milk gum, please,' he said.

I looked at his grave face. 'One kilo of each?'

His little brow furrowed. 'No. Just one of each sweet, please,' he said with impeccable manners.

'Oh.' I realised he was being serious. 'Right.'

'Is that OK?' His mum's hand tensed on her purse.

'It's fine.' I bit my lip to stop a giggle escaping. Where was Josh? He really ought to be hearing this.

Sebastian's mum handed over her twenty pence, praising her son for being a sensible boy, and they left the shop hand in hand.

'Josh!' I called, when they'd gone. 'I've had a new customer, and he's adorable,' I said, moving through to the stockroom. 'But we'll never get rich, because he only wanted . . .'

My words trailed off. Josh wasn't in the stockroom. The door was ajar, light streaming in, catching fragments of dust. I stepped outside, blinking in the sunshine slanting between the rooftops. Josh was at the end of the street, talking to someone standing by a blue van parked there. There were several boxes on the pavement, and Josh was signing what looked like a delivery form.

As I shielded my eyes, the figure he was talking to sharpened into focus. I recognised the belly pushing over the belt of his jeans, and I recognised the van.

Both belonged to Rob Hancock.

Chapter 15

I sloped back inside, heart racing.

Why was Josh taking a delivery from Hancock? And why was it being conducted at the end of the street, when Rob normally strolled in as if he owned the place and deposited his boxes in the stockroom?

Because he knew he shouldn't be here, that was why. I'd *fired* him. Josh must have gone out for some fresh air, or to make a call, and got suckered in to signing for a delivery I hadn't ordered.

I moved behind the counter, feeling a bit wobbly.

I didn't want to have a go at Josh, but he had to know Rob was off-limits, no matter what story he'd spun. He had as much finesse as a hippo at a tea-party and I had no doubt he'd ridden roughshod over any objections Josh might have made; probably told him to keep schtum, and hoped I wouldn't notice his name on the delivery note. Perhaps he hoped once his stock was on the premises, I wouldn't bother returning them.

I closed my eyes and indulged in a vision where I sprinted after Rob's van, shot his tyres out, then dragged him from the driver's seat and gave him a good pummelling.

'Everything alright?'

My eyes snapped open to meet the curious gaze of Paddy, Celia's neighbour. I hadn't realised he was in the shop.

'I'm fine!' I said, rather forcefully. 'Is Celia OK?'

'As far as I know,' said Paddy, his walnut-like face softening at the mention of my grandmother. 'I'll be taking her for her physio appointment tomorrow.'

'What about your job?' Paddy worked as a groundsman at a country house hotel a few miles away.

'They won't mind,' he assured me in his gravelly voice, though I wasn't so sure. Mr Hudson, who owned a string of country house hotels, was – not to put it too mildly – a bit of a bastard. He'd given a talk when I was a student, about how to succeed in business, and although he'd claimed to have modelled himself on Richard Branson, his attitude was more *Wolf of Wall Street*.

'I could take her,' I offered, though I quailed at the thought of getting Celia's ancient VW out of the garage. It didn't even have power-steering, it was so old. How she'd managed to get around in it I had no idea, but it explained why she had superior body strength and could beat me in an arm-wrestle.

'No, no it's fine, I want to do it,' Paddy said, keenly. He had leathery skin and a fleece of greying curls.

'Your usual?' I said, reaching for the jar of liquorice allsorts, not feeling in a chatty mood.

'I think I'll have some pear drops for a change,' he said, and in spite of myself I smiled. Celia must have converted him.

'Do you think she'd go on a date with me?' he blurted.

I almost dropped the jar. 'I – I really don't know,' I said, tipping out too many pear drops.

The thought of Celia dating hadn't crossed my mind, and I was fairly sure she hadn't considered it either. Since Gramps died, she'd thrown herself more vigorously into work, and seemed happy enough. I couldn't imagine her wanting another man – especially one younger than her.

I risked a quick glance, and caught the brightness of hope in Paddy's brown, Malteser-like eyes. For as long as I'd known him he'd just been Paddy-next-door, even though he lived in the cottage adjacent to Celia's. Not long after he moved in, Mum somehow found out he wasn't married, had a son from a past relationship, and had lost his little finger in a lawn-mowing accident.

I'd never seen him with a woman, but he certainly liked Celia, and I doubted he'd lived a monastic existence all these years.

'Well, you could ask her,' I said, wondering if she would be furious with me.

'She's been so good with Muttley,' he went on, hands bunched into the pockets of the combat trousers he always seemed to wear. 'He hasn't, um, entertained any lady dogs since she encouraged me to have his . . . I mean, get him neutered, like. He comes back as soon as I call him now, provided I stick to the training plan and give him a little treat. He loves his treats, even more than he likes bitches, see?'

'I see,' I said, sliding his pear drops into a bag. Maybe it was why he'd bought a dog in the first place – to get Celia involved in his life.

He plucked a heart-shaped lollipop from a display and held it to his nose, like a rose. 'Think she'd like one of these?' His eyebrows quivered. 'As a thank you for helping with Muttley.'

'Take it if you want to,' I said. 'I'm sure she'll appreciate the gesture.'

As he left, the lollipop sticking out of his pocket, there was the sound of the door smacking in its frame, and Josh came through, carrying a box which he deposited on the counter.

I stared at it, as though it was a hand grenade.

'What's up?' he said with mild alarm.

'What is that?'

He looked at it, head cocked. 'Um, let me think. A dressing table? No, wait.' He squeezed his bottom lip with two fingers, thinking. 'Is it a china pig, wearing a bowler hat?'

'Not funny, Josh.' My voice was chilly. 'Where did you get it?'

The laughter left his face. 'It's a surprise,' he said. 'Do you want to see?'

'I know what's in there, Josh.'

'No you don't.' He grabbed a pair of scissors and cut through the tape. Swimming his hands inside, he pulled out a smaller box, of mint humbugs.

'We've got plenty . . .' I started to say.

'Look.' He shifted his gaze to two words in a bubble on the box: *sugar-free.*

'So?' I said coldly.

His grin faltered. 'I had this genius idea, after that protest the other day,' he said. 'You can buy diabetic sweets, that don't contain sugar, so I thought I'd order some.' He waggled his hands in a 'tah-dah' gesture. 'So you don't need to make your own, see?'

'I already have a selection of diabetic sweets, if customers want them.' I was still using my new, cold voice. It *was* a nice gesture, and he did look super-cute when he was excited, but he definitely should have asked me first.

'I didn't know.' Crestfallen, he looked around. 'Where are they?'

'I keep them in here,' I said, yanking open one of the drawers behind the counter to reveal a paltry selection. 'I only have two diabetic customers, and they both like barley sugar. The chocolate and the éclairs are just in case anyone asks.' I gave him a pointed look. 'Which they never have.'

'But you don't have to sell them as diabetic, just sugar-free,' he said, brightening. He was proving to be one of those people who always looked on the bright side. 'It's symbolic.'

'But they're full of sweeteners, which aren't necessarily good for people who aren't diabetic.' I pressed my fingers to my temples. 'People want homemade things these days and anyway, I've *promised*.' The word *promised* was almost a whine. 'Those will have to go back.'

'Are you sure?' He stuck out his bottom lip. 'Couldn't we still put them for sale?'

'No, Josh, we couldn't,' I said, my temper fraying. 'And *why* did you order them from Rob Hancock, when I told you I wasn't buying from him any more?'

He looked at me, stricken. 'I forgot,' he said, passing a hand over his mouth. 'Does it matter that much?'

'Yes, Josh. It matters,' I said, enunciating clearly. 'I do not want to buy anything from Rob Hancock, ever again.'

He took a step back, as if my words had hit him in the chest. 'Bit harsh,' he muttered, stuffing the humbugs back in the box and attempting to stick the tape down. 'If you feel that strongly, I'll get him to pick them up.'

'No.' It came out sharply. 'I don't want him here.'

Josh's eyebrows rose. 'He's not that bad, is he?'

For a moment, I couldn't speak. I was remembering the time my grandfather had a rare day off and I was in the shop on my own, the other assistant on her lunch break, and Rob Hancock had butted up against me as I signed for a delivery in the stockroom. I could still feel his damp breath on my neck as his chubby fingers scuttled across my cheek.

I hadn't told my grandfather, but made every effort to avoid Rob after that. He'd never tried it again as the years had passed, but always gave the impression he wanted to, and sometimes said things like, 'I saw a great pair of tits this morning . . .' pausing to look at my chest, 'in the tree outside my window,' but only when Gramps wasn't there.

'I told you I've changed supplier,' I said. 'Please don't order from him again.'

'Marnie, I'm sorry,' he said, taking a step towards me. 'I didn't mean to upset you.'

'I need some air.' I whipped my apron off and tossed it onto the stool. 'Will you be OK for ten minutes?'

'Marnie, wait. I . . .' he began, but I was already through the door

I'd walked down the beach for a full five minutes before I felt able to breathe. I stopped at the water's edge and eased my sand-filled shoes off, letting the ice-cold waves lap at my toes.

I couldn't work out whether I was angrier at Rob's shady behaviour, or at Josh for going behind my back. Were my instincts about him wrong?

I wondered what Gramps would have made of him. He'd liked Alex a lot, expressing his approval through the ancient ritual of back-slapping, but then again he'd seemed to like Rob Hancock. Or at least, he'd never indicated that he hadn't. They weren't great friends or anything. I suspected it was more from habit that he kept placing orders with him, having known Rob's father. Both my grandparents were sticklers for habit and routine, just like Uncle Cliff was. Only my mother had seemed stifled, desperate to escape.

The breeze coming off the sea whipped my hair around and cooled my overheated cheeks. I glanced about, seeing the place as if for the first time – the curve of beach, the towering blue sky blooming with cotton-wool clouds, and the glimpse of the castle across the bay.

The setting had seemed enchanted to me as a child, exploring the shore with my cousins. Even during the winter months the place had its own magic, especially when the sand was coated with a layer of snow. But the drip-drip of Mum's restlessness had filtered down until – like her – I'd longed to get away.

People who had lived here all their lives couldn't understand why anyone would want to leave.

'There's nowhere more beautiful on earth than the Jurassic Coast,' Celia would say, making me think of dinosaurs as she stroked my hair when I couldn't sleep. 'It's in my blood.'

But it wasn't in Mum's blood, nor mine.

Yet here I was, almost thirty, and still here. Taking on more responsibility, since the award.

My toes curled into the wet sand.

But Mum was settled in Italy now, and it looked like Celia might be on the verge of a romance, if Paddy got his own way. Soon, Beth would be enveloped in motherhood, and although Alex was returning briefly, he'd be going back to his new life in America with Bobbi-Jo.

There was nothing to keep me in Shipley, apart from the sweet shop.

And Gramps would understand if I left, he'd want me to be happy; just like he'd wanted Mum to be happy, even though he'd missed her when she wasn't around.

I slid my sandy shoes back on and made my way up the beach.

I would go to Alex's parents' party, I decided, and say a proper goodbye, to show him I was moving on, and once my sweet-tasting day was over I was going to make a proper travel plan.

Next year I could be on a desert island, in a palm-thatched beach hut, snacking on watermelon. Or tripping around the Mediterranean, sampling local delicacies. Or in the savanna, a leopard sizing me up from a shady tree . . .

Or I could start by visiting Mum in Italy, and tell her that my real life was starting at last. She might even want to come with me, if she needed a little break from Mario. She could show me all the sights she'd seen on her travels.

I indulged in a little daydream of us browsing a market stall in Delhi, and my mood was magically transformed by the time I got back to the shop. Josh was sitting behind the counter when I bounded in, startling a pair of girls looking at chocolate bars with names piped on in white icing.

'I'm sorry,' he mouthed, looking genuinely remorseful.

Any lingering annoyance melted away. 'It's fine,' I mimed back, around a smile.

He pressed his palms together. 'Thank you.'

The girls watched our silent exchange with open curiosity.

'Can we have a photo with you?' one said shyly to me. She looked about eleven, her blonde hair woven into neat cornrows.

'We saw you on the news,' said her friend, with a dimpled smile. 'We want to run our own business like you, one day.'

'How nice,' I said, touched. 'My hair's a bit of a mess.' I'd also trailed in sand, and the hems of my jeans were soaked – hardly a typical role-model – but the girls didn't seem to mind. They came to stand either side of me, each holding up a chocolate bar with their names on – Amy and Emily.

'I'll take it,' Josh said, leaping from behind the counter as Amy struggled to attach a selfie-stick to her phone, and when he'd taken several shots plus 'one for luck' – probably because I'd shut my eyes when the flash went off – the girls thanked me politely and went to pay for their chocolate.

'You can have them on the house,' I said.

They looked shocked. 'You'll never make a profit if you give away your stock,' said the blonde one, taking a sequinned purse from her little handbag. 'We insist on paying full price.'

I left Josh to it, aware, like me, he was hiding a smile, and went into the office.

First, I logged onto my phone and checked the shop's bank account, which was the healthiest it had ever been, thanks to the prize money. No problems there. Then I clicked over to my personal account and scanned my latest statement. The salary that went in each month had mounted up, and the figure made my eyes widen to twice their normal size.

There was more than enough to fund an escape.

I had no excuse not to go.

Chapter 16

'Good god, it actually looks edible,' Beth declared. Round-eyed with awe she viewed my peanut brittle as if it was a dinosaur egg. 'I can't believe it.'

'Rude,' I said benignly. Beth was as hopeless in the kitchen as I was, a fact her mother blamed squarely on 'our generation'.

'I wonder what it tastes like,' I said, secretly chuffed that what I'd made resembled the image in my head.

It hadn't even been that hard. I'd roasted some peanuts and combined them with brown rice syrup, a little cane sugar and butter, then boiled the gooey mess. Once it was bubbling, like a volcano about to erupt, I poured it onto baking trays and pressed it down carefully.

'Should we try some?' I said, picking at a corner and snatching my hand away. It was dangerously hot.

'You have to wait for it to harden,' said Beth, with a dirty grin. 'What's next?'

'Well, I thought I could make some coconut ice . . .'

'Which you will *not* put in the oven.'

'Which I will *not* put in the oven,' I agreed, 'some salted caramel cups, which I'm going to try now, and maybe some Turkish delight.'

'Yummy,' said Beth, rubbing her bump. If anything, it seemed to have grown. She looked like she had a space hopper stuffed up her shirt.

In a fit of optimism that had lasted all afternoon – in addition to my healthy bank account, I was a role model for at least two eleven-year-old girls – I'd decided to take Beth up on her offer of using the oven at her in-laws' while Steven and Jacky were away.

'Sure you'll be OK?' I'd asked Celia, phoning her as I locked up the shop.

'Of course,' she said, seeming baffled I would think otherwise. 'Paddy's here, keeping me company.' Her voice dropped an octave. 'He bought me a lollipop to say thank you for training Muttley,' she said. 'I don't think he realised it was shaped like a heart, bless him.'

I shook my head, relieved she'd taken it as a friendly gesture, but feeling a bit sorry for Paddy. Celia clearly wouldn't recognise a romantic proposal if it wagged its tail in her face.

When I arrived at the Fairfaxes' Grade 2 listed town house, Beth had greeted me with wild enthusiasm, claiming that constantly re-searching Katherine Parr was doing her head in.

'Thesis is a ball-breaker,' she groaned. 'And I can't believe I'm still pregnant.'

'Watch me cook,' I'd instructed – three words I never imagined leaving my lips – and she descended with a forceful plonk at the breakfast bar in the Fairfaxes' sleek kitchen, while I got busy with the ingredients I'd purchased in a health store before catching the bus to Wareham.

Now, enthused by my success with the peanut brittle, I commenced preparations for the salted caramel cups, bringing up the recipe on Beth's tablet.

'I thought you were using Ye-Olde Worlde recipe book, á la Appleton,' Beth said, propping her chin in her palm.

'I was, but most of it's too old-fashioned, and everything's crammed with proper sugar.'

'Fair enough.'

She'd spread her legs to accommodate her massive belly, two pencils pinioning her curls to her head, but my wave of affection for her was swallowed by a prickle of guilt. I wasn't sure Beth would approve of my escape plan. She seemed pleased that I was focused properly on the shop for once.

As I lobbed medjool dates into Jacky's flamingo-pink Kenwood food processor, and added cold water, I found myself thinking back to my one and only serious argument with Beth, straight out of university, when I kept banging on about leaving once I'd saved enough money, and she'd asked why I thought running away was such a good idea.

'Just because *you've* got your Shipley future mapped out, doesn't mean we all want to stay here,' I'd said, hurt. 'And anyway, it's not running away, it's called Exploring the Big Wide World.' I'd made quotation marks, which I wasn't proud of. 'I take after my mum.'

When I ended up staying, working at the sweet shop full-time to help support Mum through a break-up, and because Gramps had developed glaucoma and was refusing to have an operation, I think Beth thought I'd forgotten about going away.

I know she missed me when I finally went with Alex, but she'd seemed thrilled I was finally realising my long-held dream – even if it did end up being cut short and put on hold.

I decided to put off mentioning anything until after she'd had the baby – which couldn't be much longer judging by the way she kept wincing, rolling her eyes to the back of her head, and clawing at her lower back.

'I seriously don't think I can do this labour thing,' she said, as I took a break from trying to figure out how to make the food processor work.

'You'll be fine,' I said, in my most reassuring voice. I swivelled the lid onto the processor and pressed start. Nothing. I prodded the button again, then removed the lid and peered in. Everything was where it should be. 'Why isn't it working?' I muttered.

'I'm starting to think my labour-chanting might not be enough to take my mind off the pain,' Beth said, casually plugging the processor into a socket on the wall.

Immediately a horrible whining started up, and watery dates spewed in the air.

'Bloody hell!' I cried, expertly catching a couple before they landed.

'Oops,' grimaced Beth. 'Forgot to put the lid on.'

I rinsed the dates, plopped them back in, and as the processor got to work properly we clapped our hands to our ears. It sounded as if someone was drilling a hole in the wall.

'Jesus,' I said when it stopped. 'What a racket.'

'I'm serious though,' Beth said. 'What if I can't do it?'

'You don't have a choice,' I pointed out, scooping a handful of date paste and rolling it into a ball. It felt and looked disgusting, like something that might erupt from Chester's bottom. 'Imagine you're Katherine Parr,' I added.

Beth brightened. 'She *did* have a daughter, aged thirty-six.'

'That's old, for a baby. They usually come out much younger.'

'Ho ho,' said Beth. 'She died soon after.'

'The baby?'

'Katherine Parr.' Her face became wreathed in worry.

'In that case, don't imagine you're her.'

'My mum said I only took forty-five minutes to be born.'

'There you go then,' I said, smashing up chocolate and placing it in a bowl over a boiling pan of water to melt.

'But she was in labour for three days with my brother.'

'Look, it's fear of the unknown,' I said, trying to remember what the midwives on *One Born Every Minute* had said when Beth made me watch an episode. 'You just have to remember to breathe.'

'I think I know how to breathe.' She clamped her hands over her breasts and gave them a jiggle. 'My pretty duckies are massive,' she said.

'Please don't call them that.' I added some coconut oil to the melted chocolate and stirred it with a spatula shaped like a guitar.

'That's Steven's,' Beth had said when I checked it was OK to use it. 'He's learning to play one. I think he's having a mid-life crisis.'

I remembered his early morning chat with Celia a few days ago. 'How's the dog?' I said, looking round for the bright-eyed Alsatian.

'She's great, thanks to your gran,' said Beth. 'She kept pooping everywhere, but that was ages ago.'

'Celia?'

Beth gave me a narrow stare. 'The dog,' she said. 'They've taken her away with them.'

Before I could ask Beth if she knew of an ongoing dispute between her father-in-law and Celia, she said, 'So, are you going to this party on Saturday?'

My heart jolted. 'I wasn't going to, after Alex told me he was bringing his new paramour,' I said, pouring a layer of chocolate into the cupcake tin Beth had found in a cupboard. 'But I've decided I should. You know.' I flicked her a glance. 'To get closure.'

She smiled impishly, her worries about childbirth seemingly forgotten for now. 'You want to see what she looks like.'

'Yes, I want to see what she looks like,' I admitted, dropping a ball of date-caramel goo over the layer of chocolate, and adding another layer.

'And you're happy leaving Josh in charge of the shop, even though you hardly know him?'

'I am.' I thought of his *faux pas* with Rob and the sugar-free sweets. He'd made a mistake, but his intentions were good, and he was brilliant with customers. 'Anyway, Agnieszka will be there,' I said. 'And so will I for most of the day. The party doesn't start until five.'

'Maybe seeing them together will help.'

'Josh and Agnieszka?' I said, sprinkling Himalayan sea-salt over my caramel cups and standing back to admire them.

'You know what I mean.'

'Maybe you're right,' I said. 'You have to take a photo of this, it looks brilliant.'

She picked up her mobile and clambered off the American-diner-style stool. 'I want to be in it,' she said, lumbering around to stand on tip-toe beside me to make herself taller.

I picked up the cupcake tin and held it out, while she angled the phone to get everything in.

We did the universal selfie-smile, that looked like we had a sweet in our mouths we were trying not to suck, and she took the picture. 'I'll put it on Instagram and tag the shop,' she said, just as Harry strode in.

'Evening.' His eyes skimmed over me with the usual flash of dis-appointment – as if his wife was being monopolised by a tiresome neighbour. His paint-speckled baseball hat had slipped back, trapping his hair. 'Roof's on and the floors are finished,' he said, kissing Beth's ear. 'We should be able to move in by the end of the month.'

'That's brilliant,' she said, lifting her face to his. 'Though your mum won't be pleased. I think she's hoping to keep us here forever.'

As they rubbed noses, Harry rested his hands on her bump, and I felt a twinge of envy at the intimate vignette. I tried not to think about Alex and Bobbi-Jo, and immediately imagined them wrapped in each other's arms.

'I'd better go and catch my bus,' I said, shoving the tray of caramel cups in the fridge. 'Feel free to scoff these, by the way.'

'Still not got yourself a car?' Harry eased his work boots off and crossed to the sink. 'You're the only person I know under eighty who still gets the bus.'

'Doing my bit for the environment,' I said lightly, noticing the mess I'd made on the worktops. 'Should I load the dishwasher?'

'I'll do it in the morning,' Beth said, waving a hand.

'If you had a car you'd find it much easier to drive away from Shipley.' Harry was focused on scrubbing a particularly stubborn stain from his wrist underneath the tap. 'I'm surprised you never replaced yours when you came back from Timbuktu.' He turned and met my gaze, but I couldn't read his expression.

'I didn't think I needed one.'

'How's Alex, by the way?'

'Harry.' Beth's voice held a warning and, as I looked from her to Harry, it struck me that they must have discussed my break-up with Alex, and that Harry had a view Beth hadn't shared with me.

'A lucky escape,' he muttered so quietly I almost didn't catch it.

'What's that supposed to mean?'

'Take no notice,' Beth beseeched.

Harry gave a humourless laugh. 'The apple doesn't fall far from the tree,' he said, even more quietly.

'Harry!' Beth threw him an angry look.

'If that's a slur against my mum you'd better take it back.' I took a step towards him, not even sure what I would have done next if Beth hadn't ordered him to apologise.

'Sorry,' he muttered, but he didn't look round, or even sound as if he meant it.

'Here, take this,' Beth said to me, handing me the cardigan she'd removed earlier. 'It'll be chilly out now, and you haven't got a coat.'

'Are you practising for when you're a mum?' I said, pushing my arms in the sleeves, unwilling to let Harry's words go but not knowing what to say. 'It's a bit short.'

'It'll do,' said Beth, fussing with the sleeves.

Harry began whistling, a tuneless sound that grated on my nerves.

'Laters,' he said, without looking round as Beth ushered me into the hall.

'Take no notice of him.' She reached up to tuck a strand of hair behind my ear. 'He's grumpy because he's not been allowed access to my pretty duckies for a while.' She dropped me a saucy wink. 'If you know what I mean.'

'You're disgusting,' I said with a laugh, but as I walked down the drive in the growing darkness, Harry's words reverberated around my head, and I couldn't help wondering what he'd meant.

Chapter 17

Before catching my bus I walked down a couple of winding roads to Church Street, and the mid-terrace house where I'd lived on and off with Alex.

I'd been there a few times since he left, drawn like iron filings to a magnet. On the last occasion I'd stood on the pavement in the pouring rain, crying silently as I pictured the oddly shaped little living room where we'd made love, plans, and once, a chest of drawers from a flat pack that fell apart when we tried to open the drawers.

I'd stood there so long, in my sweatpants and hoodie, the new tenants called the police, convinced they'd acquired a stalker.

Now the lights were on upstairs, and a shadow passed across the bedroom window. The thought of them sharing the brass bed Alex and I bought once we were officially an item seemed all wrong, but so did everything about another couple living there.

Alex's mother, Helen, kept an eye on the place, but clearly hadn't noticed the grass in the front garden was badly overgrown. Alex had loved to cut the grass, charging up and down with the petrol mower, while I sat on the doorstep with a glass of wine and judged his performance, like Simon Cowell.

'You know what, you've really made that grass your own.'

'You've absolutely blown me away, Alex.'

Leaning over the wall I plucked a blade of grass, jealousy swirling in my stomach. Would he bring Bobbi-Jo here and show her around, while he was back? He owned the house, after all. What if one day he decided to move back with her – or sell the house to pay for a Hollywood wedding?

Thank god I was leaving soon, and wouldn't have to think about this sort of thing. Once the anniversary party was out of the way, and I'd found a manager for the shop, and Beth had given birth, I'd be on my way.

Suddenly, the upstairs window was violently thumped open.

'Arianne!' called a man's voice. 'Come here!'

I dropped to my hands and knees and scuttled away from the circle of light spilling from the house.

'I think there's something by the gate,' the man said urgently. 'Go and have a look on the badger-cam.'

There was the sound of a woman's excited squeal and I shuffled down the pavement, hugging the shadows like a cat-burglar. Without looking back, I straightened and hurried away before Arianne discovered it wasn't a badger outside the house, but the owner's disgruntled ex-girlfriend.

The last bus back to Shipley was empty apart from a snogging couple near the front. I tried not to stare as the man's hands brazenly frisked his boyfriend's body, as though checking for hidden weapons.

The driver slowed to let someone or something cross the road, and I looked out of the window to where a man was standing beside a campervan in a lay-by. He was pacing around, a mobile pressed to his ear, his other arm flailing about as he tried to get his point across. Clearly the person on the receiving end was getting a proper rollicking. Either that or the campervan had broken down, and the man had forgotten to renew his AA membership.

A car passed in the opposite direction, catching him in the beam of his headlights, and recognition shot through me.

It was Josh.

I knocked on the window, but the bus was pulling away, and he was too intent on his conversation to notice. As he faded from view, I began to doubt what I'd seen. Josh hadn't mentioned a campervan, and why would he be parked in a lay-by near Wareham, when he was staying with friends in Shipley?

I remembered I still hadn't got his payment details, and resolved to sort it out first thing in the morning.

Friday. The day Alex was flying back to England.

I had a splitting headache by the time I arrived back at Celia's, and my heart dropped when I saw Paddy's work boots on the mat in the hall. I wasn't in the mood to be sociable, and was surprised Celia was still up. She normally turned in about nine, to read one of her spine-cracked thrillers.

A rumble of laughter emerged from the living room, and I peeped around the door. Celia was holding a dried pig's ear aloft while Muttley danced on his hind legs.

My vision swam and I blinked a couple of times.

'I can't believe you've got him to do that,' Paddy was saying. 'I tried for ages last night and got nowhere.' He wasn't bothering to hide his admiration, which seemed to encourage Celia to greater heights. She trotted in a circle – using her stick, I was pleased to see – still holding the treat out of reach so the dog had to follow her movements as if they were dancing.

Chester was in the corner, growling low in his throat. He hated competition, and Muttley was younger and more agile.

'You should take him on *Britain's Got Talent*,' Paddy gushed (there was no other word for it) leaning forward to pat Muttley's rump as he finally got his treat and swallowed it whole.

'I think dancing dogs have been done to death,' said Celia, with a hint of disapproval. She didn't care for dogs being paraded on television and had predicted an early grave for Pudsey, due to the perils of fame.

'Had a nice time with Beth?' she said, catching sight of my hovering head. 'No baby yet?'

'Not yet,' I said, smiling at Paddy.

'Alright?' He scrambled up and shuffled his feet with the embarrassed air of a schoolboy in front of the headmistress.

I noticed Celia's cheeks were strawberry, and there was a spark in her eyes. Not so immune to the possibility of romance after all. 'Sorry I missed dinner,' I said.

'Don't worry. Paddy stayed for a bite.' She gave him a look that was as close to flirtatious as I'd ever seen, and the world seemed to tilt a little. 'Have you eaten?'

I nodded, though I wasn't sure the dates, chocolate, and peanuts I'd picked at during my sweet-making session counted.

Muttley came over to investigate and I fussed his silky ears while Chester craned his head and barked a protest.

'I'll leave you to it,' I said. 'It's been a busy day.'

'I was going to make some hot chocolate.'

Celia only drank hot chocolate if she had a cold, or the temperature had fallen below freezing.

'Not for me, thank you,' I said, backing into the hall. 'Night night.'

I wasn't used to a male presence in the house, since my grandfather's death; even if it was only Paddy-next-door.

'I'd love one,' he was saying keenly, as I let the door swing shut and headed up to the bathroom.

My headache had eased by the time I'd showered and blasted my hair dry. I slid beneath my duvet, certain I wouldn't sleep, but the burr of conversation downstairs – interspersed with some aggrieved whining from Chester – was oddly comforting, and I drifted off straight away.

Paddy wasn't at the breakfast table the following morning, as I'd feared, but Celia was non-committal about what time he left. 'After the dogs had been out for a wee,' was all she was prepared to say, busy with her first appointment of the day – a rescue dog, destroying its owner's house one cushion at a time.

Apparently Paddy was dropping Celia off there, before taking her to her hospital appointment.

As I left for work, Isabel Sinclair emerged from her house, swinging baby Fitzgerald in a car-seat. She loaded it into a hulking SUV, of the sort I'd seen on *Ice Road Truckers* ploughing across deepest Alaska. Clearly downsizing didn't extend to her mode of transport.

She drew her head from the car and spotted me approaching.

'Hello,' she drawled, shielding her eyes from the sun with an angled arm. She looked dressed for the gym, her fuchsia sports bra visible beneath a couple of layered vest-tops. Her tousled hair was pinned back beneath a headband, and her trainers looked box-fresh. And very large. Doris was right, she had massive feet. 'Got step 'n' pump this morning,' she said in a sing-song voice – as if she hadn't recently staged a protest and threatened to ruin my grandfather's legacy.

'You should see a doctor about that,' I couldn't resist saying, as I drew level.

'You won't be joking when you see the paper this morning.'

I looked at her smug, beautiful face and wanted to slap it. '*The Examiner* doesn't come out until tomorrow.'

'Try *The South-West Recorder*,' she said, plugging her baby's mouth with a heart-shaped dummy. 'You look desperate, I look classy, end of story.'

Shit. That paper would reach a wider audience than *The Examiner*.

Before I could react, she turned to wave at a thick-set man, standing on the doorstep behind her. With his close-cut hair and bullish features he looked like a nightclub bouncer, but was wearing a towelling robe with matching slippers, and cuddling a snow-white dog.

'Gerry, don't forget to feed Pollywollydoodle before you put the breadmaker on,' Isabel called in a high-handed way.

'It's top of my list,' said Gerry through a yawn – as if it was the most boring sentence he'd ever uttered. I imagined the transition from publishing magnate – or whatever he'd been – to dog-sitting house-husband was proving less than enthralling, and that being married to Isabel was something of a challenge.

'Have a super day!' I said, matching her tone, but as I marched away my heart was hopping about like a startled rabbit. Had she really seen the paper, or was she playing mind games?

Doris was in her garden already, trimming her billowing lavender bush with a large pair of secateurs. 'Celia says hi!' I fibbed, scurrying by before she could accost me.

The sun mysteriously vanished and a bank of grey clouds scudded across the sea, turning it a steely grey. I shivered, wishing I'd brought a jacket. As I approached the shop, something on the window caught my eye, and as I drew closer the black smudgy mess transformed into a spray-painted skull and crossbones. Beneath it, the word 'POISON' dripped with macabre menace.

'What the *hell*?'

'It was there when I got here,' Josh said, coasting around the corner on his newly fixed skateboard, hair quivering in the breeze. 'I couldn't believe it,' he said, rolling to a stop beside me. 'I was going to ask the owner of the guesthouse if she had something I could clean it off with.'

My eyes felt hot. 'No,' I said sharply. 'The fewer people that see it the better.'

'Who do you think did it?' Josh scratched his stubble. 'Local art students?'

I attempted a laugh. 'Probably Isabel Sinclair.' I pulled my keys from my bag, averting my gaze from the window. My grandfather would be turning in his grave.

'There'll be something in the stockroom I can clean it off with,' I said, unlocking the door. Inside, I switched off the alarm, and saw that my fingers were trembling.

'I'll do it while you open up,' Josh said, hot on my heels. 'By the time any customers turn up, they won't know it was there.'

'*I'll* know it was,' I said, heading to the stockroom to find the white spirit I'd bought along with several tins of emulsion, as part of a New Year's resolution to repaint the shop. 'How can people be so mean?'

Any remaining pleasure I'd felt at winning my award slipped away. If anything, it had brought nothing but trouble.

'Hey, don't cry,' Josh said, stilling my hand as I fumbled about for a cloth.

I hadn't realised I was crying, but as I passed my other hand over my face it came away damp. 'This wouldn't have happened if my grandfather was alive,' I mumbled. Somehow, my face was pressed against Josh's chest, and his arms were tight around me. I could feel his heart pumping against my cheek, and smell his musky scent.

A flare of attraction shot up my spine and I nuzzled closer as his lips pressed the top of my head. I hadn't realised he was so much taller than me. Or that his chest was quite so firm.

'It'll pass,' he murmured, his breath warm on my scalp. 'Don't let her spoil what you've achieved.'

'But I haven't achieved anything,' I said, and then I was sobbing in earnest, bubbling snot all over his Superman T-shirt. 'This is my grandfather's shop and it always will be. All I've really done is keep it open.'

Pulling back, he lifted my chin with his finger.

'But that's everything,' he said, his voice tight with emotion. 'You could have sold the place when the old man popped it, or got someone else in to run it,' I remembered that was my plan and felt a flicker of guilt. 'But you didn't and you're doing great.' His eyes glowed with sincerity, while mine were puffing up. 'You're finding your own way of doing things,' he said. 'This is just a blip, believe me.'

I badly wanted to. But I kept seeing Isabel's self-satisfied, asymmetrical face in my mind – as if she knew something I didn't.

I wriggled reluctantly out of Josh's arms, and could have sworn he looked disappointed. After smoothing my hands down my cheeks, I wiped my face on the first cloth that came to hand. Luckily, it was clean.

'Can you go and get a copy of *The South-West Recorder* while I clean the window?' I said, attempting to claw back some semblance of professionalism. 'I think I'm in it, and not in a good way.'

Chapter 18

As Josh jogged up to the high street to fetch a newspaper from Mr Flannery's, I sloshed white spirit onto my cloth and stepped out to tackle the window.

A passing car slowed, and the driver – who looked old enough to know better – lowered his window to take a picture on his phone.

'Nice artwork!' he shouted, before roaring away in his sports car, the sound of his exhaust attracting attention from some teenage boys, perched on the railings opposite like giant seagulls.

'Smile, miss,' one shouted, aiming his phone at me before I could turn away.

Great. I would probably be on YouTube now. Hopefully, no one would be interested in a red-faced woman, dangling a cloth beside some graffiti outside a Dorset sweet shop. Although it did have a certain pathos when I thought of it like that.

Ignoring the soft drizzle that had started falling, I began to scrub at the skull and crossbones, smearing black paint across the glass so it was impossible to see the display of sweets inside.

Wiping rain off my cheek with the back of my hand, I was vaguely aware of a van door sliding open, followed by a clack of heels on the pavement.

'Miss Appleton!'

I spun around as Sandi Brent pounced. 'What do you want?' I squinted as my eyes were speared by a blinding light, positioned above a camera resting on the shoulder of the cameraman.

'Switch that off, Kyle!' Sandi hissed from under her golf umbrella. 'The existing light suits the tone much better.'

'Why are you here?' I said, though it was obvious she'd been tipped off. I made an effort to conceal the graffiti with my body. 'Please don't film this.'

'Why do you think it's happening, Miss Appleton?' The exclamation marks were gone. Sandi Brent was in full investigative reporter mode, head tilted, eyes hungry for drama. She was even dressed soberly, in pin-striped trousers, trench coat, and low-heeled shoes, and her hair had been twisted into a chignon. I doubted the lenses in her tortoiseshell glasses were anything but plain glass.

'Just vandals, messing about, that's all,' I said. I felt my hair expanding in the rain, adding to my peasant-woman look. 'It doesn't mean anything.'

'Really?' She exchanged a disbelieving look with the cameraman, who had the grace to look slightly ashamed.

'Do you want to borrow an umbrella?' He lowered the camera. 'I've got a spare in the van.'

'Absolutely not,' Sandi snapped, Stormtrooper style. 'We're trying to tell a story here.' She turned to me again, her face softening into the sort of expression a counsellor might wear. 'A story of one woman's fight to keep her business afloat amid stiff opposition, and dirty dealings,' she added, as Kyle raised the camera with an apologetic shrug.

'I'm not Erin bloody Brockovich,' I said, recalling how much I'd loved her when I was fifteen; wished I *was* her.

'We'd like to hear your side of the story,' said Sandi, as though I hadn't spoken. 'About how you're planning to respond to your detractors.'

'My detractors are a handful of people, one of whom has her own agenda, and I'm planning to carry on as I've always done, just as my grandfather did.' Turning my back, I frenziedly scrubbed at the window with a cloth more sodden with rain than white spirit, my hair flopping wetly forward.

'But what about the sugar issue?' Sandi's voice was a hushed whisper of sympathy as she ducked her head to meet my gaze, her subtly made-up eyes – still with perfect eyeliner flicks – awash with understanding.

'I've addressed that already,' I said, stubbornly smearing paint around the window in graceful swirls. My hand was completely black.

'So you're going to come back fighting?' Sandi seemed intent on urging me towards the ending she had in mind.

Seized by an urge to be decisive, I faced her fully. 'Yes,' I said. 'That's *exactly* what I'm going to do.'

'How?' she persisted, reminding me of Chester with a particularly juicy bone.

'I'm introducing a line of homemade sweets with less sugar.' I sounded like the Queen addressing the nation. 'You should come along on Monday, and judge for yourself.'

I shook out my cloth, spattering her cream coat with black blobs. She looked down, her mouth a perfect circle of drop-dead horror. 'Oops, sorry.'

'You . . . you . . .' For once, words seemed to desert her. She rubbed her coat with the palm of her hand, spreading the dark stains. 'Look what you've done,' she wailed.

Kyle smothered a grin.

'Let me help,' I said, and began dabbing at her with the filthy cloth, which stank to high heaven.

'Get off me!' she shrieked, reeling away, catching Kyle with her umbrella. As he stumbled back, the camera began to topple.

'Don't drop it, you fucker,' she spat. 'We don't want to lose the footage.'

Fortunately – for him – Kyle managed to catch it before it hit the pavement, its waterproof casing dripping water over his shoes.

Releasing air through her teeth, Sandi gathered herself and arranged her face into something resembling compassion. 'Well, we wish you the best of luck with everything, Mandy,' she said, mustering a terse smile. I couldn't be bothered to correct her. 'We are on your side, you know.'

'You could have fooled me,' I muttered as Kyle helped her into the van before driving away, offering me a sympathetic smile while Sandi checked her make-up in the rear-view mirror.

'What was all that about?' said Josh, turning up as the van disappeared round the corner. Rain glistened in his hair, and his damp clothes hugged the contours of his body.

'Sandi Brent somehow got wind of this,' I said, indicating the horrible mess I'd made on the window. At least it no longer resembled a skull and crossbones – more a deformed butterfly, with the letter P underneath. 'I reckon whoever did it must have called her.' Suddenly shaky, I didn't object when he placed a hand at my elbow and ushered me back inside. 'Did you get a paper?'

He nodded, lifting his top and tugging it from the waistband of his faded jeans. 'It's not too bad, actually.'

'You must be kidding.' In the photo on the front page, I was gazing at Josh with a rapturous expression, as though I'd encountered a Greek

god – or Tom Hiddleston in his pants. My fringe had turned outwards
at the sides, giving the impression I had horns. 'It's a disaster.'

'You look cute,' he said, examining the picture closely with a smile.

'I look like a brainwashed cult member,' I said, snatching the paper out of his hands and reading Chris Weatherby's article.

The Sour Taste of Success . . .

**Award-winning Marnie Appleton (39) of The Beachside
Sweet Shop, was targeted by protestors this week, led by prolific
blogger** hardly prolific **Isabel Sinclair (29),** had he switched our
ages deliberately? **wife of Gerry Sinclair, publishing CEO,** *former*
publishing CEO. **When asked how she planned to tackle the issue of sugar addiction in this country,** 'in this country?' I said.
'I'm not the bloody health minister,' **Miss Appleton announced
that on Bank Holiday Monday she'll be inviting customers to
sample her handmade low-sugar sweets. Whether the public will
swallow this** 'ha!' **blatant business ploy, or vote with their feet
and stay away, remains to be seen. Readers can find Ms Sinclair's
blog at www.izzywizzymummysbusy.co.uk**

I shoved the paper at Josh and stood shivering in my damp shirt.

'Do you have a staff-training notice?' he asked.

'What?' I shook my head. 'Never needed one,' I said.

'Wait there.' He moved to the counter, found a sheet of paper, a
pen, and some Sellotape. 'There,' he said, when he'd finished writing, sticking the makeshift notice to the door and locking it. 'Now
you have.' He grabbed my hand. 'Come out the back and have some
coffee.'

'I saw you last night,' I said, letting him lead me to the kitchen, the touch of his hand radiating warmth through my veins. 'Near Wareham.'

He let go of my hand, to fill the kettle with water. 'Where were you?' he said, taking a fresh jar of coffee from the cupboard above the sink, not disputing it was him.

'On a bus,' I said. 'I went to see Beth.' Was it my imagination, or had his shoulders stiffened? 'I didn't know you had a campervan.'

'It's a friend's,' he said, spooning coffee into mugs. 'We were supposed to be going for a drink out that way, but the stupid thing broke down.'

'I thought it must have,' I said. 'You looked quite angry on the phone.'

He glanced at me and away again, before I could see his expression.

'No breakdown cover?' I guessed.

He nodded, adding milk to the mugs and handing me one. 'Shall we drink in the stockroom?' He flourished an arm.

'Why not?' I said. I glanced into the shop, but couldn't see any customers waiting to come in. The sky outside was gunmetal grey, and rain threw itself against the window, washing away the remains of the paint.

I couldn't remember the last time I'd closed the shop on a week-day, and was filled with a naughty-schoolgirl feeling as we perched on one of the wooden pallets in the stockroom that Gramps had planned to 'do something with', though he'd never made clear what.

It was cosy, the only light coming from the rays filtering through from the shop. The air was filled with the sugary smell of sweets, and the sound of the rain cascading down the guttering outside added an air of intimacy. I began to feel a bit better. 'I think we'll weather the storm, if you'll pardon the pun,' I said to Josh.

'I don't doubt it for a minute,' he said. He scooched back on the pallet until he was leaning against the wall. Bringing his knees up to act as a shelf, he rested his mug on one of them. In the half-light, his face looked serious. 'I really am sorry about yesterday,' he began.

I waved my hand. 'You've already apologised,' I told him. 'It's in the past.'

For a second he looked stricken, and seemed about to say something else.

He loudly cleared his throat. 'Did you always want to join the family business?'

I half-turned so I was facing him properly, drawing my legs underneath me. 'I didn't really think about it, to be honest. I used to help out when I was little, then worked here as a teenager, for pocket money. After I studied business at uni, it made sense to be here full-time, I suppose.'

His brow wrinkled. 'So it wasn't a career plan as such?'

I puffed air into my drying fringe, guessing it looked horrendous. 'Well, I didn't *not* want to work here,' I protested. 'I mean, it suited me over the years, but I always thought of it as convenient, and a stop-gap before . . .' *before what?* 'I was saving up to go travelling.'

He gave me a considering look. 'And yet, here you are.'

I took a gulp of coffee and rubbed at a spot of paint on my sneaker. 'After my grandfather died, it seemed like the right thing to stay.'

'You were the natural heir,' he said, putting on a theatrical voice. 'The successor to the family empire.'

It sounded quite good when he put it like that. 'I suppose so.' I paused. 'No one else in the family wanted to take it on, but I couldn't bear for it to be sold.' Every time I said the word 'sold' there was a pinching sensation in my chest. 'It wouldn't have felt right.'

'Your boyfriend didn't fancy running it with you?'

'I don't have a boyfriend,' I said quickly. 'My ex was a sound engineer, though he did love the sweet shop. He was good at coming up with ideas, like guess how many jelly beans in a jar, and . . .' I broke off. I didn't want to discuss Alex with Josh. Apart from anything, mentioning his name reminded me he'd be on a plane right now with Bobbi-Jo, and within hours would be introducing her to his parents. 'Do you have a girlfriend?' I said, rather desperately.

'Nah.' He pushed a lock of hair back. 'Well, I did for a while, last summer.' He rested his head against the wall. 'We went to loads of music festivals, but at one, these guys started pissing in cardboard cups and flinging them into the crowd.'

'Ew, that's gross,' I said. Mum had invited me to Glastonbury once, to see a tribal musician she was dating. He was playing in an area called The Common and the performance involved ritual paint-throwing and tomato fights. It had been fun to spend time together, in spite of the biblical rain that weekend, and the musician boyfriend sloping off with a groupie.

'I know,' Josh said, making a sucking-lemon face. 'She went ballistic, said all men were animalistic bastards, and she never wanted to see me again.'

'Charming.'

He took a sip of his coffee. 'It's OK,' he said with a shrug. 'I mean, I was really into her at the time, but I got over it.' When he looked at me again, there was a tinge of shyness in his eyes. 'She was hot, like you,' he said, unexpectedly. 'All dark hair and eyes.' He made a shape with his hand, presumably demonstrating a shapely figure, though he could have been swatting away a spider. 'Long legs, nice boobs, and all that.'

A wave of heat attacked my face, and I was glad he couldn't see me clearly. 'That's nice,' I said, ridiculously flattered.

'And a great personality,' he added, as an afterthought.

A smile tugged at my mouth. 'Not that great, considering she dumped you in case you threw wee at her, one day.'

'I know, right?' He looked mildly indignant. 'What a bitch.'

'Exactly.'

There was a moment of charged silence. Even the rain had eased. There was just the occasional plop of water dripping off the roof.

'I could show you a card trick,' Josh announced, at the same time as I said, 'I suppose we should get back to work.'

'Card trick first.' As Josh shifted a buttock to pull free his pack of cards, his mug toppled from its perch, spilling coffee across the pallet and seeping into my jeans.

'Oh shit, sorry,' he said, lunging forward. He grabbed the mug and set it upright, then tried to stem the flow of liquid dripping through the slats with his hands.

'It's fine, I've been soaking wet all morning one way or another,' I said, realising too late it sounded smutty.

Josh obviously thought so too.

His eyes locked with mine, our faces so close our breath mingled hotly. His coffee-scented hands were suddenly on my face and my fingers had tugged up his T-shirt and were roaming across his stomach of their own accord. His lips grew closer, eyes deepening with desire . . .

'What in the name of Barbara Windsor . . .?'

We sprang apart as if we'd been tasered, light flooding the stockroom with the force of a helicopter searchlight.

I turned to see Doris in the doorway, hands on her hips, eyes twice their normal size, as if she'd found us in the act of copulation which – to be fair – a couple of seconds later she might have.

'There are customers outside,' she went on, before I could mount a defence. 'This shop has never been closed on a weekday in all the years I've lived here, and what do I find?' She glanced at Josh, who'd grabbed a box of sweets and was holding it in front of his crotch, then back at me. I realised a couple of shirt buttons had come undone, revealing the white lacy bra I hardly ever wore, and must have put on by mistake. 'I find the pair of you, at it like rabbits, ripping each other's clothes off like, like . . . beasts in the wild . . .' She paused, breathing rapidly. As I buttoned my shirt I caught a manic glint in her eyes, and a hectic flush on her cheeks, and remembered overhearing her boasting to Celia once that she and her husband Roger had enjoyed a 'robust' sex life and that she 'missed that side of things'.

'How did you get in?' I said, heading over to close the stockroom door that led outside.

'It was unlocked.' Her eyes hovered around Josh's midriff. 'Not very security conscious at all.'

Not daring to make eye contact with Josh, I linked my arm through Doris's and shepherded her into the shop. 'I'm sorry you had to see that,' I murmured, positioning her in front of the counter. 'We've had some bad publicity, I'm afraid. Josh was, um, comforting me.'

'I could see that,' she said, puffed up with something I didn't want to think about. 'But did he have to do it with his shirt off?'

'It wasn't off,' I started, then changed tack. 'I don't suppose you saw someone spray-painting a skull and crossbones on the window earlier, did you?'

To my relief, she snapped back into being the Doris Day I knew. 'That's vandalism,' she tutted, producing a spiral notebook and biro from her handbag and scribbling something down. 'Do you have CCTV?'

'I'm afraid not.'

She sucked in her breath and adopted her Miss Marple expression. 'I'll ask around, see what I can find out,' she said, tapping the side of her nose with her pen. 'I saw the paper this morning,' she added, putting the notebook away. 'Don't let them get you down.'

'I'm trying not to,' I said, smacking away a vivid image of Josh's lips approaching mine in slow motion. 'But it's difficult.'

'What would your grandfather do?'

'This wouldn't have happened in his day,' I pointed out. 'It's because of winning that award.'

'Well use it as an opportunity to exercise that brain of yours, and come back and be better than ever.'

I remembered the sweets I'd made the night before, which had turned out better than expected. 'I'm trying,' I said, feeling a flicker of pride.

Doris's face collapsed into a smile. 'You always were brighter than you let on, Marnie Appleton. Your granddad used to rave about how brainy you were, not like that lazy mother of yours.'

'She wasn't lazy,' I protested. 'She just wanted different things.'

Josh's thighs are so strong, his stomach so hard, his . . .

'What is it, dear?' Doris's alarmed voice brought me out of my trance.

'Nothing!' I looked past her to see that the window was finally paint free, and fingers of sunlight were poking through the clouds.

'Customers,' I added, as Josh headed to the door with the keys, throwing me a loaded glance. 'It's time to open the shop.'

Chapter 19

'Wow, Mar, you look great!' said Phoebe, rising from her seat at the bar to give me a bear-hug. 'I'm loving the denim jacket and the hair,' she added, with a grin, though my cousin's tawny curtain made mine look as if it had been styled by a tipsy chimp.

I'd texted her on impulse after work to see if she was free that evening, remembering she was going to be in Bournemouth visiting Uncle Cliff. She suggested we meet at The Anchor, a favourite haunt years ago, that had transformed from traditional spit 'n' sawdust to trendy pub and bistro.

'You don't look so bad yourself,' I said, though charcoal shadows cradled her hazel eyes, as if she'd not slept for a year.

'I'm knackered,' she confirmed, in her usual forthright way. 'Burning the candle all the way through and forgetting to light it again.'

At the tender age of eighteen, Phoebe had been the first Appleton to move to London, and landed a job as a waitress in a Mexican restaurant, much to Uncle Cliff's horror. He'd clawed at his hair, imagining all kinds of horrors befalling his beloved daughter; most of them involving drug cartels and the Mafia.

But when a fiery relationship with her manager ended, and he fled back to his native country, Phoebe ended up running the place. She brought in a new chef, a young and as yet unknown talent, and within a couple of years El Mirador was one of the most sought after restaurants in London, attracting celebrities from around the globe.

Phoebe invited Beth and me to stay once, and we spotted a tiny Kate Moss with some friends, drinking sparkling water and smoking a cigarette, and when Alex and I went there he swore he saw a Kardashian going into the ladies.

Since then, Phoebe had opened another, equally successful, restaurant in the city. I was in awe of her success, but it had come at a price. She hadn't had a relationship in years, and her last visit to Shipley was to attend our grandfather's funeral.

'So what's been happening in your life?' I said when we'd collected our drinks and moved to the only available seating area – a leather-covered alcove next to a party of women celebrating a birthday, judging by the 'Happy 40th' balloons, and the empty cocktail glasses littering their table.

After bringing me up to date, making me laugh with her stories – one involving a cat-fight at El Mirador after a double booking between rival reality shows – we were halfway down our second bottle of red wine when she said, 'I heard you were having some problems at the shop since winning that competition.'

'How did you know?' I said, shrugging off my jacket and getting comfy – though someone had been at the seat with Mr Sheen and I kept sliding forward.

'Celia keeps Dad and my brothers informed, and they let me know.' She showed me her iPhone. 'We have a WhatsApp group called Family Matters.'

'Sensible,' I said. 'You probably know more than I do about what I'm up to.'

'I like to stay in the loop.' She flashed the wicked grin I remembered from when we were children. Two years older and bossy with it, she'd loved having a younger cousin to impress but was fiercely protective too, and used to become quite motherly whenever my mum vanished to pastures new, or turned up with a new boyfriend. 'It sounds like you've got your work cut out,' she said, swilling her wine around her glass.

'You could say that.' I gulped the rest of my drink. I needed it. After Doris had left earlier that day, with a complimentary bag of pineapple cubes, there'd been a steady flow of customers into the shop. Several had wanted more details about the makeover, while others wanted to know why I'd become the target of a hate campaign.

Dealing with them had left no time to dwell on what had almost happened in the stockroom, and to my relief Josh hadn't alluded to it – other than letting his fingers linger near mine when we both dived for the till at one point.

'I'd better go and do the banking,' I'd said around four, escaping to the office and then to the building society, wondering whether the butterflies rampaging around my stomach were due to lust, anxiety, or hunger.

As I went to lock up, he'd looked at me with a troubled expression, as though about to apologise, and I'd briskly said, 'Let's go then, Josh. I'll see you in the morning.'

He gave me a rueful smile, grabbed his skateboard and pushed off down the road, hitching up his jeans as they slipped around his hips.

'I might be getting away from it all soon,' I said to Phoebe, slightly slurring my words.

She paused in the act of opening a packet of peanuts. 'Away?' she said, screwing her face up. 'What do you mean, *away*?'

'I mean *away* away.' I jabbed my finger in the direction of the door, wine sloshing about in my almost empty stomach. I'd only managed half my dinner, too scared to turn on the television to watch the local news. 'Across the sea to Skye.'

'You're going to *Skye*?' Phoebe looked perplexed. 'But why?'

'No! It's a song,' I said with a giggle. 'You *know*.' I began to warble the words, but couldn't remember them all and segued into, ' . . . *country ROADS, taaaake me home . . .* '

'Have some nuts,' ordered Phoebe, grabbing my hand and tipping some into my palm.

I shovelled them in and chewed obediently. 'I *need* to get away,' I repeated, spraying crumbs on the glossy black table between us. 'It's what I always wanted you know, to leave Shipley.'

'Well, you did get away.' Phoebe sat back and crossed her legs, her black-booted foot swinging. She'd stopped smiling, and suddenly looked like Celia when she was about to tell Chester off – which admittedly wasn't very often. 'You went down the Amazon with the gorgeous Alex, if I remember rightly.'

'That ended up being more of a holiday,' I said, helping myself to more peanuts, and washing them down with a slug of wine. 'We were going to stay away longer, but Gramps got sick.'

'I know,' she said. 'But you were glad to be back, as I recall.'

'I was very glad I made it home to say goodbye.' I swallowed hard at the memory of his slight figure in the hospice, worn thin by the cancer that swept through him with frightening speed, only weeks after his diagnosis. 'But I never intended to stay.'

'Bollocks,' scoffed Phoebe, tearing open a bag of crisps with her teeth. 'You could have left again, but you didn't.'

'There was too much to do,' I said. 'Celia was grieving, Mum had just met Mario and was distracted, and Uncle Cliff had to get back to prising rotten teeth out.'

She finished a mouthful of crisps. 'So?'

'So, someone had to take care of the business.' Annoyance swept through me. 'Why is it so hard to understand?'

'You could have . . .'

' . . . sold the shop or got in a manager,' I parroted. 'So everyone keeps saying.'

'That's because it's true.'

I thought of Celia and Gramps, who'd done so much for me – parents and grandparents rolled into one, never begrudging a single second.

'I wanted the sweet shop to stay in the family, for Gramps,' I said, studying my empty glass to quell a surge of tears. 'And Alex and I needed to save up before we could go away again.'

'So why not take the opportunity when he was offered the job in New York?'

'What is this, the Spanish Inquisition?' I snapped, rearing out of my seat. The room tilted like a galleon.

'I was just saying.' Phoebe looked unfazed. 'No need to go feral.'

'Sorry.' I thudded down again. 'It's been a really odd week.'

'I heard he's coming back today,' she said. 'For his parents' anniversary party.'

'WhatsApp?'

She nodded. 'Ben's in the band they've booked to play,' she said, referring to her younger brother. 'I guessed Alex might be there.' She gave me a sly little look. 'Are you going?'

'He's met someone else,' I mumbled, looking around for a waiter. They seemed preoccupied with the birthday party, which was descending into chaos. One of the women was weeping into a napkin, while her friend rubbed circles on her back. 'You're not too old for a baby, Sal,' she was saying, over the hubbub of noise. 'You could try another round of IVF.'

'Oh Marnie, I'm sorry.' Phoebe slid round to sit beside me, her musky perfume provoking a wave of nausea. 'I didn't know.'

'It's fine,' I said. 'But I think I need to get away to move on.'

'Do you think if you'd gone with him . . .?'

'I couldn't go because Celia broke her leg,' I said, chopping the air with my hand.

Phoebe looked sceptical. 'You could have joined him when she was better,' she said. 'From what I heard, you practically told him to go and he was heartbroken.'

'For Christ's sake!' I shouted. 'Is nothing sacred around here?' Seeing shocked stares from the birthday table, I dropped my voice. 'This is why I want to leave,' I hissed. 'I hate everyone knowing my business.'

Unperturbed, Phoebe patted my knee. 'Going away's fine, but there's nothing wrong with coming home,' she said sagely. 'I should know.'

'But you're happy in London.'

She sagged against the leather upholstery, as though her bones had melted. 'Not really,' she said. 'I'm a bit sick of being a high-flyer.' She beckoned the waiter with a click of her fingers, and he trotted over as though glad to escape the mania now sweeping through the birthday party. Two more women were crying, one threatening the other with legal action if she didn't return a petrol mower she'd borrowed six months ago. 'More wine, please,' Phoebe ordered. 'And do you have any Scampi Fries?'

'So you're thinking of giving up the restaurant?' I said, when he'd trotted off.

She wound a strand of hair around her fingers. 'I quite fancy coming back and opening an arts and crafts shop, or a flower stall.'

'There's already a flower stall,' I said. 'Ruby's Blooms in the square?'

'Hmmm,' she said, not really listening. 'I could help Dad on reception at the surgery, or just do nothing for a bit.' She sighed. 'I've so many good memories here.'

I couldn't believe this was Phoebe talking. Phoebe, who'd met George Clooney and his wife at the restaurant, had holidayed in Dubai, and employed a personal shopper to buy her clothes.

'All your good memories are in *Shipley*?'

She pouted a little drunkenly. 'Don't tell me you don't have any.'

At once my brain was swollen with them, and I seemed to be laughing in them all.

'Do you remember that rope swing in the park?' she said. 'Every time we jumped on it, it snapped and we'd end up with mild concussion?' She exploded into laughter. 'Oh my god, you looked so funny lying there while Ben tried CPR!'

'Memories can be made anywhere,' I said, trying to keep a straight face. 'There's a big wide world out there.'

'Why do you think Auntie Laura never took you with her on her jaunts?' Phoebe loomed forward, wagging a bejewelled finger. 'So she always had a reason to come home, that's why.' She slumped back. 'She never really wanted to escape after she came back from India, but she'd said it so many times she started to believe her own bullshit.'

'Pheebs!' Shock pierced the wine-induced haze in my brain. 'I'm sure that's not true, or she'd have stayed around.'

'Oh come on, Mar.' Phoebe slid even down further down in her seat. 'I mean, I love Auntie Laura but she's hardly a feminist role-model, constantly waiting for some lover-boy to sweep her away.' I tried to concentrate, certain what she was saying was of great importance, but her face was dipping in and out of focus. 'I doubt even *she* knows what she wants, but you do, Marnie.' She gave me a mock-menacing look, her chin almost level with the table. 'You just don't know it yet.'

'How the FUCK did you get to be so *wise*, Pheebs?' I shook my head in admiration. 'What?'

Her shoulders were heaving. 'I'd forgotten you swear and shout when you're drunk,' she managed, hoisting herself up. 'It's bloody *hilarious*.'

'I'm *not* drunk, and I'm *not* fucking SWEARING,' I said, separating my words very carefully. 'I just think you're so fucking CLEVER.' Reaching out, I squidged her pink-apple cheeks with my fingers, enjoying hearing her giggle the way she used to.

Her gaze rolled past me. 'Sweet baby jay, is that YOU?'

I swivelled round to see a familiar face on the television behind the bar. 'Fuck!' It was the late edition of the local news, and there I was in glorious HD, bloodless lips moving soundlessly. I looked like a flood victim with my rain-flattened hair and my shirt plastered to my breasts, while Sandi Brent resembled Sandra Bullock playing a news reporter.

In the next shot I was bending over, scrubbing furiously at the shop window, my denim-clad bottom displaying a spreading brown stain that only I knew was coffee.

'Oh my GOD,' cried Phoebe. 'It's like a scene from *EastEnders*.'

Suddenly we were choking with laughter, and Phoebe had slipped completely under the table. The birthday group looked on in tutting disapproval, which only made us laugh harder.

'I'm fucking starving,' I said, when we'd recovered. 'Let's go and get some fich and ships.'

Chapter 20

I shot out of bed the following morning, like a vampire released from its coffin.

'Christ,' I mumbled, catching my reflection. I had a pillow-creased face and blood-shot eyes, while my hair looked as if someone had backcombed it on one side. Bizarrely, I was wearing my denim jacket back to front.

A memory crashed in, of scoffing fish and chips with Phoebe on the beach, then paddling in the freezing sea, before weaving our way arm-in-arm back to Celia's. I dimly recalled Phoebe crashing out at the foot of my bed, giggling when I asked if she remembered how, when we were young, I was convinced my dolls would spring to life while I was sleeping.

She'd already left, but had torn a page from a paperback and scrawled a message in eyeliner. *Had fun cuz gr8 to see you. Enjoy your party. Spk soon xx* She was clearly more used to writing texts. I'd forgotten she didn't suffer hangovers; unlike me. My skull felt as fragile as an egg, while my stomach churned like a washing machine on a spin cycle.

Rummaging my phone from under my pillow, I noticed a message from Beth.

Harry and co will be at the shop 7.00 am Sunday. Ate nearly all the caramel cups, spent the night trying not to throw up!!! X PS does this mean Bunty will be addicted to healthy sweets??X PPS marzipan popular in Tudor times – worth a try??

A further text read Look forward to seeing you later. Alex X

My heart gave a juddering wallop. In my sleep-addled state I'd forgotten he was back on British soil. For the first time in almost a year we were in the same country, and only one thought was flashing in neon lights.

What the hell should I wear?

I began rifling through my wardrobe like Gok Wan.

Definitely not the blue thing I wore on our first date, or the skirt I was wearing when we met – the hem was ripped anyway – and not the green top that Alex said brought out my eyes, or the jeans he thought made my bum look great, or the wraparound cardigan that emphasised my boobs.

The pounding in my head increased as I tossed things behind me, like Chester kicking up earth when he buried a bone in the garden.

I really needed a trip to the charity shop, and to buy some new clothes.

Eventually, I settled for a flowery, fitted dress I'd bought on a whim, that wouldn't look out of place at a summer fete. It screamed fresh, wholesome and non-threatening. Or maybe I should go to the opposite extreme, and wear something to show Alex what he was missing.

I grabbed a white jumpsuit with a plunging back and neckline that Beth had passed on – an impulse purchase, too long in the leg for her, and not really her style. It wasn't mine either. It was the sort of thing Katy Perry might wear to the MTV music awards.

I slung it back in the wardrobe. Better stick with the frock.

After a quick shower – though there wasn't such a thing at Celia's, with the terrible plumbing producing a trickle more suited to water torture – I got dressed, rolling on some old Spanx to ensure a smooth outline under the dress, and applied a light layer of make-up. I even attempted an eyeliner flick, á la Sandi Brent, that didn't look too bad. I resisted the urge to trim my fringe, knowing it would result in a wonky line, reminiscent of the school photos Celia had scattered around. Instead, I swept it to one side and fixed it in place with a silver hair slide Mum had bought me for Christmas.

Not bad, I decided, scrutinising the result through half-shut eyes. Less like something from *The Walking Dead*, and not too matronly.

'You look nice,' Celia said, as I slunk into the kitchen to make tea, and to eat something to settle my stomach. She was coming through the back door with Chester on a lead, her stick in her other hand, wearing her favourite cowboy boots over geometrically patterned leggings.

'Thanks,' I said. My voice sounded croaky and dehydrated, as if I'd been shouting all night. That happened to me sometimes after drinking wine, it affected my vocal cords.

'I've got a trilby hat in the closet that would go with your dress.'

'How's your leg?' I said quickly, burying an image of the time she'd worn it to one of my school plays, prompting a teacher to ask – straight-faced – if Celia was a fashion designer.

'The physio said I'm doing so well I don't need this any more.' She banged her stick on the flagstones. 'I've got to keep doing my exercises,' she added, sticking out her leg and dancing her foot in the air.

'Just take it easy,' I said, bending to give her a hug. 'Maybe you should hang onto the stick, just in case.'

'Paddy said we should have a ceremonial burning session in his back garden.'

'Did he now?' That sounded dangerous to me. And completely unnecessary. Not the sort of behaviour Celia would condone. But looking at her closely, I noticed a gleam in her eye. 'What's it got to do with him?' I said, cutting an avocado in half and eating it with a spoon.

'I thought it would mark the end of your gran's recovery. Symbolic, like, you know,' said Paddy, stepping into the kitchen behind Celia and stamping his feet on the mat.

'Morning,' I said with a guilty smile, while Muttley shot past to snuffle around Chester's bottom.

'I bumped into him in the lane,' said Celia, her gaze dropping to the dogs who were circling each other warily. Thinking back, I couldn't remember whether she'd been awake when I got in. I dimly recalled yelling good night, but she hadn't responded. Assuming she was asleep I'd crept upstairs, which seemed to take an age as they kept moving like an escalator.

A thought too horrible to contemplate crept in: had she spent the night at Paddy's? But my grandmother wouldn't do that. *Would she?*

Her cheeks were cherry red, as if she knew exactly what was running through my mind. I put down my spoon, stomach curdling.

'I'll put the kettle on,' she said, at the exact moment I said, 'Well, I'd better get to the shop.'

Paddy remarked, 'You do look very nice, Marnie. Much better than you did on the news.'

Oh god. 'You saw that then?'

He exchanged a look with Celia, giving the impression they'd watched it together; in bed.

'You came across very well,' she said loyally, slotting some bread into the toaster. 'I can't stand that Brent woman, always trying to catch people out.'

'What did I say?'

'Well, you couldn't really get a word in edgeways, because that woman kept going on about duty, and women having to fight to succeed in business and—'

'Sounds like she's on my side then,' I said optimistically, taking a slurp of scalding tea.

Another meaningful glance in Paddy's direction.

'Not exactly,' he murmured, bending to grab Muttley's collar as he attempted to mount Chester by the Aga. 'She started waffling about the cut-throat world of the food industry, and the nanny state, and that with a local blogger raising public awareness about healthy eating, you'd be lucky to survive.'

My mouth fell open. 'She said that?'

'More or less,' he said, looking as guilty as if he'd voiced the opinion himself.

'Take no notice,' said Celia. 'Whoever that blogger is, they're not going to reach too many people around here. There's barely a broadband signal in some parts.'

'And in a way, they're doing you a favour,' said Paddy. 'It's more publicity for the sweet shop.'

Bad publicity.

'Who is this blogger anyway?' Celia snapped to attention. If she'd had antennae they would have been twitching. 'Anyone we know?'

'Yes, who is it?' Paddy echoed.

'She was probably talking generally, not specifically,' I said. I didn't want Celia to know it was Isabel Sinclair. She would probably give her a rollicking, and give her something else to blog about. 'Anyway, I'd better go,' I said, relieved when Chester turned on Muttley and made a grab for his tail. 'I don't want to be late!'

I left them trying to calm the dogs with the aid of a rubber bone and hurried down the hill.

Isabel was unloading a box of misshapen vegetables from her boot as I passed. I was going to ignore her, but she gave me a lofty smile, and said, 'Making some smoothies to put on my blog.'

'Won't that be a bit messy?'

'Funny.' She swished her hair. 'I've a lot more followers since the piece in the paper came out.'

It was true. They'd flooded in after the newspaper article linked to her latest blog post, which was entitled *Making a Stir, for a Good Cause!* It was illustrated with a picture of her running along the beach, pouting into the camera with the caption, 'Sugar free and lovin' it!' Alongside the gushing comments from The Perfect Mums, some old friends had popped up asking, *When are we going to see you again, sweets?* And *Loving your top in that picture babe, where's it from?* Another wondered if baby Fitzgerald was out of nappies yet, and there was a rather heart-breaking appeal from her mother: *How's darling Fitzy? Please get in touch sweetheart, Daddy and I are missing our only grandchild.* Another commenter called HealthyMum had written, *You go, Izzy. Sweets should be banned, I nearly choked on a barley sugar once.*

'You might as well give up,' Isabel sniped. 'My book deal's imminent, and soon I'll be on all the news shows spreading the word, and no one will want your nasty little sweets.'

'Talk about delusions of grandeur,' I growled. 'We'll see about that.'

I made myself breathe deeply, and drink in the view to calm myself down. There was a water-skier cutting through the clear blue sea, and the benches along the old stone pier were dotted with spectators.

I'd tried water-skiing once, with Alex, but spray had whooshed up my nose and nearly choked me, and I'd tumbled into the water.

Agnieszka and Josh were waiting outside when I arrived at the shop and as I watched him lean towards her, an odd sensation washed through me. *Jealousy?* Ridiculous. Just because we'd had a clinch didn't mean he was falling in love with me. *More's the pity.* STOPPIT! I ordered the voice in my head. I was too old for him anyway, whereas Agnieszka was a tall, sun-kissed twenty-two-year-old, with a sheet of white-blonde hair, and lively brown eyes.

Spotting me, she gave a little wave. ''Allo, Marnie!' She grinned at Josh. 'He's magic man,' she said, and I realised he was showing her a card trick.

'He certainly is.' I flushed as he caught my eye. He looked particularly handsome, in a green-and-white checked shirt.

'I like the dress,' he said to me, putting the cards away and tucking his skateboard under his arm. 'Very *Downton Abbey.*'

'Hardly,' I said, unlocking the shop. 'Have you ever watched it?'

'Er, no,' he admitted. 'My mum did, though.'

Agnieszka led the way inside, shedding her white furry gilet on the way. She wore it whatever the weather, just as she wore the same buttock-moulding jeans, so tight it was obvious she wasn't wearing any underwear. I wondered if Josh had noticed, though doubted he worried like I did that she might get thrush.

'I've got an . . . *event* later on, so I'll be leaving early,' I told them, trying to ignore my pulsing headache. For a crazy second, I contemplated inviting Josh. But I couldn't leave Agnieszka, however capable she was, and it would look too much like tit-for-tat in front of Alex if I turned up with a good-looking – younger – man.

Agnieszka positioned herself behind the counter, and Josh began juggling some lollipops, attracting passers-by. A couple came in to watch, and he charmed them into trying some different sweets with their eyes closed, challenging them to guess what they were.

'You're a natural at this too,' I said, as they left, smiling. 'You should be running the shop.'

'No way,' he said, vehemently. 'This is your baby.'

His words sent a ripple of pleasure through me, even though it wasn't strictly true.

'It could be yours one day,' Gramps had said to Mum, years ago.

'I'm not interested in business,' she said. 'I can't be pinned down to one thing.'

'The *business* bought your home, paid for your upbringing and your travelling, and has made your father, and a lot of other people, very happy.' That was Celia, furious with Mum.

She was right, I thought. It wasn't fair of Mum to have dismissed it like that. Seeing the smiling faces of the customers just leaving was proof that we'd brightened their morning – or at least Josh had.

The rest of the day passed with agonising slowness. I busied myself with paperwork and tried not to think about Alex and what to say when I saw him.

Josh brought me coffee and gave me a speculative look.

'What's this event then?'

'Oh, just an anniversary party,' I said. Even the words made my palms tingle with nerves. 'Do you have your bank details, so I can pay you at the end of the month?'

'Listen, about yesterday . . .'

'It's fine,' I broke in. 'I'm sure Doris won't say anything.' I wasn't sure at all. Probably the whole of Shipley knew I'd been cavorting with my new assistant.

'I wasn't worried about that.' He leaned against the doorframe. 'I wondered if you wanted to . . .'

'Bank details, Josh?' I looked away, my head still full of Alex. 'You do have an account?'

'Not really.'

I shot him a look. 'You don't?'

'Well, yes, it's just . . .' He broke off, colour rising in his cheeks. 'Actually, no I don't,' he said. 'Stupid, I know but . . .'

'It's fine,' I said, wondering how someone got to the age of twenty-five without opening a bank account. 'Maybe you could open one next week?'

He hesitated, and seemed on the verge of saying something else when Agnieszka called for assistance, and the moment passed.

'Will you be OK to lock up?' I said, when the time finally crawled to five o'clock.

'Of course,' Agnieszka and Josh said in synch and exchanged a smile. They'd been getting on well, to the point where I'd heard Agnieszka giggle several times – a surprisingly rich sound I'd never heard before.

'You see your man?' she asked, doing a pouty thing with her lips, though she knew Alex and I were no longer together.

Josh gave me a quizzical look that warmed my cheeks. 'Your man?'

'No man.' I needed a panic wee, but couldn't face wrestling my Spanx down. Instead, for the second time that day, I said, 'I've got to go, or I'll be late.'

Chapter 21

Alex's parents lived just outside Weymouth, in a detached, white-fronted house framed by beech trees and bordered by a picket fence.

As the taxi drove off I lingered on the pavement, the evening sun warm on the back of my neck, and debated whether to run away.

Jazzy music drifted from round the back, mingling with voices and laughter. No one would miss me if I didn't turn up.

My phone buzzed. Beth.

Thinking about you. Stay strong, Crumble-face XX

I smiled at the nickname, invented by a bitchy girl at school, who tried to make something of my surname and came up short. '*Apple-ton, apple-pie, . . . apple . . .* crumble-*face.*'

I looked at the house again, its sparkling windows mirroring the cloudless sky. I'd eaten Sunday lunch inside, countless times. I'd admired the sea view from the orchard at the bottom of the garden, and the antiques his parents had collected. I'd watched television in the front room, and helped comfort his sister, Rebecca, when she moved back after a relationship break-up. But I hadn't visited since Alex went to New York. It wouldn't have felt right without him, and although they hadn't said so, I worried his parents blamed me for our break-up.

I adjusted my Spanx beneath my dress, feeling as if my spleen was being dissected, then stalked through the rose-covered archway at the top of the path leading to the front door. No one answered the bell. Probably all in the garden.

I made my way round the side, heart beating like a jackhammer, still rehearsing in my head what to say to Bobbi-Jo.

'How do you do?' Too Jane Austen.

'Good to meet you, Bobbi-Jo. Alex has told me so much about you.' Except he hadn't.

'Yo, bitch. Wassup?' Maybe not.

I headed straight for the marquee in the middle of the lawn, managing to avoid eye contact with anyone. It was hot inside, holding the warmth of the day, and I felt perspiration break out on my forehead. The band was playing cover versions, and recognising my cousin Ben on the saxophone, I waved.

He winked, and inclined his head to where Alex's dad was helping himself to a mountain of food from the buffet.

'Hi, Max,' I said tapping him on the shoulder.

He swung round, his broad face lighting up. 'Marnie!' He drew me into a hearty, one-armed hug. 'So glad you came, lovely girl,' he said. 'We've missed you.'

'Happy Anniversary!' I carolled, giving him a squeeze. I'd missed him too, and Helen. They were the sort of parents everyone should have; safe, supportive, and reassuring. They'd both retired from teaching now, and did a lot of voluntary work in the local community.

'You might find them dull,' Alex had said, after his memorable introduction to my mum, but I hadn't. I liked that they had heated discussions around the dinner table, but never fell out.

I'd imagined Alex and me being like his parents one day – comfortable in each other's company, still holding hands, still in love.

Sometimes, in Peru, when I thought about never going home, I'd felt a pang at what we would be missing.

'Come and see Helen,' Max was saying, dashing crumbs from his shirt-front. He led me out to the dappled shade of an apple tree, where Helen was chatting with a clutch of friends, sipping a glass of champagne.

'Happy Anniversary!' I said again, handing over the card I'd brought, and a little decorative bowl I'd bought off Etsy. 'It's inlaid with pearl,' I explained as she unwrapped it. 'You know, because it's your pearl anniversary.'

'It's beautiful!' She smiled radiantly, holding it up for her friends to admire. 'You really shouldn't have.'

'Yes, it's lovely,' Max agreed, looking a little baffled. He probably couldn't see the point of a decorative bowl.

'Thank you, Marnie,' Helen said, warmly. She was a tiny, compact woman with neat auburn hair, but her eyes and smile were just like Alex's.

'Congratulations on your award!' she said, slipping a hand round my middle. The waist of my Spanx rolled over, creating a rubber-band effect, and I hoped she couldn't tell. 'And take no notice of all that nonsense in the paper,' she said sotto voce, so her friends couldn't overhear. 'You just keep doing what you're doing.'

I gave her a grateful smile. 'I'm trying a couple of things,' I said. 'Moving with the times.'

She gave me an appraising look. 'Well, good for you.'

'You're made of strong stuff,' said Max, through a mouthful of coleslaw. 'You'll be fine.'

As Helen nodded her agreement I was touched by their misplaced faith. They clearly weren't holding any grudges about me not going to America with Alex.

'He's here,' Helen said, as if she'd read my expression. 'Why don't you get a drink and say hello?'

But I didn't want a drink. A headache prodded at my temples from the night before, and my stomach was doing cartwheels. I wanted to grill her about Bobbi-Jo; ask if she was pretty, clever, did they like her?

It struck me like a punch that, as Alex's potential wife-to-be, she would get the same heartfelt treatment that I had.

'I just popped by to wish you all the best,' I said, shaking my head at a waistcoated waiter, hovering with a tray of drinks. 'I can't stay.'

'Oh, Marnie you must,' said Helen, removing her hand from my waist as my Spanx rolled over again. 'I know he'd like to see you.' She brought her head closer, her sparkly earrings catching a ray of sunlight. 'Between you and me, I'm not sure about his new girlfriend,' she whispered.

'Really?' This was unprecedented. The Steadmans liked *everyone*. My imagination ran wild. Had she accidentally killed a patient, or dropped the F-bomb over breakfast?

I was hijacked by a horrible thought. *She'd shared a bed with Alex.* Probably the one in his childhood bedroom which, despite being updated since he left home, his *Baywatch* posters banished, still contained the *essence* of him.

'She's a bit too perfect,' Helen said, with a little eye-roll.

'Oh.' Compared to murdering your family, or mugging a pensioner, it wasn't much of a criticism. 'Could be worse,' I said, managing a strangled laugh.

'There he is,' Max boomed, making me jump about a foot in the air. 'Alex, over here!'

My heart rate rocketed, and I suddenly felt on the verge of a panic attack. I grabbed a glass of champagne from the circling waiter and knocked it back in one, then sneezed three times in a row.

'Hello, Marnie.'

I pivoted round, jogging Helen's elbow and sending her drink cascading down Max's shirt.

'Oh god, I'm so sorry,' I said.

'Don't worry, I've got it,' she laughed, flapping her hand. 'Come on, you.' She steered a soaked and bemused Max towards the house, so I had no choice but to lift my snotty-nosed face to greet Alex.

'Hi,' he said again, and it was as though everyone else had been blasted off the face of the earth leaving just the two of us, locking eyes for the first time in nearly a year. Every emotion I thought I'd buried pounded back to the surface, and the force of it made my legs wobble.

How can he not feel it too?

For a blazing, heart-soaring second I thought he had, as his eyes burned into mine. He might look a bit different to the Alex who'd walked out of Celia's house all those months ago, but underneath the longer hair he was the same man I'd fallen in love with.

Then his lips started moving (the lips I'd so badly missed kissing) and I tuned in to hear him saying, ' . . . this is Bobbi-Jo.'

The world zoomed into garish focus, and I saw a woman at his side, holding onto his arm and studying me with open curiosity.

She was perfect, small and curvy with an air of maturity that probably came from being a nurse. And a mother. The laughter lines around her wide, blue eyes hinted at a fun personality, as did her discreet nose-piercing.

Ungluing herself from Alex's side, she swept a strand of shiny, conker-brown hair from her cheek and thrust out her hand.

'Lovely to meet you, Marnie,' she said in a Jennifer Aniston accent, her smile uncovering a kooky gap between her two front teeth. 'I've heard *so* much about you.'

Grasping her palm I pumped it firmly, noting that her strappy, camisole top showcased a tattoo of a tiny bird on her shoulder.

'Good to meet you too, Blobbi-Jo. I mean, Jobby-Blo.' Alex's face was gripped by a spasm of laughter. 'Sorry, I mean, Jo . . .'

'Hey, it's OK,' she said with immense kindness, and it was easy to see her in a hospital, administering a drip, or shoving a thermometer up an old man's rectum. Or would it be in his ear? I wondered if Alex liked her to wear her nurse's uniform outside work, and felt a bit sick. 'Just call me Bobbi,' she urged, releasing my hand. 'Everyone else does.'

I could feel another sneeze building. It erupted before I could stop it, and my hair slide unclipped. As it flew out, my fringe flopped down, and a bubble popped out of my nostril. 'Oops,' I said, mortified. I fished a tissue from my bag and blew my nose, eyes scanning the grass for my slide.

It was nestled in the grass by Bobbi-Jo's sandal-shod feet. Too late, I realised she was bending to retrieve it too, and as we bobbed down our heads crashed together.

'GODDAMMIT your skull is like GRANITE!' she cried, clutching her forehead, her face crumpled with pain.

'Here,' said Alex expressively, handing me the hair slide.

Perspiring and confused, I managed to squash it back in, and almost fainted when I pressed the emerging lump on my scalp. 'Thanks,' I mumbled, wishing the ground would open up.

'Hey, it's OK, I'm fine,' she said, though her watering eyes were slightly less friendly.

A heavy silence fell. I was still holding my champagne glass, and brought it to my lips before remembering it was empty. I took a pretend sip anyway, and Alex clamped his teeth to his lower lip.

'How have you been?' he said at last, and his toffee-coloured eyes were warm as they rested on my face.

'Oh, fine, fine, you know.' I grinned maniacally. 'Busy, busy!'

'I'm glad,' he said simply.

He was wearing a navy polo-shirt over stone-coloured jeans, and my heart twisted that he'd bought them without me knowing.

'You?'

Something flickered across his face. 'OK,' he said quietly, raising his beer bottle as if in a toast. 'My contract's just ended, but there's something else in the pipeline.'

I hate this. Talking as if we were strangers.

My brain cells lumbered about, seeking a fresh topic.

The gentle music floating from the marquee suddenly switched to a blistering Rihanna cover, and a couple of kohl-eyed girls sprang to life and started twerking.

'You look good,' Alex said, and I switched my gaze back to see if he was joking. Apart from my crazy hair and red-rimmed nostrils, my Spanx had rolled over so many times it felt like I'd stuffed a hula-hoop up my dress.

'Thanks,' I mumbled, aware Bobbi-Jo was looking from me to Alex with a fixed smile.

I cast a quick glance at her generous hips, encased in the sort of tapered trousers that would make me look like a businessman, and when I looked up, Alex was wearing an expression I'd last seen in Iquitos, after our Amazon trip. We'd left the hostel to grab some food at a café close to the river to watch the sunset. There'd been music playing, soft and sensuous, and I hadn't been able to resist getting up to dance, moving and swaying to the beat, and when I opened my eyes, Alex had been looking at me just like he was now; as if I was rare and precious.

'Hey, I hear you own an award-winning candy store!' Bobbi-Jo said, snapping the moment in half. Appearing to have recovered from our collision, she gave a gap-toothed grin. 'If Adam was with us I'd take him there, for sure.'

'Where *is* your son?' It came out wrong; more hardened social worker than polite enquiry.

Bobbi-Jo's smile calcified. 'He's with my parents,' she said, looking at Alex, as if for confirmation, and as she rested her hand on his forearm I spotted the ring on her wedding finger and my heart did a triple backflip.

How hadn't I seen it before, when a diamond that size was probably visible from space?

A klaxon was going off in my head. *They're engaged, they're engaged, they're engaged!*

Why hadn't anyone told me?

I tried to speak, but my vocal cords felt broken. I attempted what I hoped was a facial movement, to indicate I had to leave, terrified I might throw up.

'Marnie, what's wrong?' called Alex as I streaked away, elbowing guests out of my path. As I flew past the marquee I spotted Max wearing a fresh shirt, standing beside Helen. He looked about to make a speech, but I couldn't bear to hear a toast to his long and happy marriage.

I had to get away, even if it meant walking all the way back to Shipley.

'Marnie, please, just wait a minute.'

I paused and turned, chest heaving. I didn't dare lift my eyes from the toes of his loafers. When had he started wearing loafers? Is that what stepdads wore? He'd probably started eating muesli too. Did he even go swimming in the sea any more, or was that off the agenda for health and safety reasons?

Aware my thoughts were spiralling out of control, I made to leave.

'Marnie, please can we talk?' Seeing his hand reaching out, I took a step back.

'Not really,' I said, still staring at the grass. 'I hope you'll both be happy.' My tone was more suited to offering commiserations at a funeral, but I couldn't muster the energy to make it sound more convincing. 'Say goodbye to your mum and dad for me.'

Chapter 22

I leapt onto a bus at the bottom of the road with seconds to spare, puffing as if I'd just completed a triathlon. I slumped in a seat at the back, the view back to Shipley misted by a veil of tears.

My phone buzzed a couple of times.

How's it going? X Phoebe.

What's she like? Beth. Hope she looks like this . . . She'd attached a picture of an orang-utan, which under different circumstances would have made me laugh.

As I tried to compose a reply another message appeared, from Alex this time. Are you OK? Can we meet? Really need to talk to you. Maybe he was going to break the news that Bobbi-Jo was pregnant.

Feeling sick, I deleted the text and switched my phone off.

The shop was peaceful when I let myself in, and the first thing I did was yank my Spanx off and toss them on the floor. I drew air into my lungs, for what felt like the first time all day, and felt fractionally less sick.

Josh had forgotten to set the alarm, but had left a handwritten note on the counter, with his mobile number, and a message to call if I needed a hand with anything the following day.

Money in my pocket, ha ha, not really, it's in the safe, he'd added in a loopy scrawl. *Loads of customers, two said they wouldn't be back because of that woman appearing on Morning, Sunshine! and going on about how evil you are, but Aggie said they bought twice as much as usual!!* Aggie? And what was Isabel doing on *Morning, Sunshine!?* I rarely watched breakfast telly, but lots of people did.

With a nugget of dread in my chest I turned the computer on, and waited for it to judder to life. After finding the website, I pressed the link to that morning's edition. It immediately cut to Isabel, seated on a citrus-yellow sofa in the studio. She was in full 'earth-mother' mode, as if auditioning for one of the channel's family dramas, her beautiful face made up to look make-up free, her hair in a tousled pony-tail. A simple, open-neck blouse was tucked into a tiered skirt that floated to the ground, leaving only a glimpse of her giant feet, encased in espadrilles.

'If you read my blog,' she was saying with a meaningful glance to camera, 'you'll see I'm a passionate advocate of sugar-free eating, especially where our children are concerned.' She pressed a manicured hand to her chest. 'They really *are* our future.'

Vom.

'And you have a particular issue with . . .' The weekend presenter, Donal Kerrigan, a bandy-legged Irishman who'd recently been nominated 'weird crush of the year' by *heat* magazine, glanced at his notes. 'The Beachside Sweet Shop in Shipley, which recently won an independent business award?'

'Yes, I do.' Isabel's chest inflated with indignation. 'People shouldn't be rewarded for encouraging unhealthy eating,' she said, switching from earth-mother to Sunday school teacher. 'It *has* to stop, and it has to stop NOW.'

'Isn't that a bit strong?' said Donal, hitching up an eyebrow. 'I mean, I loved my sweeties as a kid, back in Ireland.' He fired off a throaty chuckle. 'My favourites were Acid Drops,' he said, shaking his head at the memory. 'Do you remember them?' He grinned. 'I felt quite daring ordering a quarter of those, I can tell you!'

Yesss! *In your FACE, Isabel Sinclair.* I remembered Alex had met him at a couple of industry award dos, and they'd hit it off.

'Yes, but that was the *past*,' Isabel said in a syrupy tone, making a quick recovery. 'Times are a'changing, and what *I* want to see,' she jabbed her breast with a slender finger for emphasis, 'is more people adopting a responsible attitude, like mine.' She paused, lowering her eyes and bringing them up again, but Donal seemed unmoved.

'*Everyone* loves a good sweet shop,' he drawled, with a lop-sided smile that didn't even look practised. 'I might check out The Beachside Sweet Shop myself!'

'Please do,' I said to the screen. 'I love you, Donal.'

Isabel looked like she wanted to throttle him, and I wondered how she'd landed the gig. Some contact from her modelling days, undoubtedly. 'I do agree that they used to have their place,' she said, lightly touching his knee, in a clear attempt to ingratiate herself. 'But times are different, Donal.'

'So if your plan is to close down this sweet shop and it works, what then?' He made his eyes go big. 'There are hundreds in the UK alone. Do you plan to close them all?'

Isabel's back straightened. 'That's a *brilliant* idea, Donald.'

'Donal.'

'I could be the woman who made a difference to the entire nation,' she said, almost to herself, and I could almost see the cogs turning. If she hadn't been sure about her agenda before, she certainly was now.

Bloody Donal had given her a USP.

She gave a quick shake of her head. 'In my blog,' another look to camera, 'I mention *new* pleasures we can all enjoy, like . . . like, nature, and walking, and only eating food that comes out of the earth.'

'Oh, I love potatoes too,' said Donal, closing his eyes in apparent rapture. 'Mashed, boiled, roast, baked, chipped . . .'

'I think Isabel has a point.' The camera swung to Donal's co-presenter, a broad-shouldered woman in a zig-zag patterned top that made my eyes burn. 'We shouldn't be stuffing our gobs with sweeties, and I for one will be checking out Isabel's blog and buying her book for suggestions about how to replace sugar with something healthier.' Her tone was reproving, and Donal dropped his head like a scolded schoolboy.

'Thank you so *much*, Norah.' Isabel made cow-eyes at the woman, eliciting a smile of solidarity. 'I don't like to think of myself as a crusader,' she said, her martyred expression suggesting the exact opposite. 'I think once people read the book of my blog – a book deal is imminent, by the way – they'll see that I'm an ordinary mother, wanting the best for families and, and *people*, everywhere.'

'And this book will be called?' prompted Norah.

Donal glanced at his watch and swallowed a yawn.

'Busy Izzy . . . my Transition from Model to Model Mum,' she obliged, adding, 'One Woman's Mission to Make the Nation a Healthier Place. To Live. In.'

'She made that up!' I shouted.

'By closing every single sweet shop in the country?' Donal suppressed a smirk. 'That could be your tagline.'

He shot up in my estimation again.

'I really want to get my message out there,' Isabel said, darting him a filthy look.

Donal caught her look and returned it. 'And what is your message, in a nutshell?'

For a fleeting moment, Isabel seemed flummoxed. She opened her mouth, closed it again, then quick as a flash, said, 'You'll have to buy the book and find out!' She gave an evangelical smile that brought my hackles up, and the section cut away to a weather report.

I logged off and sat for a moment, staring at my hands.

Whether she really believed in her 'mission' or not, Isabel had managed to have the last word, and that was what people remembered.

And, to be fair, her book title was pretty good. Apart from the bit she made up.

I clicked on her blog, but was reassured to see it was no more well-written or informative than before, though she'd written a new post about how she hoped her protest about The Beachside Sweet Shop had resulted in fewer people shopping there.

My blog to book is shaping up nicely, she gushed. *I'll be very much focused on eating clean, as well as being a good mummy to my baby boy, and a good wife to my darling husband, Gerry.*

Her mother had commented, *That's all very well, darling, but WHEN can we see Fitzy?? And as I recall, you were always in the sweet shop as a girl, you used to spend all your dinner-money on Galaxy Counters.*

Isabel hadn't responded.

I checked my emails, half-expecting a barrage of hate mail, but there was nothing of note. I switched off the computer and pushed my hands through my hair, dislodging my hair slide. In a sudden frenzy, I dived into the office and grabbed the scissors off the desk. Snatching a handful of fringe I sawed at it, letting the hair fall in clumps to the floor. There was quite a lot of it. I'd be avoiding my reflection for the foreseeable future.

I jumped with fright when the phone rang, almost stabbing myself in the eye. I looked at the clock. How was it only eight-thirty? I felt like I'd been up for days.

'Yes?' I barked into the handset, flinging the scissors into the desk drawer for my own safety.

'Ah, this is Radio South-West, Ms Appleton, sorry to phone you so late on a Saturday. We tried your home, but couldn't get hold of you there.'

'Radio who?'

'South-West. I'm Jeremy Taylor.' The soothing voice continued, 'We're covering local affairs on our show tonight, and wondered whether you had a quote for our listeners, in response to the uproar following your recent award?'

'I'm sorry?' I couldn't seem to quite grasp what he was requesting. 'A quote?'

'After Isabel Sinclair's interview on *Morning, Sunshine!* We thought you might have a response.'

I pressed my fingers to my temple. 'Not really.'

A heartbeat passed. 'I read you were going to create a low-sugar brand of your own.'

'Mmm,' I said. I couldn't muster the energy to sweep up my fringe, never mind embark on another sweet-making spree. And I still hadn't prepared the shop for Harry and his helpers.

'So, you're clearly taking the public's concerns seriously.'

'S'pose so.' I scratched my nose. My face felt hairy from my snipping session. 'Yeah, I guess.'

'Is that your quote?' The voice grew sarcastic. 'You *suppose* so?'

I caught my grandfather's eyes, smiling from his photo above the desk, innocent of the campaign to ruin his sweet shop.

'Well of *course* I'm going to respond,' I said, straightening my shoulders. 'The Beachside Sweet Shop has been through a world war, a battle with a developer in the eighties who wanted to build a casino, and a small fire in a bin that could have been a disaster if my grandfather hadn't had an extinguisher to hand. It'll take more than a bunch of,' *frustrated bitches* 'protestors to close me down.'

'That's the spirit.' His voice warmed up. 'Thank you so much, Ms Appleton. I have to say I've been in your shop before, but I wish you'd bring back Spangles, they were always my favourite.'

'I'm afraid I don't have that power.'

'No.' Jeremy Taylor cleared his throat. 'Well, anyway, the show goes out at nine and we'll be sure to include your quote.'

As the owner of the voice hung up, I fought off an image of Alex's eyes, and Bobbi-Jo's engagement ring. I wondered if he'd intended to tell me when he phoned my mobile the night I spoke to Mum, but I'd cut him off before he could muster the courage.

'Bloody HELL!' I said out loud.

I thought about phoning Beth, or Phoebe, but couldn't face their sympathy. And they'd been so supportive when Alex left. It wasn't fair to put them through it again.

I wandered into the stockroom, switched on the light, and stared at the coffee-stained pallet. I wondered what would have happened if Doris hadn't burst in on Josh and me. Maybe a no-strings attached fling was what I needed. Only I wasn't very good at 'no-strings'.

On impulse, I rushed back to the computer and found a website for wannabe gap year travellers I'd looked at hundreds of times. I scrabbled my debit card out of my bag, and within minutes had booked a one-way ticket to Thailand at the end of July. I had no idea what I'd do when I got there, or where to go after that, but would somehow figure it out.

I had plenty of time to find a new manager for the shop, and teach him or her how to make my healthy sweets. Once I'd learnt how to make them myself.

Feeling slightly better, I made a mug of coffee, and helped myself to a handful of fruit pastilles for energy. I tuned the old transistor in the office to a dance station, and set to work clearing the shop floor, starting with the pick and mix sweets, then heaped the jars in a trolley and wheeled them into the stockroom. I'd thought it might feel weird – like displacing history – but as I worked a sense of optimism took hold.

It would be much easier to attract a manager, once the place didn't look like a throwback to the fifties.

I carried on as dusk fell, keeping the lights off as I didn't want to draw attention to the fact that I was alone in the shop. And anyway, the moon had risen, throwing enough brightness in to see what I was doing.

It sounded fanciful, but I had a feeling Gramps was with me, keeping a watchful eye on proceedings, and I hoped he would approve.

I tried not to think about Alex and Bobbi-Jo, smooching at his parents' party, drunk on champagne and each other. I remembered the time we'd smooched, at a leaving do for one of his colleagues at the TV station, when he pulled me into the hotel garden, and told me he loved me by the ornamental fountain.

I blinked away tears, and when 'Uptown Funk' came on the radio I turned the volume to maximum. I moonwalked behind the counter, then violently pumped my hips and swung my arms above my head to the pounding bass. After attempting a slut-drop that almost dislocated my knee, I switched to some Beyoncé-style krumping, which felt wanton without my Spanx on, and concluded by karate chopping the air, and executing a couple of kung-fu kicks. My shoe flew across the floor, so I kicked off the other, and as one tune segued into another, shimmied up and down doing jazz hands. As I unfurled my fingers above my head, stamping my feet like an angry bull, endorphins flooded my brain. I wondered if it was possible to dance myself happy.

I continued to boogie, until disco lights danced across the ceiling. Closing my eyes I spun in a circle, faster and faster, head tipped back, arms outstretched . . .

Someone was thumping on the window.

I stopped twirling and crashed against the counter, shielding my eyes from the glare of a torchlight shining in. A figure was peering through the window, hand cupped over his eyes.

'Please open the door!'

My heart crashed against my ribs, as my spinning head registered a vehicle parked outside. The disco lights were the flashing blues and reds of a police car.

Breathing like someone in the final stages of emphysema, I staggered to the door, unlocked it and peered out.

'We had a call that there was a burglary in progress, and someone was fighting him off,' said a lanky police officer, urgently scanning the empty shop. 'Madam, are you hurt?'

Still high on endorphins, I was overcome with a wild desire to drag him inside and attempt a jive, but as he swept his torch around, taking in my demented appearance, and the Spanx lying on the floor, his expression changed to alarm.

'I own the shop,' I panted, wiping an accumulation of dust and sweat off the back of my neck, suspecting my fringe looked a lot worse than I suspected. 'Just preparing for a paint job tomorrow.'

He didn't bother asking to look around. I wouldn't have been surprised if he'd vaulted over the bonnet of his car like a seventies TV cop, such was his haste to get in it and drive away.

It wasn't until I'd locked up behind me and was scurrying home, barefoot, in the moonlight, that I realised I hadn't tuned in to Radio South-West and, what's more, I didn't care.

Chapter 23

I set my alarm to go off early the following morning, keen to be at the shop before Harry turned up.

As I stumbled downstairs I heard voices in the kitchen. Spotting a suitcase in the hall, a memory stirred of being roused from sleep in the early hours by the sound of a key in the door. I'd quickly sunk back into a dream, where Bobbi-Jo was listening to my heart through a stethoscope as I tried to pluck out her nose-stud with a pair of tweezers.

'Marnie, what on *earth* happened to your fringe?' Mum greeted me, as I entered the kitchen.

'I gave it a trim,' I mumbled, blinking sleep from my eyes. I'd got showered and dressed without troubling the mirror.

'Well, it looks quite . . . avant-garde,' she said, which was mum-speak for terrible. 'Very Uma Thurman in *Pulp Fiction*.' She got up from the table and pulled me into her arms. She smelt of her usual patchouli oil, with a tang of train carriage.

'More like Jim Carrey in *Dumb and Dumber*,' I said, tightly returning her hug and breathing her in.

'Silly.' She cuffed my arm. 'You do look tired though.'

'So do you.' I stepped back to study her face. She didn't look as robust as usual, her eyes too big in her heart-shaped face, her tumble of hair escaping its tortoiseshell clip. It was a shock to see strands of grey among the black. 'What are you doing here?' I said, looking around for a swarthy Italian. 'Where's Mario?'

'Not here,' said Celia, who was perched on the arm of Chester's armchair in her dressing gown. 'Your mother's left him.'

'What?'

'I haven't left him,' Mum corrected, huddling deeper into her woollen cardigan, even though it was warm in the kitchen, weak sunlight already streaming through the window. 'I needed some space to think about things, that's all.'

'I thought he was The One; the earthbound guide to your free spirit.' I crossed to the fridge and took out a carton of orange juice. 'What about the Tuscan villa, the sunshine, the wine, the pool . . .?' *the chest hair I saw you winding your fingers through.* It was when she'd managed to get Skype working, not realising I could see a lot more than just her face. She'd been sprawled on Mario's lap on a leather sofa, absently fondling him. He'd thrown back his head in apparent ecstasy, an indecent bulge in his boxer shorts, and I'd wanted to scrub my eyes clean afterwards.

'It's just *stuff,* darling,' Mum said. 'You know it doesn't matter to me.'

It was true she didn't care for material things; hence her having none of the trappings most women her age had. No home, no car; even the chain she wore round her neck she'd inherited from her grandmother, and her slim-gold watch was a gift from me on her fortieth birthday, bought with money I'd saved from my job at the sweet shop.

'I was planning to visit you,' I said, disappointment flowing through me.

She came over and squeezed my waist. 'Well, now you don't have to.'

'She'll be wanting to stay here,' Celia said, directing her words to me. She often did when we were in the same room, as though Mum required an interpreter. 'It's a jolly good job she has a home to return to.'

'Oh, stop it,' Mum said mildly, crouching to gather Chester in a hug, her dove-grey chiffon skirt pooling around her bare feet. Chester adored Mum, much to Celia's annoyance. I had the feeling she'd prefer him to chew Mum's hand off. 'It'll only be for a week, or two,' she murmured into his fur. 'While I work out what I want to do.'

Celia widened her eyes at me in disbelief, but for some reason I didn't believe she was that horrified. For a start, they'd been chatting before I came downstairs, and she'd gone to the trouble of making Mum's favourite peppermint tea in a pot, which she didn't bother doing when anyone else dropped in. Even Paddy got a tea-bag dunked in a mug.

'Woke me up, crashing about,' she grumbled, getting up and tightening the belt of her dressing gown.

'That might have been me,' I confessed. 'I tripped over the mat when I came in, and fell against the wall.'

'I need to move back up to my bedroom, now my leg's better.'

'We can sort that out today,' Mum said, with unusual eagerness. 'Your gran's been telling me your plans for the sweet shop,' she added to me, shoulders scrunching around her ears. 'Sounds exciting!'

I returned her grin, my disappointment yielding to pleasure that she was back. 'It's just a lick of paint,' I said, checking the time. 'Actually, I need to go in a minute.'

'And you're going to be making your own sweets, like we used to?'

I looked round from buttering a slice of burnt toast. 'I thought I'd give it a go.'

'I was telling your mum about that blogger,' said Celia, opening the back door to let Chester out. 'Doris reckons it's that woman down the road, who has the dog with the silly name.' Turning, she gave me a hard look. 'Is that true?'

Damn Doris, and her sleuthing ways. 'Possibly,' I mumbled.

'Why didn't you say so?' Celia's brow furrowed. 'I've arranged another training session. She's still whining at night and waking up the baby, and she dug up the vegetable patch.'

'Isabel?'

Celia sighed. 'The dog.'

Mum's head twitched from Celia to me. 'What's the story?'

'Oh, one of our neighbours is on a bit of a crusade about unhealthy eating,' I said, trying to make light of it. 'I thought I'd try something different, that's all.'

'Sweets aren't unhealthy, unless you eat them all the time,' Mum said, with more verve than I'd heard since Mario invited her to Italy, and she bought some art books from a charity shop and said she was going to 'get cultured'.

She crossed to the recipe books with none of her usual languor. 'I can help you make sweets, it'll be fun.'

As she found the red book and started flicking through the pages, Celia and I exchanged looks.

What's with her? she said with her eyes.

Beats me, I said with mine, but I was secretly pleased by her interest.

'Coconut ice!' she cried, glancing up with a Cheshire cat grin. 'I can start with that.'

I daren't look at Celia as I recalled my smoke-filled error. 'That's lovely of you, Mum, but I'll need to make some adjustments.'

'Adjustments?'

'The thing is, I have to use sugar alternatives,' I said. 'It's . . . complicated.'

Mum looked mildly aghast. 'Sugar alternatives?'

'I've promised,' I said, rather desperately. 'I need them by tomorrow, so once I've been to the shop and Harry's started work . . .'

'Harry?' Mum said, returning her attention to the recipe book.

'Beth's husband,' I reminded her. 'I thought I'd use some of my winnings to give the shop a facelift.'

'Can I come and have a look?' she said.

'Of course you can, but maybe when it's been painted,' I said, wanting her to see it at its best. 'I'll be going to Beth's later, to make the sweets,' I added. 'The cooker there's a bit more reliable.'

'Charming,' huffed Celia, pulling on her wellies, ready to clear up in the garden after Chester.

'They're in their new place?' asked Mum.

'Not yet. They'll be at his parents' for a few more weeks at least.' I gave her a hug and planted a kiss on her cheek, then picked up my bag and headed for the door. 'I'm not sure what time I'll be back.'

'Alex called a couple of times last night.'

I wheeled round to face Celia. 'What?'

'He wanted to speak to you.'

Mum's hand hovered, in the act of turning a page. 'I thought he was in America.'

'He sounded upset.' Celia's eyes were intent on me. 'Have you seen him?'

Perspiration broke out on my upper lip. 'I might have gone to his parents' anniversary party yesterday.'

'I thought he was seeing someone else.'

'He *is*, and they're engaged,' I said flatly, though saying the words out loud sent a shockwave through me.

'Engaged?' Mum and Celia said together. They looked appalled, as if I'd said he'd converted to Scientology, and I hurried out before either could ask for details.

Tugging my phone from my bag, I switched it on and saw I had a voicemail.

'Marnie, it's me, Alex.' I pressed the phone harder to my ear. 'I wondered if you were OK yesterday, you left in such a rush . . .' he paused, and my memory pitched back to the squashy blue sofa in his house, where he used to pull my feet into his lap and give them a massage, when I'd been in the shop all day. 'It was good to see you,' he said, his voice thick with feeling. 'Please call me.'

I switched my phone off again and ran almost all the way to the shop, not even slowing when a fully dressed and made-up Doris appeared on her doorstep and waved her notepad at me. Did the woman ever sleep?

Harry's van was there when I arrived, and there were signs of activity in the shop. I burst in to find dustsheets already down. A workman with a pair of blue overalls hanging from his waist, and a tattooed serpent curling around one bicep, was slapping white undercoat on the wall, and a woman with the same shade of russet hair, and a freckled nose, was doing the same to the other. I remembered Beth telling me Harry employed a husband and wife team, renowned for their ability to paint a room in under an hour. At the speed they were moving I imagined they'd be done by the time I put the kettle on.

Beth emerged from the office, dangling the spare set of keys from her finger. 'Hope you don't mind,' she said, taking a sip from the mug in her other hand. 'I thought the sooner they started the better.'

'You shouldn't be here,' I scolded, out of breath. 'There's paint fumes and dust and slippery surfaces.'

'I won't stay long, keep your wig on,' she said.

The workman pointed his paintbrush at his wife. 'That's Em, and I'm Toby,' he said with a friendly grin. He had an athletic vibe – a bit like Greg Rutherford.

'Nice to meet you both.' I fluttered a wave.

Em gave me a shy smile and returned to her painting.

I looked at Harry, carefully sanding the counter top in preparation for a coat of varnish, frowning with absorption.

'Should I run through the itinerary?'

With the tiniest of sighs, as though I'd asked for the moon, he pushed his goggles into his hair and removed his dust mask. He counted off on his fingers. 'Paint the walls, replace the shelving behind the counter, remove lighting, paint the skirtings and doorframes, and sand the floorboards.'

Not for the first time I wondered how I would have felt if Alex had taken a dislike to Beth. Harry was lovely with everyone else, and I'd never heard anyone say a bad word about him, so I could hardly blame her for loving him, but sometimes I wished she'd married someone else.

'Good,' I said briskly, conscious he was trying not to look at my fringe. 'Shall I leave the door propped open to let the paint smell out?'

'Obviously.'

I scuttled over to turn the sign to 'CLOSED' to deter people from coming in.

'I'll leave you to it then.'

I found Beth in the kitchen, humming under her breath. 'Honestly, you should go home,' I said. 'How come you're up so early, anyway?'

'I was worried when I didn't hear from you last night.' Her gaze drifted up. 'Why?' she said to my fringe.

'It was driving me mad.'

'I wondered why there was hair all over the floor in the office.' She studied me a moment longer. 'It'll grow back,' she concluded. 'So, come on.' Her eyebrows lifted. 'How did it go with Alex?'

'Ugh,' I groaned. As I gave her the low-down her expression veered between laughter and horror, and settled on concern when I got to the bit about Bobbi-Jo's engagement ring. 'I think she wanted me to see it,' I said, spooning three sugars into my coffee and stirring it wildly. 'She put her hand on Alex's arm on purpose.'

'Oh, Marnie.' Beth took away the spoon and squeezed my hand. 'I'm so sorry.'

'But he wants to talk to me,' I said. 'I think she might be pregnant.' I glanced at the dome of Beth's belly. 'Though not as pregnant as you are.'

'I thought she already had a child.'

'She does, but he's about five.' I removed my jacket and slung it on the worktop. 'Her clock's probably ticking, and she's latched onto Alex because she knows he's a good catch.'

'Weeell . . .' Beth looked about to protest, then said, 'Maybe he wants to invite you to their wedding.'

I almost choked. 'I bloody hope not,' I said. 'I'm not the kind of ex who'd be OK with that sort of thing.'

'Me neither,' said Beth with a shudder. 'It's not natural.'

'I'll be glad when they're back in New York, to be honest.'

'Out of sight, out of mind?'

'Something like that.' A picture popped into my head, of the pair of them pushing a buggy through Central Park in the snow. At least there'd be no chance of me bumping into them. 'So much for his plans to travel.'

'I got the impression he only went along with all that for you,' said Beth, scooping froth from her mug and into her mouth. 'And he'd never have met her if you'd asked him to stay here.'

I was about to strenuously protest that it wasn't my fault when her expression changed. 'What's wrong?' She looked as if she was holding in a burp.

'Bit of back pain,' she said, chewing her bottom lip as she put down her mug. 'Nothing to worry about.'

'Hmmm,' I said. 'Maybe Bunty's getting on your nerves again.'

'Feels like she's using an angle-grinder.'

'Ouch.' I waited for her face to relax, deciding to ignore her comment about Alex. She was just reacting to being in pain that was all. It had never suited her. 'Mum's back,' I said, to distract her.

'Oh?' Her eyes stretched. 'What's happened noooooooOOOOOW!'

'Beth?' She'd dropped to a squat. 'What are you doing?'

'I don't know.' She pressed her chin to her chest. 'It feels right, somehow.'

'O-*kay*.' She looked odd, with her gigantic belly protruding between her white-trousered knees, her lime-green stretchy top so tight I could see her belly button sticking out. She was making a noise low in her throat, like Chester when he was unsettled. 'Anything I can do?'

'Just keep talking.'

'Right.' She was puffing air through pursed lips, as if trying to blow out a stubborn candle. 'Is it still OK to come over later and make some sweets for tomorrow?'

'That's fine,' she said, sounding like Linda Blair in *The Exorcist*. 'The in-laws won't be back until late tonight.'

'Are you *sure* you're alright?'

'I'm going to die in childbirth,' she squawked, looking at me through damp eyelashes. 'I can't give birth, Marnie, I just can't. I've changed my mind.'

'Of *course* you can.' I knelt down and rubbed her back. 'It's fear of the unknown, that's all.'

'It's fear of pain and dying.'

'That as well.'

'Oh GOD!' she wailed, plopping her bottom on the floor, legs sticking out in front of her. Thrusting her back against the cupboard, she pushed her hands into her hair, squashing her curls. 'I want gas and air NOW!'

'But you're not in labour yet,' I said, confused. 'Are you?'

She gave me a mournful look. 'I'm not due for another week.'

'I know but . . .'

'Thesis won't be happy, I'm not finished yet.'

'Katherine Parr will have to wait.'

Beth's cheeks were raspberry pink. 'Take care for my soul. Save me, thy servant, which wholly trust in thee. Have mercy upon me, O Lord, for I will never cease crying to thee for help,' she intoned.

'Pardon?'

'It's a part of a prayer that she wrote. Katherine Parr. Seems appropriate.' Her eyes were roving blindly.

'Where are you going?' she said as I scrambled to my feet.

'Er, just to see how Harry's getting on.'

'Don't leave me.' She was on her hands and knees, crawling after me. 'Have you got any painkillers?'

'I think you might need more than an aspirin,' I said. 'Just wait here, I won't be a minute.'

I hurried out the front, and stopped in my tracks. Harry was rollering the ceiling white, while Toby and Em were now coating the walls with the buttermilk paint I'd had in the stockroom for months. The place looked so different already; bright and airy, the sun reflecting off the walls to dazzling effect.

'Everything OK?' I said.

Harry's face twitched with irritation. 'Everything's fine.' When I didn't move he lowered his roller with a long-suffering sigh and removed his paint-speckled baseball cap. 'What is it?'

'Beth's in a bit of a state.'

'Ah.' He scratched his ear. 'She's been in a state for a while, to be fair.' For a second, he seemed to forget it was me he was talking to. 'She was fine at the start, she'd got it all worked out, but . . .' he bit his lip. 'I dunno, she's lost the plot a bit lately.'

I looked up, as if she might be clinging to the ceiling. 'I think she's in labour.'

'WHAT?' The roller clattered to the floor.

Toby and Em looked round, eyes flaring with alarm.

'S'up mate?' said Toby.

'Carry on with what you're doing.' Harry's tone brooked no argument.

They resumed painting, like robots.

'Are you sure?' said Harry, following me into the kitchen where Beth was standing, staring at a spreading wet patch around her feet.

'My waters have broken,' she said, in an awestruck tone. 'At least, I don't think I've weed myself.'

'Her waters have broken.' Harry looked at me, animosity stripped away. His expression was a peculiar mix of unbridled panic and joy.

'Yup,' I said. 'They certainly have.'

'It is water, not wee, isn't it?' Beth said plaintively. 'It smells like straw.'

'What happens now?' asked Harry, clutching his cap to his chest like a workman in a period drama, with no idea about women's bits.

'You're the ones who've been to parenting classes,' I said, wondering whether Beth was intending to ever use a sentence without the word 'wee' in it again. 'Do you go straight to hospital, or wait for contractions to start?'

'I think they've already started,' Beth said, cupping her bump. Her eyes refocused, flipping from Harry to me. 'I'm not ready,' she whimpered. 'I haven't been practising my chanting.'

'Should I call an ambulance?' Harry seemed gripped with indecision for possibly the first time since I'd known him.

I decided I'd better take charge. Despite having months to prepare, their memories had clearly been wiped. 'I'll call the hospital and ask their advice.'

An efficient voice at the end of the line informed me Beth should come in, as her waters had broken. 'She's at risk of infection,' I said to Harry, which had a startling effect.

He burst into tears. 'We have to go! Right now!' he cried, traversing the kitchen, cap in one hand, the other raking his hair.

'But what about the shop?' cried Beth, as if it was all that mattered. 'And the baby-sling I ordered hasn't come yet, and I saw this little vintage silver spoon on eBay I was going to order . . .'

'You're not Kate Middleton,' I soothed. 'Bunty's got plenty of stuff already, you just have to—'

'And I don't think I like the colour for the nursery in the new house, it's supposed to be sage, but it looks like parsley. I hate parsley, it gives me heartburn.'

'Oh Christ, Beth, I'm so sorry.' Harry looked stricken – as if she'd announced the baby wasn't his. 'I'll strip it off before we move in, I swear, I'll get some paint specially mixed, just say the word . . .'

'Will you two chill the hell out?'

'Oh god.' Harry swiped his face with his forearm. 'It's all turning to shit.'

I placed my arm around Beth's trembling shoulders. 'Don't worry about any of that,' I said in my firmest voice. 'It's not important.'

'But the shop . . .'

'Toby and Em can finish,' Harry interjected, eyes wet and staring. 'So I'm driving her to the hospital then?'

'Er, yes,' I said. 'Go to the hospital. They're expecting you. Tell them your name. They'll know what to do.' Better to keep it simple. I handed him Beth's bag, then turned to squeeze her hands. 'This is it,' I said, seized with emotion. 'You're going to have a baby.'

'Oh my days,' she said. Her eyes were like saucers. 'Is this really happening, Marnie?'

I nodded, her face blurring. 'Yes it is,' I said, laughing and crying at once. 'Go,' I said to Harry, who seemed frozen to the spot now. 'We can't stay here crying all day.' I sniffed. 'Keep me posted, OK?'

Beth nodded furiously. 'If I die . . .'

'You won't.'

'Of course she won't,' growled Harry, flinging her bag across his shoulders and rubbing his swollen eyes. 'Don't even say that, Beth.'

As we led her through the shop, me clutching Beth's hand while Harry's arm circled her back, Josh strode through the doorway, his skateboard under his arm.

'What's happening?' He jumped aside to let us pass.

'Beth's in labour.'

'My waters broke.' She gave him a trancelike stare. 'It's all over the floor.' Her knees buckled. 'It hurts, it hurts, it hurts, it hurts, it bloody well hurts, it hurts, it hurts, oh Christ almighty it hurts,' she chanted, which definitely wasn't what she'd been practising. 'Get it out, get it out, get it OUT!'

In a sudden, panic-stricken movement, Harry yanked open the door of his van and virtually threw her onto the front seat before sprinting round the other side. Wild-eyed, he leapt in and revved the engine.

Beth buzzed down her window. 'Help me,' she said feebly, sticking her hand out.

Grabbing her fingers I leaned over and said to Harry, 'You'd better get her there in one piece or you'll have me to answer to.'

My words had a calming effect. He pulled on his baseball cap sideways, straightened his shoulders and nodded.

'What about your bag, with your birthing things?' I said to Beth.

'It's been in the back of the van for a week.'

'Good.' I unwound her fingers from mine. She was staring past me with a puzzled expression.

Turning, I saw Josh inside the shop, talking to Toby while miming a painting action. I was swept with gratitude. He was obviously offering to help.

'I recognise him,' Beth said, as if she hadn't been keening like a war widow mere seconds ago. 'Isn't he Rob Hancock's nephew?'

Chapter 24

'What are you on about?' I stared at Beth as Harry crunched the gears.

'It was when your gran broke her leg and you were at the hospital.' Her face was sheened with sweat. 'Oh no, it's happening again,' she whimpered.

'Tell me,' I ordered, my breathing as shallow as Beth's.

'Ooch! OW!' She attempted to focus. 'I took in a delivery and Hancock had someone in the van and I asked who it was and he said his nephew and it was him, that man in the shop, I recognise him, he's got the same hair and eyes and he was wearing a yellow T-shirt with "Blink if You Want Me" on it,' she said, delivering the words in a frenzied stream. 'Oh no, oh no, oh, no, oh no, oh no,' she wailed, as Harry finally found a gear and veered away from the kerb.

'AAAAARRRRGGGGHHHHHHH!' was the last thing I heard as the van roared off, and turned the corner so fast I half-expected it to swing over onto two wheels.

So much for being careful.

I stood for a moment, turning her words in my head.

She'd been out the back the first time Josh came in, and hadn't had a chance to meet him since. He probably hadn't noticed her the day Rob Hancock dropped off his delivery.

His nephew.

He'd tried to put me off Kandy Kings, and placed an order with Rob, even though I'd told him he wasn't my supplier any more. I remembered his reluctance when I said I was thinking of making my own sweets, and how he'd defended Rob.

My heart was racing, while around me life carried on as normal.

The beach was filling with people, visiting for the bank holiday weekend, erecting windbreaks and deckchairs and flapping out towels. An ice-cream van had already parked down the road.

A couple emerged from the guesthouse with a little girl.

'You can get some bonbons later,' the woman told her, flashing me a quick smile. 'You've just had a fry-up for breakfast.'

Josh was Rob Hancock's nephew.

Fury rose, and must have reached my face as the woman grabbed the girl's hand and snatched her away.

I marched into the shop and gripped Josh by the arm. 'Can I have a word?' Not waiting for a reply, I yanked him away like a wheelie bin, pretending not to notice a look of alarm shoot between Toby and Em.

'What's wrong?' Josh sounded bewildered as I shut the stockroom door behind us, before slamming my palms against his chest and shoving him hard.

'What the . . .?' His calves hit the pallet behind him, causing him to plop down. He stared at me, blank-faced with shock. 'What's going on?'

'Is it true?' My voice was a strangled croak.

His brow scrunched. 'Is *what* true?'

I snapped the light on so I could see him more clearly. 'Are you Rob Hancock's nephew?'

He dropped his head. 'Marnie,' he began, raising his eyes and looking away again. '*Fuck.*' He looked as guilty as a murderer.

'So it *is* true.' I'd known it must be, or Beth would never have said it, but the acknowledgement still cut through me.

'It's not what you think—'

'You bastard,' I butted in. 'Did he send you here?'

He rose and took a step towards me. 'Yes,' he said. 'But I can explain.'

I held up a hand. 'Let me guess. You were meant to persuade me to start buying my sweets from him again?'

He closed his eyes. 'I was supposed to give you the willies.'

'He wanted you to scare me as well?' I blasted. 'Well, that's just—'

'No, no, a box of his liquorice willies.' His eyes flew open. 'I was supposed to have ordered some as a "surprise",' he made quote marks, 'because I thought they were an amusing idea, and you wouldn't have the heart to refuse.'

'Because of your *charm*, I suppose.'

He looked at the floor again.

'Where are they then?'

'In my campervan,' he said, hooking his thumbs in the pockets of his surfer shorts. 'This place is too classy and, anyway, they look more like fingers.'

I digested that for a second. 'So, basically, he wanted you to do his dirty work.'

Josh scuffed the toe of his shoe on the floor. 'It's no excuse, but he's been losing customers since Kandy Kings opened that new production plant. They're so much cheaper, the independents can't compete.'

'That's his problem, not mine,' I snapped. 'I'm perfectly entitled to change suppliers if I want to.'

'I know, I know, and I told him,' he said. His face had paled, throwing his stubble into sharp relief. 'That night you saw me from the bus, I was telling him I didn't want to do it, that I liked you too much, it wasn't fair.'

I tried to control my breathing. 'Why do it in the first place?'

'Cos I'm an idiot.' He looked deeply ashamed. 'I'm not even close to him,' he said in a low voice. 'He's my mum's brother, but he moved away from Yorkshire a long time ago.'

'So how come you ended up working for him?'

'I wasn't exactly.' Josh sank back down on the pallet, fingertips pressed to his forehead. 'Everything I told you was true, I swear,' he said. 'About not knowing what I wanted to do with myself . . .'

'You did work in a sweet shop before?'

'Yes, and I loved it.' He looked up, Adam's apple bobbing as he swallowed, and although part of me wanted to kick him in the shins, another wanted him to continue. 'Rob asked me down to stay for a bit,' he said. 'He'd got wind that I was struggling to know what I wanted to do.' He shrugged. 'It was OK at first, just driving about with him now and then while he did his deliveries, seeing my cousins, practising my magic.'

'And then I told him I didn't want his sweets any more.'

Josh nodded. 'He was well pissed off.'

'So he told you to try to change my mind?'

'He knew you were looking for someone to replace your friend.' He stared at his feet. 'He said he'd pay me, not much, and I suppose I thought it would be a breeze.'

My lip did an involuntary curl of disgust. 'You must have been laughing behind my back.'

'No!' he said, so vehemently I jumped. 'I swear to you, Marnie, that once I met you I really, really liked you. We hit it off, didn't we?'

His green eyes held an appeal that made me falter.

'I thought we did.'

'I didn't want to go through with it, I hated how upset you were when you realised that sugar-free delivery was from him. I was intending to take it back, even though I knew he'd be furious.'

I pressed the pads of my fingers to my eyelids. 'Christ, what a mess.'

'I'm so sorry, Marnie.'

I sighed into the silence that fell. 'The other morning . . .' I cleared my throat. 'That wasn't part of the plan?'

Josh's head snapped up. 'Christ, no,' he said. 'I really fancy you.'

Maybe he was like his uncle, and couldn't resist trying it on. The thought sent a ripple of confusion through me.

'Let me make it up to you,' he said, holding out his hands in a plea. 'I am on your side, I promise.'

'I don't know.' It felt wrong to let him off.

'You don't have to pay me anything.'

There was a rap of knuckles on the door and it swung open. Toby was there, eyes cast down as if to avoid any possible nudity. 'Paint's dry, shall we put up those shelves now?'

'Yes please, that would be marvellous,' I said, switching to a jolly-teacher voice. 'Would you like something to drink?'

'I'm fine, thanks,' said Toby, smoothing a paint-smeared hand over his tousled hair. 'Em has brought a Thermos and some of her fruitcake.'

'Sounds delish,' I said. 'Anything I can do?'

'Is the boss man having his baby today?' A pair of inquisitive grey eyes met mine. 'We're trying, me and the missus.'

'That's lovely,' I said, normality slipping back as I thought of Beth. 'And yes, I think the boss man may be having his baby today.'

'Look, if you want to zip off I can project-manage for the rest of the day,' Josh said, as Toby's head dipped out. 'It's the very least I can do.'

'How do I know I can trust you?'

'I suppose you don't,' he said, getting to his feet and giving me a steady look. 'But you have my word.'

Another thought joined all the others, swirling through my head in a dizzying jumble. I wouldn't be able to make my sweets at Beth's in-laws; not with her in hospital. And I still hadn't bought my ingredients. Or found a recipe for Turkish delight and marzipan.

I spun around on the spot. Why was everything happening all at once?

Josh looked on, a flicker of hope in his eyes. 'Please let me help, Marnie.'

'OK, you can stay because you owe me, big time,' I said. His face illuminated with relief. 'But after tomorrow, you don't work here any more.'

I left, before I gave in to his stricken expression, and outside the shop I rang the hospital and asked to speak to Harry.

'It could be ages yet,' he said breathing hard, as though he was the one in labour. 'She's only two centimetres dilated.'

'How's she doing?'

'Screaming for an epidural.'

'I thought she might be.'

'I knew she would be.'

A moment of mutual understanding passed between us.

'Everything OK at the shop?' he said, as if suddenly remembering the day had started quite differently. 'Toby and Em are the best, you know, they won't let you down.' It was the most heartfelt thing he'd ever said to me.

'They're doing a great job.' No point mentioning Josh's revelation.

'Right then,' he said. 'I'd better get back.'

'Keep me updated, if you can.'

'I will.'

There was nothing else for me to do but go to Tesco's.

Chapter 25

'What's all that?' said Mum, jumping up from the table when I staggered in under the weight of several carrier bags.

'Stuff to make sweets with.' I dumped it all on the floor. 'I thought I'd better crack on if I don't want to be up all night.'

'Aren't you meant to be at the shop?'

'They don't need me,' I said, curious what she'd been doing since I'd left. It looked like she hadn't moved from the kitchen. 'Are you OK?'

'Fine,' she said vaguely. 'I thought you were going to Beth's to make your sweets.'

I filled her in on what had happened.

'Don't you want to be at the hospital with her?' Her brow crinkled. 'She *is* your best friend.'

'She only wants Harry.' My eyes stung with sudden tears. It did feel odd that my oldest friend was having her baby without me. I'd been there for so many milestones: holding her hair back the first time she got drunk and threw up on her mother's dahlias; when she confessed she loved Harry-next-door, but didn't think he would ever look at her 'like that'. When she developed a stress rash after becoming upset studying violent punishments in the fifteenth century (I'd booked us a spa day and banned her from mentioning anything historical for eight hours) and as her maid-of-honour I'd been there to celebrate every hour of her wedding day.

But I would miss her most life-changing experience.

'It's normal to want to share it with her husband,' Mum said, even though she'd given birth to me alone, upstairs in the bath – in lieu of a birthing pool – giving Celia the fright of her life when she returned to find her daughter calmly frying her placenta, with me strapped across her in a makeshift sling, and the bath like a scene from *CSI*. 'And you're going to be a brilliant auntie.'

'Thanks, Mum.' I smiled at her through my tears, and she stretched out her arms for a hug.

I slid into them, wishing I could stay there. Alex had texted again, asking to meet.

Just five minutes, Marnie. Two, if that's all you can spare X

I can't I'd replied, careful not to put a kiss. And anyway there's nothing to say, I couldn't resist adding.

There's a lot I want to say X

Stop with the kisses, they're inappropriate.

Not for you X

Two words – Bobbi-Jo.

I know how this must look, just give me a chance to tell you a couple of things X

Tell me now.

It would be better face to face XX

While I thought about it he sent another text.

Remember this? X

I'd clicked on the attachment, which was a photo of two retriever puppies, cuddling.

Why? I typed, refusing to look at them directly.

Because you always said it's impossible to be cross or upset if you're looking at puppies X

I was wrong.

I'd switched off my phone before I could weaken, my head instantly piling up with thoughts of Beth, and the shop, and Isabel Sinclair and her 'crusade', and the revelation about Josh. Would he ever have told me, if Beth hadn't recognised him?

My brain was still churning like a cement mixer as I pulled away from Mum.

'Why didn't you take me with you on your travels?' I said, surprising myself. I'd long ago come to terms with it, but the question had popped out of its own accord.

'Oh, Marnie, it was for your own good,' she said, paling. 'You needed a stable home, like I'd had, and who better to give you it, than my parents?' She tilted her head. 'I wasn't cut out to look after you full-time.'

It was what Celia used to say whenever I asked why Mummy wasn't there all the time, like other mummies. 'You could have tried,' I said, slipping my jacket off.

'Oh, *Marnie!*' To my utter amazement, she flung herself down at the table again, and burst into noisy tears.

My jaw dropped. First Harry, now Mum. I'd seen her cry a bit before – usually after one of her boyfriends left – but nothing like this. 'I'm so sorry,' I said, dropping my jacket. 'I shouldn't have said anything.'

'You're so much more forgiving than I deserve,' she wept, pushing the heels of her hands into her eyes. 'Why don't you slap me, or banish me, or tell me you hate me?'

'Because I don't hate you, silly.' I dragged a chair beside her and sat down. 'You did what you could when you could, and when you couldn't there was Celia and Gramps, and my cousins and Uncle Cliff.' Her shoulders shook even harder. Was she ill? I wondered suddenly. 'Mum, why *have* you come back?'

She gulped back a sob. 'I've been doing some thinking lately.'

'Oh?'

'My life has started to seem empty,' she said, her voice thick with tears. 'I mean, I do love Mario, but when I saw what you'd achieved with the shop, it made me realise how little I've done with my life that has any meaning, apart from giving birth to you . . .' her voice stuttered into sobs again.

'But it's not really *my* achievement,' I said. 'I'm just carrying on what Gramps started – what *his* grandfather started.'

'You won an AWARD!' she said, bringing her fist down on the table. 'And you're *clever*, you went to university, and all I've ever done is shag around and go on ho . . . holiday.' She hiccupped. 'I'm so . . . *silly*.'

'Mum, stop it,' I said, shocked. 'Here.' I passed her a length of kitchen roll. 'I've been marking time at the shop, you know that,' I said. 'All I really want to do is go travelling, just like you did.' I cupped my hand over hers, anticipating her reaction. 'I'm going to Thailand at the end of July.'

'What?' She turned to face me, and I couldn't help noticing that even when her cheeks were tear-blotched and her nose bright red, she still looked stunning. 'Why would you want to go away?'

I stared, taken aback. 'Well . . . *you* did.'

'Oh, Marnie, that wasn't really travelling, it was . . .' she paused, and nibbled her lip, her eyes wide and worried. She looked so unlike the mother I knew I felt a twinge of alarm.

'It was what?'

Before she could reply the back door shot open and Chester padded in, followed by Celia, who was wearing another of her Fair Isle sweaters, with a tartan pleated skirt and pink-spotted wellingtons.

'Still here then?' she said to Mum, and there was quiet satisfaction in her eyes. 'You could have got some dinner on.'

'I didn't know what you'd want to eat,' Mum said, passing her soggy kitchen roll over her face. If Celia noticed she'd been crying, she didn't comment.

'There's some Dover sole in the fridge,' she said, dropping in the armchair and tugging off her boots. 'A piece for Chester too, he likes his poached in milk.'

'Of course he does,' said Mum, and we exchanged a smile. I was relieved to see she looked much more like her old self.

'Oh listen, I need to use the oven,' I said, standing up in a sudden panic. 'I've got sweets to make for tomorrow, hundreds and hundreds of them.'

'Ooh, can I help?' Mum brightened. 'It'll be like old times.'

'I thought you didn't approve of my cooker,' Celia said, with a glimmer in her eye.

'I haven't got much choice now, Beth's in hospital, and it could be hours before she has the baby.'

'You only took forty minutes, from start to finish,' Mum remind-ed me. 'And I did it all without drugs.'

'Women go to hospital too early these days,' said Celia, pushing out of the armchair using her stick. I got the impression there'd be no burning ceremony – she liked it too much. 'Look at dogs, they just go into a corner and get on with it.'

'Well, Beth can hardly do that,' I said.

'I was in labour with Cliff for four days, before I called the mid-wife,' she continued. 'By the time she'd cycled here, he was already on the breast.'

Mum and I looked at each other. 'Did midwives still use bicycles in the sixties?' she said.

'Around here they did.' Celia sounded offended. 'The cord was round your neck and your father had to come in and untangle you.' She frowned, remembering. 'Always was good with knots.'

'It was an umbilical cord, not a length of rope,' said Mum. 'They don't get knotted up.'

I bit back a giggle, surprised I had the ability to laugh after the day I'd had.

'Anyway.' Celia slapped a purposeful hand on her thigh. 'I suppose we could go and eat at Paddy's,' she said to Chester. 'He invited us just now, but I thought you might want some company.' She glanced at Mum.

'I think we'll be fine, if that's OK,' Mum said, looking at me to check.

'Of course it's OK with me.' I started to unload jars and packets onto the worktop, still puzzled and a little hurt by Mum's reaction to me going away. I'd expected her to approve, not look at me as if I'd announced I was going to prison.

'I need to get on,' I said.

'Good.' Celia gave a firm nod, and after sliding her feet into a pair of lilac Crocs she slipped out again with Chester.

I watched her cross the garden to the lane that led to Paddy's, her stick tucked under her arm, and the little bubble of worry that I'd carried in my chest since her fall finally popped.

'Right.' Mum removed her cardigan, and fastened Celia's apron around her tiny waist. 'Where shall we start?'

Putting my worries about everything else aside, I spent the next few hours in a flurry of mixing, melting, whisking, boiling and pouring, with a sprinkling of inventive expletives from me as Mum didn't like the F word.

'How the fanjita is this ever going to look like Turkish delight?' I cried, scraping a wooden spoon around an unappetising mix of water, xylitol, beetroot powder and arrowroot. 'More like Shipley Horror.' I wiped my cheek with my forearm, and it came away white. Arrowroot powder seemed to get everywhere. 'Isn't the mixture supposed to be thick and stretchy?'

Mum glanced over. She was flushed and sparkly-eyed. 'Have you put too much rosewater in?'

'No,' I said. 'I measured it properly.'

She came over and peered in the pan. 'It should firm up once it cools.' She whipped it off the hotplate and stood it in a bowl of cold water in the sink.

'Leave it there, and get on with your peanut brittle.'

She'd already produced three trays of coconut ice, using the ingredients I'd bought, and some chocolate truffles using a bizarre combination of avocado and cocoa powder. Her efforts looked like *Bake Off* showstoppers, whereas Mary Berry would have consigned my marzipan crunch to the bin.

'They taste delicious,' Mum assured me, popping a chunk in her mouth. I knew she meant it, because she'd once said she found it physically impossible to swallow anything she didn't love the taste of.

She'd fired a meaningful look at her boyfriend at the time, but I was only ten and thankfully missed the double meaning.

'If you've got ripe bananas and cinnamon I can make some low-sugar fudge,' she said, after finding a recipe in the old red book, and looking on my laptop for ways to adapt it. I was surprised and pleased by how wholeheartedly she was embracing the endeavour.

'Here's the cinnamon,' I said, sliding the jar across. 'There are plenty of bananas in the fruit bowl, we hardly ever eat them.'

'And have you got any ginger for your balls?'

I sniggered. 'In the bag.'

'It's a shame we can't use the ingredients in the book, so you can say the sweets are based on a family recipe.'

'I could say they've been *adapted* from family recipes.'

'Good idea.' Mum beamed, her cheeks glowing pink.

I checked the pan. Thankfully, the mixture was taking on the consistency of knicker elastic, which immediately made me think of Beth's nether regions. I wondered whether she'd had her epidural, and if she'd remember to listen to the history podcast she'd downloaded, to relax her if the chanting didn't work.

'Your mixture's boiling,' Mum said.

I lurched across to the Aga and gave it a stir.

'Do you remember our cooking song?' she said, a smile tweaking her lips.

'"Beans, beans, Are good for the heart. The more you eat, The more you fart!"' I sang, conducting an imaginary orchestra with my spoon. 'Classy choon.'

Mum giggled. 'I'd forgotten that one,' she said. 'I was thinking of . . .'

' . . . "Jambalaya on the Bayou",' we said together, and broke into a rousing chorus that brought back those precious afternoons in the flat above the supermarket, when Mum would put Hank Williams on the CD player to accompany our sweet-making. She often listened to country and western, rather than what was in 'the hit parade' as Celia still called it.

Her voice was sweet and husky and made me want to stop what I was doing and listen, but she'd become self-conscious if I did, so I'd hum along, watching her face instead.

'That one never made much sense either,' I said, when we'd finished. 'Goldfish pie, filly gunboat? What the f . . . blinking heck?'

Mum's shoulders vibrated with laughter. '*Craw*fish pie, filé gumbo,' she said. 'Filé's a spicy powder.'

'I think I prefer my version.' I looked at the clock. 'I should really pop back to the shop and see how they're getting on,' I said, slotting my cooled peanut brittle into the fridge, which was rapidly filling up.

'Go,' Mum said, wafting a hand. 'I'm fine here.'

She looked it. In fact, she looked happier than I'd seen her in a while. 'Are you missing Mario?' I said as I washed my hands.

'He can be a little . . . intense, but yes I am.' Some of the laughter left her face. 'Do you miss Alex?'

We'd never had the sort of heart-to-hearts about boyfriends some mothers and daughters had. It was Celia who told me the facts of life, after we'd attended a local dog-show she was judging and a spaniel took a liking to a startled-looking dachshund. The rest I'd picked up from friends, school and *Hollyoaks*.

'It doesn't matter if I do,' I said firmly. 'He's with someone else.'

She looked sceptical. 'You should fight for him, if you want him back.'

It was odd that Doris had said the same thing.

'I had my chance,' I said, pushing my arms into my jacket. 'It's too late now.'

My phone buzzed as I picked up my bag.

'It's from Harry,' I said. 'Beth's nine centimetres dilated!'

'That was nice of him to let you know.'

'I know.' Maybe becoming a father was changing him.

I couldn't help hoping it would last.

Chapter 26

Toby and Em were clearing up as I arrived at the shop. Both had the radiance of a job-well-done, and my jaw swung open as I surveyed their handiwork.

The paintwork looked warm and light, and the freshly sanded floorboards drew my eye to the front of the counter, which was newly painted in yellow and white stripes. Tiny gold lights adorning the edges of the shelves added a fairy-tale sparkle.

'We've put the empty tins out the back for recycling, is that OK?' asked Toby, flushed with pleasure at my response.

'Everything's perfect,' I breathed, tears pricking my eyes. They'd even hung my chimes back over the door, and my award certificate had been framed and was hanging beside the photo of Gramps behind the counter.

'Your man did that,' Em said, seeing me looking at it. 'Josh?'

'Oh, he's not my man.' Touched, in spite of myself, I wondered where he'd got the frame from.

'He popped out for a bit, and came back with it professionally done,' Em continued, as if tracking my thoughts.

'Is he still here?'

'Yeah, he's around,' she said. 'He's done quite a lot actually, and said you'd probably need help putting the stock back out.'

'Oh,' I said again, overwhelmed. I hadn't expected to feel so . . . *emotional*. It was probably the fallout from seeing Alex with Bobbi-Jo, and Beth going into labour, not to mention Mum's outburst, but still. The shop looked wonderful.

'We can help too, if you like?' offered Toby.

But in spite of their helpful smiles, I imagined he and Em were gagging to get home for a shower and a bite to eat.

'You've done more than enough,' I said. Overcome, I grasped hold of Toby and aimed a kiss at his cheek. Unfortunately, he turned his head at the last moment and I ended up planting a smacker on his lips.

'Oops,' I said, as he flushed to the roots of his hair.

Em gave a soft giggle. 'Awkward!'

I held out my arms to her. 'Do you want one too?' I joked, and managed to peck her flushed, paint-freckled cheek. 'I'm going to recommend you to everyone,' I added, before remembering with a pang that I wouldn't be around in a few months. 'Honestly, you've done a brilliant job.'

I presented them with a family-sized box of chocolates as an extra thank you, and after they'd gone I stood for a moment longer, soaking up the atmosphere. The paint smell was barely detectable, and I liked the lingering aroma of sanded wood.

Taking down the photo of my grandfather, I showed him around the shop, hoping he liked the new look, my heart swelling with sadness that he wasn't there to see it.

'I think he'd approve,' said Josh, and I spun round to see him in the office doorway. 'You can make the place your own now.'

'You don't get to have an opinion,' I huffed, moving past him to replace the photograph, head swimming a little at his scent – peppery with a dash of mint. 'Let's get the sweets back out,' I said, steeling myself to not speak to him for the next hour or so.

'Listen, are you sure I can't stay on?' Josh reached out a hand, then let it drop to his side. 'I really am so sorry, Marnie.'

If only he wouldn't say my name like that, as if we were under a duvet in a passionate clinch.

'How do I know this isn't still a ploy to get me to buy from your uncle again?' I was trying to emulate the anger I'd felt before. 'It could have been you who drew that skull and crossbones on the window, for all I know.'

'Firstly, that doesn't even make sense,' he said, folding his arms and crossing one ankle over the other. 'It would hardly have been in my uncle's interests to get you closed down, and that's what the cross-bones were about.' He had a point. 'And secondly, there *is* no ploy.' He rubbed his chin. 'I won't be going back to my uncle's, whatever happens,' he said. 'In fact, I'll probably never speak to him again.'

That took the wind out of my sails. 'Even so,' I said, tugging down the cuffs of my jacket in an effort to look more business-like, before catching my reflection in the window. I still had a dusting of arrow-root powder on my face. Combined with my unfeasibly short fringe, I looked like a medieval king. 'You were here under false pretences and I can't forgive that.' I cringed at my own pomposity, but Josh nodded, as if he'd expected nothing less.

'Fair enough.' He lifted a shoulder. 'I've been a dickhead.'

'Yes, you have.' Before my resolve slipped completely, I inched past him and switched on the radio in the office for some distracting background noise. Toby and Em must have been listening to it while they were working, and it was tuned to Radio South-West. Some rather dull show was in full flow, but with Josh's eyes boring a hole in my back I couldn't face changing stations. Instead, I shot through to the stockroom.

As if sensing our conversation was over, Josh refilled the pick and mix, then put the till back on the counter and plugged it in. 'I found some Brasso and polished the scales,' he said, carrying them through carefully as if they were a box of kittens.

'Thank you,' I said primly. I noticed he'd changed his T-shirt since earlier. It was marshmallow-pink with the slogan *I've Got Your Back* atop two hugging stick figures. Surely he couldn't have had it printed, especially? Perhaps when he'd had my certificate framed. There was a printing shop on Main Street.

To hide my confusion, I crammed a box of Drumsticks into a shelving cube. It was too big so I yanked it out again, and immediately thought of Beth.

'Hey, what's this?' Josh danced over and mimed a hand movement by my ear.

Alarmed, I ducked my head. 'What are you doing?' I said, then did a double take as he opened his palm to reveal a love-heart sweet.

Forgive me pleaded the message.

'How do you *do* that?' I plucked it from his hand and brought it to my nostrils, inhaling its sweetly powdered scent.

'It's a talent,' he said with contrived loftiness.

My mouth twitched. 'I'm not going to forgive you that easily,' I said, popping the sweet in my mouth.

'But you might?'

'Maybe.' His eyelashes were far too luxurious for a man, framing a hopeful gaze. 'You're bloody persuasive.'

'Only because your opinion matters to me.'

As we stood, not moving, the radio presenter's dulcet tones penetrated my brain. I recognised the voice I'd spoken to the evening before.

'Just a reminder folks,' Jeremy Taylor was saying, 'that if you're looking for some entertainment this Bank Holiday Monday, why not pay a visit to The Beachside Sweet Shop in Shipley and sample award-winning Marnie Appleton's handmade, low-sugar sweets.'

'Ooh, you're famous,' Josh said, widening his eyes.

'After Ms Appleton's rousing comments on the programme last night, I think you got the message that it'll take more than a bunch of frustrated bitches to get rid of a business that survived a world war and a potential takeover!'

I froze.

'This is Jeremy Taylor, and you're listening to *Business Matters.*'

Josh shook with laughter. 'Did you really say that?'

'Only in my head.' I dropped my face into my hands. 'It must have slipped out.'

'Hopefully Isabel Thingy wasn't listening,' he said, a smile in his voice. 'But great publicity for you.'

'I don't know about that,' I fretted. 'Swearing on-air isn't really the way forward.'

He tugged my hands from my face and I knew I should pull away – probably slap him – but somehow, instinctively, I knew Josh wasn't like his uncle. He'd made a mistake, but he wasn't a bad person.

I raised my head. 'Is your surname really Radley?'

'Yes,' he said firmly. 'You can ring my mum and check, if you like.'

A smile curled my lips. 'It's OK, I believe you.'

Sounds drifted in through the open door; a swirl of laughter from the beach and the faint splash of waves, overlaid with a rumble of traffic and a cry from a grumpy seagull.

'Thank you for not mentioning my fringe.'

'It's cute,' he said. Slipping an arm round my waist he kissed my temple. 'And thank you for not, you know, kicking me where it hurts. I know I deserve it.'

'You do,' I said, leaning against him. For some reason, Alex popped into my head at the exact moment I caught a movement in my peripheral vision. Shifting my eyes I looked up and saw him, poised outside the shop as if I'd conjured him up.

He was staring right at us, his face unreadable.

I jerked away from Josh.

'What's wrong?' Concern crowded his face as I headed for the door.

Alex had jogged across the road and was climbing into his father's grey Volvo.

'Wait!' I ran out, shielding my eyes from the glare of the sun as it sank below the horizon. 'Alex!'

He lowered the window.

Our eyes met, and chunks of memory crashed in; swimming in the sea in Wareham, almost hypothermic with cold; drinking hot chocolate with marshmallows in bed; Christmas at his parents', unwrapping presents round the tree, then tea at my grandparents', with Uncle Cliff, and my cousins; a rowdy game of charades that had us crying with laughter when Alex had to mime *The Spy Who Shagged Me* and Gramps thought it was something horse related and guessed *The Dirty Dozen.* On the aeroplane to Peru, our hands entwined.

The way his hair felt beneath my fingers.

I caught my breath. 'What did you want?'

'To talk.' His eyes looked bruised. 'I was worried when you took off yesterday, and you've stopped replying to my texts.'

Was that all? 'Well I'm fine, as you can see.'

'I can.' His jaw tensed. 'I should have known from the way you were looking at him in the newspaper.'

He obviously meant Josh.

'Don't come down here being judgy,' I said. 'You've moved on, why shouldn't I?'

He rubbed his face. 'It's funny, you make out you're desperate to leave this place, but now you're settling down? I guess it was just me you didn't want to settle down with.'

I shot round the car, wrenched open the door and dived into the passenger seat. 'In case you've forgotten, *you* were the one who left.'

'Because you *told* me to.' He glowered at me. 'You were adamant, as I remember.'

'You *knew* I couldn't come, because of Celia. I didn't want you to miss your big opportunity.'

'Oh, Marnie.' He looked at me as though his eyes were hurting. 'I only applied for the job because I thought being out there for ten months would cure you of this idea that you don't want to be here.' He gestured angrily through the windscreen. 'That you'd realise how much you *love* this place.'

'What?' I stared at him. 'All I've *ever* wanted to do is to leave, like my mum did.'

'Really?' He pulled his head back, as if trying to get a better look at me. 'Even in Peru, you couldn't wait to come home.'

'That's rubbish.' I tried to hold his gaze. 'I had to come back for Gramps.'

'Marnie, I know.' He hesitated. 'But before then,' he said. 'Remember how homesick you were? You wanted me to read to you on our second night because you couldn't get to sleep. Patricia Cornwell, remember.'

I'd forgotten that. How soothing the sound of his voice was, even though the story was about a homicidal maniac with a tattoo fetish.

'And you were desperate to find an internet connection, so you could email Beth and find out how everyone was doing.'

'I missed them,' I said. It sounded childish.

'Oh, Marnie.' The way he said it – half-sigh, half groan. 'Our trip was amazing, I loved it, but I could tell you wanted to be home even before your granddad got sick.'

'You're wrong,' was all I could say.

'There's nothing wrong with wanting to be here.' His eyes briefly scanned the view. 'I thought maybe you'd got it all out of your system when you took over running the shop. That even though you were sad about your granddad, you'd turned a corner.' His face clouded. 'But then your mum cleared off again, and suddenly you wanted to leave.'

I was finding it hard to breathe. 'I thought you wanted to go travelling too.'

'Honestly?' His gaze was open. 'I didn't care where I was as long as it was with you.' It was true, he'd told me that before, but I'd thought it was the sort of thing people in love said, and didn't necessarily mean.

'I suggested you join me in New York, once your gran was better, and you *still* kept making excuses.'

'I couldn't have left her,' I said angrily. 'Not after everything she's done for me.'

He sighed. 'Anyway, I suppose that's when I knew.'

'Knew?'

'That you'd never leave Shipley.'

A panicky feeling was building. 'Actually, you're wrong,' I burst out. 'I'm going to Thailand at the end of July.'

Shock flared briefly. 'With him?'

He meant Josh. 'Maybe.'

He looked at me a moment longer. 'Then I guess I was wrong,' he said flatly. 'What about the sweet shop?'

'I'll get a manager in.' Saying it out loud made me feel sick.

Alex nodded. 'It looks good in there,' he said quietly, and I wondered how long he'd been outside before I spotted him.

'I thought it needed freshening up.'

We fell into a troubled silence.

This is Alex, I thought. We'd never had troubled silences. We barely used to argue.

Jerking forward, he turned the key in the ignition and a burst of Bon Jovi exploded from the radio.

'Dad's,' he said, switching it off.

'Still likes his soft rock.'

For a second, his face worked. He seemed on the verge of saying something, but appeared to change his mind.

'What?'

'That woman on *Morning, Sunshine!*?' He shook his head. 'Don't take any notice of her.'

I managed a half-laugh. 'I bet she's planning to sabotage my tasting day.'

'You sound like you care.'

I flicked him a look. 'It's my grandfather's legacy she's messing with.' It was almost a growl.

'And yours.'

For a second I glowed, then remembered it wouldn't be for much longer. 'When are you leaving?'

'Tuesday.' His gaze was unreadable. 'I only ever wanted you to be happy, you know.'

Tears swelled in my throat. 'I know.'

'I hope you have a good life, Marnie.'

'You too.' It was barely a whisper. I fumbled with the door and scrambled out before I broke down. 'Bye,' I managed.

As the car moved off, I realised I hadn't congratulated him on his engagement, and that neither of us had mentioned Bobbi-Jo.

Chapter 27

Phoebe called as I was trudging home.

'Maybe what he'd really wanted was to buy some chews,' she said, when I'd filled her in on everything. Well, not quite everything. I was still trying to make sense of the things Alex had said, wondering how he'd got me so wrong. 'It must have been a shock, seeing you with Josh, but he's got no right to be upset when he's engaged to someone else.'

'Exactly,' I said, with a hollow feeling inside.

'Anyway, I was thinking,' she went on, after a suitably respectful pause. 'What if I were to come and help you run the shop?'

'Sorry?'

'You know I was saying I wanted to move back to Shipley and . . .'

' . . . start weaving blankets,' I said. 'Go on.'

'Well you've said Josh can't stay, even though you obviously still fancy him, and Beth's gone, so you'll need a full-time assistant. Especially after tomorrow once people have tasted your sweets.'

'*You* haven't tasted them yet,' I said, but I could tell by the edge of excitement in her voice she'd given it some serious thought. 'Well, I will need a manager before I go away . . .'

'You're still going then?' She sounded surprised. 'Just when you've won that award, and are getting all this publicity?'

'I've booked a one-way ticket to Thailand.' The more I said it, the more unreal it was starting to feel. 'I thought it was as good a place as any to start travelling.'

'But Marnie, you've got something good there,' she said, her voice dipping into exasperation. 'You can't just walk away.'

'Well, maybe that's where you can come in.'

'I don't *want* to be a manager,' she said. 'I've had enough with El Mirador. I want to *relax* and let someone else take responsibility.'

'But if you took over, the shop would still be in the family.'

'That's emotional blackmail.'

'Of course it is,' I said. 'Will you think about it?'

'OK,' she said. 'I've thought about it, and the answer's no.'

'I hate you.'

'No you don't, you love me.'

'God knows why.'

She paused. 'A little birdie told me Auntie Laura's home.'

'She is,' I said. 'But she's in a funny mood.'

'She's been in a funny mood for thirty years.'

I replayed her words when I got home and peered in the fridge, at the colourful array of sweets under parchment, and stuffed three pieces of Turkish delight in my mouth. It really was delicious. I ate some chocolate truffles, and they were delicious too. Maybe all Mum had been missing was a vocation all these years, and once she found something to be passionate about – apart from Mario – she'd feel settled. Or maybe travelling was still her real passion, and she was feeling hemmed in by Mario.

She'd left a scribbled a note on the back of an envelope, saying she'd turned in early. *Sweets cooled and in the fridge, and your gran back in her bedroom. Xx*

Celia had turned in too, judging by the snores drifting down the stairs; as if she was nursing an asthmatic bear in her room.

As I let Chester out for a wee, exhaustion rolled over me. I gulped a glass of water at the sink and went upstairs, but the minute I lay down in bed and shut my eyes they pinged open, the day's events circling my brain.

I hadn't even thanked Josh for all his hard work. After I'd shot back into the shop, I'd just told him I had to go and herded him out.

He'd looked quietly disappointed, as though his hopes had been dashed, but hadn't said anything. It wouldn't have taken a genius to figure out my abrupt departure was ex-boyfriend related.

Giving up on sleep just after midnight, I skulked downstairs in my bathrobe. Curling on the sofa with Chester, I turned the television on low and watched a bare-breasted woman being chased through a forest by a serial-killer. I was too tired to work out why she hadn't called the police before leaving her isolated cottage, or even put a bra on.

As she conveniently tripped over a tree root and crashed into the undergrowth, I picked up my phone and scrolled through for Agnieszka's number. She normally worked on bank holidays, but I'd forgotten to check. She worked at The Anchor on Sunday night, and guessing she'd still be there I sent a text.

Ten seconds later she replied No problemo, boss, I be there.

Next, I checked to see if Alex might have texted, but of course he hadn't. Swatting away an image of him and Bobbi-Jo, grappling in his bed, I clicked on Isabel's blog, which she'd updated a few hours ago.

Below a photo of a kale and mango smoothie that looked like slurry, she'd written, *Big day tomorrow! Got my publisher friend coming to visit about turning my blog into a book, and am preparing lots of healthy recipes to feature!! A certain person, who runs a certain*

sweet shop, was mentioned on local radio last night, or so I'm reliably
informed – I don't have time to listen – and it's such a shame when
people take that attitude.

I inwardly cringed, recalling my slip-up. I honestly hadn't
meant to say it out loud, and supposed I couldn't blame her for
being annoyed.

I logged off, about to change the TV channel when I became
aware of a faint, metallic tapping at the front door.

Chester, roused from a limb-twitching dream, let out a fart.

'Thanks for that,' I said, getting off the sofa. On screen, the killer
raised a knife above his head, and I hesitated. Murderers didn't normally knock softly to be let in, and crime figures in Shipley were
reassuringly low.

Whoever was at the door sounded like they were trying not to
wake the whole house, but knew by the glow of the television that
someone was awake.

'Harry!' He'd been tapping with his phone, and his face, in the
porch light, was lit with exhilaration. 'She's here!' he said in a stage
whisper, breaking into a grin. 'Bunty's here!'

Stupidly, I glanced over his shoulder as if the baby was sauntering
up the path.

'Oh my GOD!' As his words sank in I dragged him over the
threshold and closed the door. 'How's Beth, how's the baby, how big
was she?' I blabbered in a ragged whisper. 'Bunty, I mean?' I hugged
myself into my bathrobe. 'I can't believe it!'

'Me neither!' We grinned at each other inanely, and in the half-
light of the hall I'd never seen him look happier; even when he'd
turned to watch Beth walk down the aisle, and he'd looked pretty
ecstatic then.

'She's shattered, the baby was eight pounds six ounces, and they're both amazing.'

'Do you want some coffee?'

'I'll have tea if you don't mind, I've drunk enough coffee to power the national grid.' He raked a hand through hair that looked pretty well raked through already.

'Eight pounds six ounces sounds massive.' I led the way into the kitchen and snapped the light on. Chester followed, tail wagging. 'Did she need stitches?'

'Apparently, she's really stretchy down there,' Harry said, without any trace of embarrassment. 'I thought you might want to see this.' He jabbed the screen of his phone before thrusting it under my nose.

I wasn't sure what was happening. A terrible sound emerged, like a whale being harpooned, and Chester's ears flattened.

'Sorry.' Wincing, Harry turned down the volume. 'Look!'

At first, I thought I was watching a YouTube clip of someone attending to a badly injured animal flailing, writhing and moaning on the ground.

'The epidural didn't work properly, and she took it badly,' said Harry, rubbing his eyebrow. 'She kept getting off the bed and crawling about.'

And that's when I realised I was watching my best friend give birth.

There she was, her face scrunched up in agony, the veins in her neck so prominent I feared they might fly out. 'Oh, Harry.'

'I know,' he said, equally choked. 'I felt so useless.'

The camera panned over her distended belly and zoomed in on a frizz of brown hair. For a second, I wondered why Beth was sporting a seventies-style bush, then realised it was the midwife's head. As she moved aside, urging, 'Push, Beth, push, you can do it, sweetheart, Beth screamed, 'I CAAAAAAAAAAAAAAN'T, I'VE HAD ENOOOOOOOOOOOOOOUGH, HOOVER IT OOOOOOOOOOUT, FOR CHRIST'S SAAAAAAAAAAAAKE!'

Harry and I exchanged a grimace and returned our eyes to the screen.

'GET HIM OUT!' she roared.

'She was talking about me then, but didn't mean it,' Harry said, though judging by the assassin's glint in Beth's eyes, it looked like she wanted him dead.

A minute later, after more blood-curdling screams and wobbly camera work, my breath stopped. A downy head appeared between Beth's legs, followed by a slippery rush, and suddenly the midwife was hoisting an actual baby into the air, purple, bloodied and beautiful.

'It's a girl, all fingers and toes intact,' she said, and there followed a lot of excited and relieved laughter around the bed – though Beth's soon bordered on hysteria.

Harry and I laughed snottily, heads touching as we stared at his phone as though it was the Holy Grail.

After a split-second's silence, the baby emitted some lamb-like mewls that stopped the second she was placed in Beth's waiting arms. Despite her sweat-soaked curls, tear-streaked cheeks, and badly ripped gown (I daren't ask how that happened) her expression melted into joy, prompting a flood of tears down my face.

'Hello, Bunty,' she murmured, then the camera panned to Harry's work boots and went blank.

'That was amazing,' I wept, wiping my nose on the sleeve of my bathrobe. 'You're really calling her Bunty?'

'We've got used to it, I suppose.' He dabbed beneath his eyes with his fingers. 'She's definitely a Bunty.'

'Thank you so much for letting me see that.'

'Beth wanted you to,' Harry said gruffly. 'So did I.'

'I really appreciate it.'

A peaceful silence stole over us. 'I'll go and see her tomorrow,' I said finally, turning to the kettle. I felt subtly different – as if I'd witnessed a miracle. Which, in a way, I had.

'Our folks have been there all evening, driving us mad,' he said, dropping into the armchair by the Aga as though his legs wouldn't support him any more. 'I think Beth's intending to leave first thing, and come to your sweet-tasting session.'

I whirled around. 'That's crazy,' I said. 'She doesn't have to do that.'

'Isn't that what friends are for?' He let out a giant yawn, and although I suspected his softening was due to elation and tiredness more than anything, I was grateful for the ceasefire.

His eyelids were drooping as I took a carton of milk from the fridge and ate another chocolate truffle. I was suddenly ravenous.

'What's going on?'

Swinging round again I saw Mum entering the kitchen, blinking in the brightness. 'Sorry,' I said, swallowing the chocolate whole. 'I didn't mean to disturb you.'

Chester lolloped up to her. 'Couldn't sleep?' she said, making a fuss of him. Make-up free, with her hair loose around her shoulders, and her coltish legs emerging from the hem of her silky kimono, she looked about twenty-two.

'Beth's had her baby,' I said, a smile stealing over my face. 'Harry recorded it and came to show me.'

'Harry?' She clearly hadn't noticed him slumped in the armchair. As her eyes found him, they widened. 'Harry,' she repeated, as though she'd never heard the name before. 'Harry Fairfax.'

All vestiges of sleep fled Harry's face as he got to his feet, stuffing his phone in his pocket. 'I'd better go,' he said to me.

I looked from him to Mum. Her chest was heaving, as though she'd been out jogging.

'You don't have to leave on my account,' she said, in a breathy voice that sounded on the verge of tears.

'I think I do.' Harry strode past us into the hall.

'What about your tea,' I said, idiotically. It was clear that drinking tea was the last thing on his mind. He was fumbling with the latch on the front door, swearing under his breath.

'Here, let me,' I said, rushing through and yanking it open. 'Thanks again, Harry.' But he couldn't even look me in the eye. 'Give Beth my love,' I called after him, shivering a little as the cool night air rippled my flesh into goosebumps.

Watching his van drive off, I noticed a light on in Isabel's cottage, and wondered what she was doing up. Maybe her conscience was keeping her awake.

'What was all that about?' I said, going back inside, forgetting to keep my voice down. The snoring upstairs had ceased, and there was a creak of floorboards overhead.

'What's all the racket?' Celia said, looming into view at the top of the stairs. 'I was dreaming about the dog whisperer.'

'It's nothing,' I called up. 'Go back to sleep, Gran.'

'Don't call me Gran.'

Mum was standing in exactly the same spot as I'd left her, staring at the wall.

'Why was he so upset?' I said, unsettled by her stillness. 'It's normally me he has an issue with.'

Her gaze shifted infinitesimally. 'He does?'

'Yes he does,' I said, trying to think whether I'd ever discussed it with her. But then, why would I? I'd barely liked to admit to myself that my best friend's husband didn't like me.

As she moved over to the table, like an old woman in the grip of arthritis, a thought burst into my head.

'Oh god.'

Her head jerked round. 'What?'

I registered Celia coming downstairs, but couldn't stop the words from bursting out.

'Did you ever try it on with Harry?'

It would explain a lot, and as the idea expanded I couldn't believe I hadn't considered it before. Her flirtatious introduction to Alex should have sent up a warning flare, and there'd been a boyfriend much younger than her, before she met Mario – a yoga teacher from Manchester, who had taught her how to wind her legs around her neck.

And it would explain some of Harry's barbed comments to me over the years.

'Tell me the truth, Mum.'

'Yes, Laura, tell her the truth,' said Celia.

I whipped round, almost cricking my neck. She looked like a Roman centurion, sitting on the stairs in her voluminous white nightie, holding her walking stick.

'Mum?' I looked back at her, the blood draining from my face.

Her hands were flat on the table, her head hanging between her shoulders. 'I didn't make a pass at Harry,' she said listlessly.

'Well . . . that's *great*.' Relief poured through me. The ramifications if she had didn't bear thinking about. 'Thank juniper for that!'

She lifted her eyes to mine, and they were liquid-filled pools of sadness. 'But I did have an affair with his father,' she said.

Chapter 28

What felt like a decade later I dragged my jaw shut.

'*You*? Had an affair with *Steven Fairfax*?' I wondered if I'd heard right. 'Harry's *dad*?'

Mum straightened. 'Yes. Harry's dad.'

'When?'

She shut her eyes as if to block me out. 'A long time ago, before you were born.'

I turned to look at Celia. 'You knew?'

'I knew,' she said, rising from the stair with a heavy sigh. 'I hoped it would pass.'

I rounded on Mum again. 'Why didn't you ever say anything?'

'It was years ago.' Her eyes flew open. 'And what was I supposed to say?'

I gave a disbelieving laugh. 'You said *affair*, so I'm assuming he was married?' A tightening of her jawline said it all. 'Great,' I said. 'Is that why Harry doesn't like me? Because he knew?'

Her fingers worried at her gold chain. 'Possibly.'

'But . . .' Questions pounded through my brain.

'I'll give you some privacy,' said Celia, rising. 'Tell her everything, Laura.'

When she reached the landing, I whipped round to face Mum again. She'd dropped onto a chair, elbows on the table as she cradled her head in her hands. 'I started saying something earlier, before your gran came in.'

'Yes?'

Her swathe of hair hid her face. 'That I wasn't so much travelling all that time, as running away,' she said tiredly. 'From *him*, I suppose.'

I dragged out a chair and sat opposite, feeling as if I was in a dream sequence. 'Was it . . .' I struggled for the right word. 'Consensual.'

Her head jerked up.

'The affair, I mean.'

'Of *course* it was.'

I was shocked by the pain in her eyes. 'You were in love with him.' It wasn't a question.

'Yes,' she said starkly, twisting her watch around her wrist. 'But he was married to Jacky, and Harry was only three. Steven didn't want to break up the family, so that was that.'

'So how come Harry knows?'

Her eyes darted uncomfortably away. 'I tried to forget Steven, I really did, but years later, when I was living here for a while, I bumped into him on the beach. He was with Harry, who must have been about eleven.' She hesitated.

'Go on.' I folded my arms, certain I wouldn't like what was coming.

'Harry went to get an ice-cream and Steven and I got talking.' She looked at the table, as though replaying the scene there. 'I ended up kissing him,' she said quietly. 'He pushed me away almost immediately, but Harry saw us.'

'For god's sake, Mum.' I tried to imagine how he must have felt. 'Couldn't you keep it in your pants?'

'That's disgusting, Marnie.' Her expression was pained. 'I still loved him, but he didn't feel the same about me. He really adores Jacky.' She sounded vaguely puzzled, and I could see it must have been hard for her to understand why he'd chosen Harry's plain, cosy mum over her.

'Is that why you left again, in case Harry told his mum what he'd seen?'

The air seemed to leave her body, as though now the truth was out she could relax a little. 'In a way, I'd have been pleased if he had,' she admitted. 'I wanted Jacky to throw Steven out because then he might have come to me.'

'Oh, Mum.'

'I know, I know,' she said, lifting her hands as if warding off my disapproval. 'But Harry's a good boy, and he cares deeply for his mother. He wouldn't have wanted to hurt her.'

What a horrible burden that must have been for him to carry.

'I don't know if Steven ever talked to him about it, or what he said if he did. We never spoke again.'

An even worse thought brought me to my feet.

'What is it?' Mum's face paled further.

'Is Steven Fairfax my father?'

As the words flew out my heart went into overdrive. If they'd had an affair, it made sense. It would explain why she went to India and came back heavily pregnant, and was vague about my father – why Steven had gone out of his way to be nice to me whenever he saw me over at Beth's house.

'Is Harry my *brother*?' My voice was a panicked squeak.

'Marnie, don't be silly.'

Mum's voice seemed miles away.

'Marnie?'

I couldn't breathe.

I flew to the back door and dragged it open, gulping in fresh air.

'Darling, are you OK?' As Mum placed a hand on my back I twisted away, almost falling over Chester pushing into the garden.

'Answer me.' My throat felt raw.

'Oh, Marnie.'

'MUM!'

Her face was creased in faint lines of bewilderment.

'You are silly,' she said, tentatively patting my arm. 'I was in love, I hadn't had a lobotomy, for goodness sake. And the dates don't add up, if you think about it.'

'So Steven's not my father?'

'No, Marnie, he isn't.' She sounded almost amused now. 'What an idea!'

I reeled into the kitchen and gripped the edge of the worktop. 'Are you sure?'

'Of *course* I am.' She clicked her tongue. 'Your father was Juan . . . somebody or other,' she flapped her hand, 'and I'm sorry I can't remember the details, I really am, apart from that he was *very* good-looking, but it definitely wasn't Steven.'

My lungs deflated. 'Thank *Christmas* for that.' I didn't want to be related to the Fairfaxes. The ramifications were too huge to even begin to contemplate. 'Oh god, I'm so relieved.'

'Me too,' said Celia, and I sprang round to see her emerging into the kitchen. 'I did wonder once or twice, but had no intention of opening *that* can of worms.' She padded over to squeeze my arm. 'The dates *do* just about add up,' she said to Mum, 'but I must admit, I couldn't see Marnie as a Fairfax.'

'You only had to *ask* me,' Mum said, a wrinkle between her eyebrows, as if it had all been a terrible fuss over nothing. 'We could have done DNA, or something.'

'Well I think it's probably played on Steven's mind over the years,' said Celia, her voice less stern than it might have been under the circumstances. 'He was always asking after Marnie, and about you. And he even asked me to train his dog a while ago.' She sniffed. 'He must have known that I knew about the affair, because I could hardly be civil to the man.'

'But he never asked outright whether he might be my father?'

'He probably daren't, not if it meant he might lose Jacky and the boys.'

'I think most people knew about the affair,' said another voice. We rotated to see Doris Day on the doorstep, wearing sheepskin Uggs, and a coat flung over her stripy pyjamas with a notebook peeking out of the pocket. 'It was one of those unspoken secrets among locals,' she said, stepping inside. 'Because no one wanted to see Jacky get hurt.' She threw Mum a glacial look.

'Come in, Doris, why don't you?' Celia didn't hold back on the sarcasm.

I had a dizzying urge to giggle. 'What are you *doing* here, Doris?'

'It's the middle of the night,' Mum observed, glancing at the window in mild surprise, as if she'd just noticed the inky, star-sprinkled sky.

'I was disturbed by noises from a neighbouring house,' Doris said, tipping me a wink, and I guessed she meant Isabel Sinclair's. 'Then I saw your lights were on, which was unusual in itself, so thought I'd investigate in case someone needed help, and discovered Chester in the garden.' She paused, as if building up to an Agatha-Christie-style denouement. 'And I couldn't help overhearing your conversation.'

'So you've kept it a secret all this time?' Celia asked, her nightie billowing as a breeze blew in. 'I appreciate your discretion, Doris.'

'Nobody else's business,' she said, with a bristle. 'I might not have approved of their behaviour,' another arctic glance at Mum, 'but family's family, and that little boy didn't deserve a broken home.'

'Steven was hardly innocent,' Celia pointed out, leaping to Mum's defence. 'He was the one who was married, albeit far too young, and Laura was an impressionable girl.'

Mum didn't look keen on this description. 'I knew what I was doing,' she said, as though that was a good thing. 'I was sure he'd leave Jacky for me, but he obviously regretted what happened between us. They even had another baby.' She gave a rueful half-shrug, but I remembered the look from earlier and knew he'd broken her heart. 'I just couldn't stay around here.'

We fell silent for a moment, lost in our own thoughts. I guessed Beth had no idea, or she'd have told me. Which meant Harry had kept it to himself all these years, making me the outlet for his resentment after he got together with her.

Poor Harry.

I longed for Alex, suddenly. I wanted to feel his arms around me, and for him to reassure me the way he had when my grandfather died.

'Well, I'd best be off,' announced Doris, as though she'd been round for dinner. 'I must say, it's nice to see you all under the same roof for once.'

We stared after her as she swept out, clumping across the garden in her Uggs, and there was new respect in Celia's eyes.

Chester came inside and clambered into the armchair, as if he'd had enough excitement for one night.

'When you used to come back, was it to see him or me?' I said to Mum, arms belted around my waist.

Her face crumpled. 'Marnie, you don't have to ask.' She came over and prised my arms away from my body. 'It was you, you, always you, my little bird.' She placed a palm to my burning cheek. 'But after a while I'd start thinking about him, and knew I couldn't stay.' She dashed a tear from her cheek. 'It was easier when they moved to Wareham, and then I met Mario and . . .' she paused. 'And I really think he's the one.' She gave a little wondering laugh, as if the truth had just hit her.

'Did Dad know?' she said to Celia. 'About Steven?'

Celia nodded. 'He never judged you, you know that,' she said. 'Not like I did.'

'Oh, Mum.'

'What do you think of Mario?' I asked Celia, sensing things were about to get more emotional. I'd never heard her express an opinion about him, guessing she'd assumed – as I had – that their relationship wouldn't last.

'He's what I'd call a real man,' she said, lifting her chin. 'Someone you can rely on.'

Pleasure spread over Mum's face. 'He is,' she murmured, as if re-alising it for the first time. 'How he puts up with me, I don't know.'

'Mind you, he's hairier than a Newfoundland. I half-expected him to moult when you brought him here.'

Unexpectedly, Mum spluttered with laughter and Celia and I joined in, and then we did the most un-Appleton-like thing we'd ever done in our lives.

We had a group hug.

Chapter 29

A bolt of sunshine bounced through the window and woke me at eight o'clock the following morning and, despite having barely slept, I felt recharged.

I rolled out of bed and crossed to the window. The sea glittered and danced under a faultless blue sky, and it was such unusual weather for a bank holiday I decided to hold my sweet-tasting session outside.

After washing and dressing, and arranging a hairband low on my forehead to disguise my lack of fringe, I marched outside and wrenched a trestle table from the back of the shed that my grandfather last used when he wallpapered the living room in 1979.

After dusting off the cobwebs I hauled it into the kitchen, where I was distracted for five minutes by a deluge of photos pinging onto my phone from Beth. All were of Bunty, and all identical as far as I could tell. She was lying in a little Perspex crib, wearing one of the onesies I'd bought for her, patterned with yellow rabbits.

Meet your god-daughter, crumble-face. Isn't she gorgeous? Can't wait for you to meet her xxx

I blinked back a rush of tears. She's got her mother's looks – half-alien, half bombshell ha ha. Seriously, she's beautiful. Hope you're OK. Can't wait to see you both xx

I've never been happier, though my pretty duckies are already leak-
ing like dodgy milk cartons. Might see you sooner than you think xx

'I've got some nice tablecloths you can put on that,' said Celia,
striding into the kitchen, seeming to grasp immediately what the trestle table was for. She seemed remarkably refreshed, considering the
night we'd had, and was fully dressed in a stiff-collared white blouse,
black corduroy culottes, and snow-white trainers. As she fished the
tablecloths out of a drawer, I found some card and a pen, and prepared to write out some sweet labels as Mum drifted in, as dewy as if
she'd showered beneath a waterfall.

'Shouldn't you be at the shop?' she said to me, filling the kettle.

'I open at ten on Sundays and bank holidays.'

Her eyes scanned Celia's outfit, but although her eyebrows con-
vulsed, she refrained from commenting. 'I'd like to help out, if you'll
let me.'

'Of course,' I said, amazed she was even out of bed. Mum had
never been an early riser. 'You did make most of the sweets.'

'I thought it would be nice to do something together,' she said,
pulling a band from the pocket of her white denim skirt, and twisting
her hair into a knot. 'I kind of wish sometimes I'd helped out more
when Dad was alive.'

Celia made a harrumphing noise but didn't retaliate. I had a feeling we'd turned a corner the night before, and none of us was willing
to break the fragile bond that had sprung up.

I guessed it wouldn't last. For a start, I'd need to talk to Harry at
some point, and I privately thought Mum should apologise to him
for what happened between her and his dad. And she definitely needed to let Steven Fairfax know that I wasn't his daughter.

Shoving these thoughts aside, as well as the ones of Alex that kept creeping in, I focused on writing out *peanut brittle* in my fanciest handwriting.

I felt oddly nervous as I loaded the trestle table into the back of Celia's car, now she'd decided she was ready to drive again. I wanted things to go well – particularly as Sandi Brent, and that awful reporter, Chris Weatherby, were bound to turn up in the hope things would go badly wrong.

And I had no doubt that Isabel Sinclair had plans.

'I've got my session with that dog today,' announced Celia as we kangarooed past Isabel's cottage in the car. She'd never been the best driver, even before she broke her leg.

'That's no way to talk about Isabel,' I said.

Mum gave a shout of laughter. She was sitting up front with Celia, while I flailed in the back, trying to stop the trays of sweets from sliding onto the floor.

'I'll drop you two off, but I'll be down later on.' Celia seemed to be semaphoring me a message with her brows in the rear-view mirror, but I couldn't decipher their meaning.

'Will you be bringing Paddy?' I said, with mock innocence.

'Paddy?' Mum's eyes bulged. 'Paddy-next-door?'

'We're friends,' said Celia, not rising to the bait. 'And he's working today.'

'Ooh, you and Paddy,' Mum said, nudging Celia's arm, which had the effect of making her swerve into the middle of the road.

'Christ, Mum, are you sure you're OK to drive?'

Celia responded by slamming her foot on the accelerator, while Mum squealed like a child and clutched the sides of her seat.

By the time Celia had jack-knifed the car round the back of the sweet shop my face was avocado-coloured, and we'd only been driving three minutes.

'Do you think she's safe with the old beast?' said Mum as the car roared off, belching fumes.

'Paddy's really nice and he's helped Gran a lot.'

Mum gave me a look that reminded me a lot of Celia. 'That car's an environmental hazard.'

'You know how independent she is,' I said, slipping my key into the back door. 'Anyway, the hospital has signed her off so I guess she's fine.'

'A feisty old stick, isn't she?' Mum said, as if she'd only just noticed. 'I honestly thought she'd go ballistic last night.'

'I suppose you couldn't have blamed her if she had.'

'Maybe I've not always been fair to her.'

Hallelujah, I thought as she followed me through to the shop.

'Oh wow, this looks amazing!' she said, twirling around to admire the new décor with shining eyes.

I puffed up with pride, seeing it through her eyes. 'Good, isn't it?'

She wafted behind the counter to study my certificate, and the photo of Gramps, and I left her to her thoughts while I brought the sweets in from the car.

Ten minutes later we were out on the pavement, wrestling the trestle table open. It couldn't have been simpler to operate, but somehow kept collapsing in the middle.

'I'm not sure this is a good idea,' Mum said, pink around the cheeks, but with a bit of judicious thumping the hinge finally slotted into place, and I shook the tablecloths over the glue-stained surface.

We were already attracting attention, and passing drivers tooted their horns. The little girl from the guesthouse next door was watching our progress from the dining room window, and gave me a little wave.

As the sun danced through the shop window, I found the long hook to pull down the awning, and after persuading Mum we needed to wear latex gloves, we decanted our sweets onto an eclectic assortment of plates and bowls, and a couple of tiered cake-stands purloined from Celia's cupboards.

We'd just finished when Agnieszka glided over, her hair in a sleek ballerina bun that showed off her sharp cheekbones.

'Looks superb,' she declared, kissing the tips of her fingers as she admired our efforts. 'May I?' She helped herself to a salted caramel cup and popped it in her mouth. 'Mmmmmm.' She rolled her eyes, and patted her concave stomach. 'Is very delicious.'

I introduced her to Mum, then she went inside to prepare for work.

'Ah, it looks beautiful!' she exclaimed, eyes skimming the new-look interior, and gave me a smiling thumbs-up through the window.

'Is she wearing any knickers under those jeans?' Mum squinted after her. 'I can practically see her ovaries.'

'Mum!'

I left her labelling the sweets with my handwritten cards, and went to put the float in the till – should anyone want any normal sweets – and fetch some chalk to write on the board I used for promotions.

Try my handmade, low-sugar sweets. Free today!

It wouldn't win the Man Booker Prize.

'What if no one's interested?' I said, looking up and down the street. There were quite a few people about; mostly local dog-walkers, looking longingly at the beach, or taking in the air along the pier.

'I suppose it's still early yet,' said Mum, though it was pushing eleven o'clock.

'I'll get the tongs,' I said, rushing back into the shop.

'No Josh?' said Agnieszka, in an overly casual way, as she slipped her gilet off.

'No Josh.' I was slightly surprised he hadn't put in an appearance. Perhaps he'd taken me at my word and decided to stay away – especially after seeing me sprint after Alex the day before.

I noticed Agnieszka was wearing a jewel-green top that looked new. She normally wore the same plain long-sleeved T-shirt, like a uniform . . .

'Aprons!' I said. 'We're all wearing them from now on.' That was a laugh, when I wouldn't even be here in a couple of months.

I ran to the stockroom to retrieve some fresh ones, having completely forgotten to wash the others. Mine was crumpled in the corner, and Josh's was hanging from a shelf. I couldn't help thinking, in spite of everything, I'd prefer to see it on him.

'What's this?' Mum held hers up, nose wrinkled, as though I'd offered her a wetsuit. 'Do I have to put it on?'

'It makes us look like a team,' I said, feeling my ears redden.

'Didn't your granddad order these, but you refused to wear one?'

How the hell had she remembered that? 'Well, now I want to,' I said, slipping it over my head and fastening it tightly. For a second, it felt like he was giving me a hug.

Mum did the same, with an obvious air of reluctance. 'Good old Dad,' she murmured, a smile curving her lips. 'He just wanted a peaceful life.'

'Nothing wrong with that,' I surprised myself by saying. 'He loved this place, and the shop, and had a lot to be proud of.'

'You're right, sweetheart.' Mum leaned forward and tonged a chunk of coconut ice into her mouth.

'Don't eat the stock,' I said, swiping at her hand.

'But it'th tho good.' She picked up another and squeezed it between my lips.

Several cups of tea later, the pavement in front of our table was jostling with people keen to try our sweets.

'Only one each,' I improvised, realising belatedly that I hadn't factored in running out by midday. There were more in the fridge, but once they were gone that was it.

'We should have charged fifty pence each,' Mum murmured at one point. 'Might have deterred the freeloaders.'

She looked in her element, at one point coyly refusing to reveal what made the marzipan crunch (pistachios). 'It's a family secret,' she said with a wink, when asked by a crop-haired woman with a vegan vibe.

'I think you'll find it's in the public interest to display the ingredients, especially when the goods are homemade,' the woman said sternly, before striding away without trying anything.

'Shit,' I muttered. I went back to the board and wrote **All ingredients organic, including eggs, flour and beetroot powder where used. Sugar alternatives are medjool dates, rice and maple syrup, and stevia.** It didn't sound very sexy, but then I wasn't penning the next *Fifty Shades*. Should I include almonds? Could people be allergic to almonds, or just peanuts? *Oh god, the peanut brittle.*

Let us know if you have a peanut allergy, I added. There was hardly any room left on the board.

'Talk about a buzzkill,' Mum said.

'Better than actually killing someone.'

'Ew beetroot,' said a little boy with a head of tight curls, from his pushchair. Surely he wasn't old enough to read? 'I don't want a horrid sweet, Mummy, I want a real one.'

'Who the hell's Stevia?' said someone else.

'I think I know his cousin.'

I rubbed out what I'd written with the hem of my apron. 'We'll just tell people when they ask,' I said to Mum. 'That way, we can make them sound more appealing.'

She nodded. 'Good idea.'

Some of the older regulars eyed my efforts with suspicion, as if they were deep-fried sheep's testicles.

'I've managed all these years without sugar alternatives, and I prefer my beetroot pickled and in a jar,' said the butcher, who closed his shop on a bank holiday, and was dressed for a day on the beach in sunhat, shades and sandals. 'I think I'll stick with my usual.'

At least people were buying from the shop, its fresh new appearance drawing favourable comments.

'About time you did away with that turgid brown,' said Mr Flannery, emerging with a bulging bag. He must have been dying of curiosity as he rarely left the newsagent's, and saw me as competition. 'I'll have some of that peanut brittle, it looks nicer than the stuff in there.'

A compliment indeed. I'd used my little hammer to smash it up earlier, and placed a generous sliver in his outstretched hand.

'I'll have some too,' said someone else, and suddenly there was a sea of waggling hands, and the peanut brittle had gone.

'I'll fetch the rest,' Mum said, and slipped into the shop.

The street was crowded now, and it seemed everyone wanted to try a handmade sweet.

Comments varied from 'Surprisingly nice, considering how horrible it looks' to 'Are you going to sell these regularly, they're yummy?' and 'Never thought sucking on a ginger ball would be the highlight of my day!'

And there was still no sign of Isabel.

'Mum, I could use my award money to refit the kitchen and make the sweets on the premises,' I said when she came back, getting carried away, in spite of a little voice in my head, reminding me I was going to Thailand soon.

'That's a brilliant idea.' She sounded just as enthused. 'They're a real hit, Marnie, I'm proud of you.'

'Aw, thanks, Mum.'

I was half-expecting to see Phoebe, but when I checked my phone, there was a message. There'd been an emergency at the restaurant, and she'd had to rush back. I smiled. She'd find it harder to escape than she imagined – if she even wanted to, deep down.

Every now and then I scanned the sea of faces, looking for Alex. His dad was probably firing up the barbecue under the gazebo, while Bobbi-Jo entertained them with tales of all the lives she'd saved during her nursing career.

And where was Josh? He'd seemed determined to win back my trust, and although I couldn't blame him for not showing up, I'd been certain he would.

'Only one,' I said, to a stout woman with reddening freckled shoulders, reaching for her third piece of Turkish delight. I was wondering whether to ask Mum to nip back to Celia's and make some more when I became aware of a commotion.

'I feel so sick,' said a woman, with more rolls of fat than the Michelin man. She was clutching her stomach, looking green around the gills, and staggered across to the gutter where she began to retch.

There was a sudden sense of danger in the air.

'How do we know this stuff's fresh?' The crop-haired vegan woman was back, pushing her way to the table. 'You could have poisoned these people.'

A terrible hush fell, apart from the sound of a child sobbing, and a flare of hip-hop from a passing car. People were drifting over from the beach to see what was happening, and an opportunistic seagull dive-bombed the sweets and took off with some marzipan crunch.

'Should I call for help?' I said, as the fat woman retched again.

'There's the St John's ambulance over there.' Mum pointed it out. 'They always turn up when it's busy in case someone drowns or gets sunstroke.'

'It's coming over,' said an onlooker.

'Shit,' Mum murmured. 'This isn't good.'

Vegan-woman leant on the table, bringing her cabbage-breath to my face. 'What have you got to say for yourself?'

Before I could reply, a News South-West van pulled up, and Sandi Brent stepped into the chaos, brandishing a microphone.

Chapter 30

'Looks like things aren't quite going according to plan.' Sandi's trauma-nurse expression didn't fool me for a second. She was clearly in her element. 'Would you care to tell viewers what's going on?'

'Isn't it obvious?' Mum stepped over to stand between Sandi and me. 'My daughter's sweets have been a great success.' She gestured at the almost empty table behind her. 'As you can see, nearly everything has been eaten.'

'And is currently being regurgitated,' Sandi said silkily, keeping her eyes averted. She looked poised and polished in a simple, beige silk dress and flat jewelled pumps. 'Kyle!' She turned to the cameraman, who'd been focusing on Mum's delicately flushed face, and he swung the camera to where the vomiting lady was slumped on the kerb, hands pressed to her stomach.

'Uuuurghhh!' she groaned, pushing her face between her legs. Her skirt rode up to reveal vast thighs and a glimpse of gusset.

Kyle swiftly lowered the camera.

'It's not appropriate to be interviewing me,' I said shakily. Although the woman had stopped being sick, I wanted to check she was OK. 'Excuse me.'

But before I could move, a high-pitched voice streamed out above the gathering. 'Was there peanuts in them sweets?'

I revolved to see a lanky teenager clutching his throat, lurching towards me like a drunk.

'Dear god, what now?' Mum muttered.

'What now, indeed?' Sandi echoed with thinly disguised glee, angling her microphone for maximum effect.

'The peanut brittle,' I croaked, unpeeling my T-shirt from my back where I'd started sweating. 'It's the peanut brittle.'

'But surely it was obvious what it was?' said Mum, exasperated. 'It's in the name: *peanut brittle.*'

'Exactly.' My eyes swept around, but no one would meet my gaze. All eyes were on the staggering boy, and several people were filming his swaying progress on their phones.

'Irresponsible attitudes get people killed.'

I should have known Chris Weatherby would be there, talking in bloody headlines.

'Someone get the paramedic,' I called, and word passed down the group like Chinese whispers.

Chris snapped a photo of me grabbing the boy as he stumbled into me.

'Do you have one of those pens?' I said urgently, lowering him to the ground. He was gasping, trying to pull air into his lungs. 'Oh god,' I whimpered. 'Somebody help.'

'I can do a tracheotomy,' announced Celia, appearing as though teleported. 'I'll need a straw and a biro.'

'No one uses pens any more,' someone said.

'Are you a nurse?' Vegan-woman asked Celia.

'No, but I've done one before, on a Maltese.' Misinterpreting the silence, she explained impatiently, 'It's a toy dog, like a feather duster with eyes.'

'Why would you perform a tracheotomy on a toy dog?' Vegan-woman looked understandably confused.

'Not that sort of toy,' scoffed Celia, rolling up her sleeves, but I was spared having to rush inside to hunt down either a straw or a biro as a paramedic appeared and dropped to her knees beside us.

She pulled out an epi-pen and efficiently jabbed the boy in the thigh.

'OW!' he howled, glaring as if she'd shot him with a bow and arrow. His colour faded from puce to vanilla and he scrambled to his feet, dusting his hands on his shorts.

Chris Weatherby sprang towards him. Freed from its pony-tail, his middle-parted hair draped untidily around his face. 'What do you have to say to Ms Appleton?' he asked, in a provocative manner, giving me a sideways look.

'Who?' Confusion crossed the boy's face.

'She made these so-called sweets.'

As Sandi Brent and Kyle closed in to record his answer, he puffed up with self-importance.

'Well, I fort it might be good to have more 'elfy sweets, but it shows they can be just as dangerous in the wrong hands.' As his thick brows beetled in my direction, everyone turned to stare.

I fanned my burning face with the hem of my apron.

'Sounds like he's been coached to say that,' muttered Mum. Half her hair had come loose, and there was a smear of chocolate on her cheek. I shoved my hairband up off my eyebrows, trying to look concerned but in control.

'Maybe,' I said. 'But look how everyone's lapping it up.'

'You should be thanking that paramedic for saving your life, you ungrateful sod,' shouted Celia. There was a swell of agreement, then everyone began clapping and the mood shifted slightly.

Not in my favour.

'I warned you earlier,' said Vegan-woman, who I was beginning to hate with a passion. 'You should have listened.'

'What was that?' Sandi Brent pounced. 'Are you saying Ms Appleton didn't make clear the ingredients in her sweets?'

'IT SAID PEANUT BRITTLE ON THE LABEL!' Mum yelled, and I jumped about a foot in the air. I'd never heard her raise her voice. 'People can read, can't they?' She suddenly looked like Angelina Jolie in *Changeling* and I heard the whirr of the camera zooming in. 'People do have to take *some* responsibility for their health and safety,' she went on, waving the little card as proof. 'My daughter is a responsible and caring member of this community.'

'Good girl,' approved Celia, rolling her sleeves down. 'About time she made a stand about something important.'

'Who *is* that?' Chris Weatherby asked no one in particular.

'My mum,' I said, proudly.

His eyes flicked from her to me, as if seeking a likeness, and finding none, looked suspicious.

The teenager was refusing to give his name. 'I'm supposed to be studying for exams and my mum thinks I'm in my room,' he said, looking shifty. 'I can't be on telly, but you can put me in the paper as long as I stay 'nonymous.'

'Well now that's a shame, as these dramatic events will make a great piece on this evening's news,' gushed Sandi Brent, frowning as a gust of wind pushed a strand of hair across her face. 'And you come across so well on camera,' she lied, peeling hair off her lipstick.

I could see the boy was torn.

'Nah, gotta go,' he said at last and strutted off, clearly revelling in the many back-claps and cries of 'Take care son' that followed his departure.

'I'm so glad you're OK,' I called, marvelling that minutes ago he'd been at death's door, and now seemed so thoroughly alive. Thank god for the St John's ambulance.

Aware Sandi was searching for a new victim to interview, I was tempted to slip away. I glanced through the shop window to where Agnieszka was still serving customers, as though there wasn't a real-life episode of *Casualty* unfolding outside, and behind my reflection saw a familiar SUV screech to a halt by the kerb.

Isabel dismounted in a hurry, and dragged a placard from the back seat, almost braining her husband who was driving.

'Go and fetch Fitzy from the babysitter and then come back,' she ordered, before careering round the back of the TV van to artfully tousle her hair with her fingers, and adjust her cream, off-the-shoulder dress, so it was mostly off.

'Oh, thank goodness you're still here,' she cried, sashaying through the still gossiping crowd, to where Sandi and Chris were attempting to talk to the vomiting woman being examined by the paramedic. 'I've been *so* busy with my publisher this morning, I almost didn't get here,' Isabel continued loudly.

'Rubbish,' spluttered Celia. 'There was no publisher, I was there.'

Isabel wagged her 'SUGAR IS POISON' placard, to which she'd added a photo of the shop, struck through with a crude red cross. 'I was determined to make the most of this opportunity to . . .'

' . . . promote yourself,' said Celia, frowning heavily.

' . . . express my dismay that sweet shops continue to thrive in this day and age,' Isabel went on, flashing her luminous eyes to full effect. The sun glanced off her exposed tanned shoulder, and turned her dress almost invisible.

'I can see her nipples,' Mum whispered.

'How did she even get out?' said Celia, at the same time as I said, 'She used to be a model.'

'But why is she doing this?' Mum enquired.

Isabel began handing out flyers again, stepping about delicately in strappy gold sandals that made the most of her gym-toned calves.

'There's more information on my blog,' she was saying, aiming her words at Chris Weatherby, who was photographing her at an angle, like Mario Testino. She did an automatic supermodel pose, shoulders jutting forward, before remembering where she was. 'I'm asking people to sign a petition to close down sweet shops everywhere.'

'What do you mean, how did she get out?' I whipped round to face Celia. 'What did you do?'

Isabel suddenly spotted us, lurking by the shop doorway, and hurried over with Chris's gaze fixed to her swaying backside.

'I know what you did,' she hissed, her eyes slitty. 'And it didn't work.'

'I've no idea what you're talking about.' Celia assumed an innocent expression that fooled no one.

'She knew Gerry wasn't home, and somehow trained Pollywollydoodle to guard the door so I couldn't get out.'

'Gran!'

'Mum!'

Under the weight of our glares, Gran straightened the collar of her blouse.

'Nonsense,' she said. 'And if the dog *was* guarding the door, at least you were in the kitchen.' She fixed Isabel with an icy stare. 'You didn't have the child there, and had access to food and water,' she said. 'You were hardly in mortal danger.'

'I had to climb out of the window, which is tiny,' Isabel blasted. 'Luckily, I'm very flexible, but I've a good mind to report you.'

'You should stop interfering in matters that don't concern you.'

'Health is a matter that concerns us all,' said Isabel in righteous tones, and there was a ripple of agreement from those eavesdropping closest to us.

'I *am* concerned about health,' I started to say, but she hadn't finished. 'I'm hoping to raise awareness with my book.'

'Say what?' Sandi Brent bounded over. 'Hey, you're the campaigner from *Morning, Sunshine!* Imogen . . .?'

'Isabel Sinclair,' said Isabel, turning on a sickly-sweet smile. 'And I'm pleased to see that even the *handmade* sweets didn't meet with the public's approval.'

How the hell did she know that, when she'd only just turned up? Probably the sick in the gutter.

Suddenly, it was all too much. All I wanted was to run inside, lock the shop and never come out. Or, failing that, run all the way back to Celia's and get into bed, or time-travel to Thailand. But escaping wasn't an option, and Sandi Brent wasn't done. Clearly hungry for more drama – or perhaps not wanting to be seen on screen with someone not only more attractive than her, but better at applying flicky eyeliner – she turned to face the goggling crowd.

'Does anyone have anything they'd like to say to support this campaign, especially in light of today's near miss with the supposedly healthier sweets?'

'Yes,' said a voice I recognised.

I stopped trying to edge inside the shop as Beth materialised, cradling a swaddled bundle. She radiated regal vibes in a sky-blue dress that swept the ground, and her curls were heaped up in a bun. Far from giving birth, she looked like she'd been on a retreat where she'd been taught how to meditate.

Harry was by her side, hands extended, as if worried Beth might drop the baby.

'Whatever's happened here today, we all love Marnie, and know that she's a good person,' she said in her warm, clear voice. 'And as long as we all eat our veggies and clean our teeth, I think it's OK to eat sweets now and then.' Her beatific smile made me wonder if there were some labour drugs still in her system. 'I've sampled Marnie's handmade sweets, and lived to tell the tale.'

'Copy that,' said Harry, eyes still pinned on his daughter. I doubted he'd notice if a spaceship landed, never mind that Mum was trying to hide behind me.

'You can always rely on Beth to cut through the bull-crap,' Celia said approvingly.

'Thank you,' I managed in a wobbly voice, stealing a glimpse of Bunty that took my breath away as Beth sailed past.

'I'll go and put the kettle on,' she said.

'None of that changes what nearly happened here,' Chris Weatherby butted in, just as I'd sensed a slight warming from the crowd. 'People were *ill*.'

'I liked the lady's sweets and *I* didn't vomit,' said an educated voice. 'I thought the Turkish delight was equal to, if not better, than that in Istanbul, and I should know because I've tried it.'

It was the young violin prodigy, looking super-smart in tailored trousers and an open-necked shirt.

His mum squeezed his shoulders. 'I wasn't sick either,' she said shyly. 'I loved the coconut ice.'

'Me too,' said someone else.

'And it wasn't the sweets that made me sick.' We turned to look at the vomiting woman who was on her feet now, looking bashful.

'I didn't want to tell anyone until I was past three months, but I'm actually pregnant!'

A cheer went up, and she clapped her hands to her doughy cheeks. 'It all seems so real now!'

'Still a near death with the peanut allergy,' intoned Chris, like the Grim Reaper.

'Look,' Celia interjected. 'He didn't read a clearly written label. Hardly my granddaughter's fault,' she said. 'All's well that ends well.'

'And I'm really very sorry,' I added.

Isabel had busied herself with the straps on her sandal, and Sandi appeared to be arguing loudly with Kyle.

'We're going to have to fucking well scrap everything we've filmed,' she said viciously, but no one was listening as their attention had been diverted.

Following the source of their interest I noticed a black Mercedes with tinted windows purring to a standstill.

'No one's taking a blind bit of notice of parking regulations,' Chris Weatherby muttered darkly. 'There's an article in there somewhere.'

As the side door slid open, I glimpsed a man in big sunglasses in the front passenger seat, next to a uniformed driver, and craned my neck along with everyone else for a closer look, but he ducked his head.

A tiny, crop-haired woman in jeans and a stripy shirt stepped onto the pavement and closed the door. 'Marnie Appleton?' she said, consulting a clipboard through black-rimmed glasses.

'Is she from social services?' asked Mum, sucking her finger. She'd trapped it, trying to pick up the trestle table.

'I doubt it.' Celia snorted. 'Not unless they've smartened up a bit.'

'Could be environmental health,' I said with a sinking feeling.

'Travelling in threes?'

'Who else could it be?' I stuck my hand up. 'I'm Marnie Appleton.'

'Where are the handmade sweets?'

'This way,' I said, leading the woman inside the shop with the air of someone about to face a firing squad.

'But the council wouldn't send their staff in fancy cars,' I heard Mum say.

Beth was in the kitchen, breast-feeding Bunty while Harry looked on, sipping a mug of coffee.

'They did a great job with the shop,' he said. He didn't look at me, but his voice wasn't unfriendly. 'Toby and Em.'

'They did,' I murmured, leaning past him to open the fridge.

'I'll take whatever you have left,' said the woman, scribbling something on her clipboard.

Beth glanced up. 'What's going on?'

'I'll tell you later,' I said, close to tears as it hit me the shop was probably about to be closed down.

'Is that everything?' The woman eyed the foil trays, and looked like she was attempting to frown.

'That's all that's left,' I said dully. 'Shall I put them in a carrier bag?'

'Please,' she said, looking at her clipboard again. 'And do you have any Acid Drops?'

'Sorry?'

'Acid Drops.'

'Er, I think so.'

'Excellent!' Her elfin face broke into a smile. 'I'll take the lot.'

Backing out of the kitchen, I exchanged puzzled looks with Beth.

'Agnieszka, could you give this lady all the Acid Drops we have, please?' I said. 'And a carrier bag.'

'Of course.' She smoothed her apron, as if drawing attention to how smart it looked, then shared the jar of sweets between two paper bags. 'That will be ten pounds thirty please.'

'Oh, we're not charging her,' I said quickly.

'I insist,' said the woman, handing over a fifty-pound note. 'Keep the change,' she added with a breezy smile.

'I don't understand,' I said. It was like a bribe, but in reverse. 'Please, just take them.'

'I'm afraid I can't do that.'

Agnieszka looked at the note with puzzled eyes, as if it was Monopoly money. I had to admit it had been a while since I'd seen a fifty-pound note, and wondered if this could possibly be another of Isabel's tricks.

'Lovely to meet you, Marnie.' The woman flashed another smile, and swept out to the waiting car.

I trotted after her, and rested my hand on the door before she could close it. 'Will you call me to let me know what happens next?'

Once again, she attempted to pull her eyebrows together, and I realised she must have had Botox. 'I don't think so,' she said politely.

'But surely I need to have something in writing?' I moved my hand as the door slid shut, but not before the man in the front seat removed his shades and turned to face me, and I caught a flash of familiar blue eyes.

Stepping back as it glided away, I tuned into the excited buzz around me.

'*That was definitely Donal Kerrigan in the front!*'
'*I thought I recognised him before, when the woman got out!*'
'*Oh my god, I love him so much!*'

'*Did you see him on* Morning, Sunshine!*? Didn't he mention the sweet shop?*'

OH. MY. GOD.

'Donal Kerrigan was in that car!' I turned to Mum, who jumped and looked at Celia.

'Donal who?' they said.

And I'd thought *I* was out of touch with modern culture.

Everything fell into place. The Acid Drops. Of course! He'd said on the show how much he loved them.

'It was only Donal bloody Kerrigan, buying my sweets!' I cried as Beth emerged, rushing over to sneak a better look at Bunty.

'Oh my days!' she squealed, uncharacteristically. 'I *love* that man!'

Word had got round, and the fizz of chatter and hormonal female laughter was deafening.

'*I voted for him as my weird crush in* heat *magazine.*'

'*My girlfriend thinks he's lush, can't see it myself.*'

'*Wish I'd asked for a bloody selfie.*'

'*Wish I'd got in the bloody limo, he wouldn't know what had hit him!*'

'I can't believe I missed seeing Donal Kerrigan.' Sandi wasn't even bothering to hide how hacked off she was. Even her shiny hair was drooping, and her eyeliner had smudged. 'Why the *fuck* didn't you tell me it was him?' She gave Kyle a withering stare. 'You know how much I'd love to work on *Morning Sunshine!* you complete and utter moron.'

'Fuck you,' said Kyle, striding to the TV van and bundling his camera equipment inside. 'You can make your own way back to the studio.'

'Kyle no, wait! I'm sorry, I'm sorry,' she said, scuttling after him. 'You know how much I love you.'

He let her clamber into the passenger seat before taking off, scattering a clutch of seagulls tearing apart a bin bag in the road.

'Donal Kerrigan's not all that,' said Isabel sulkily, holding her placard like a shield. 'He was actually quite rude to me.'

'Good for him,' I murmured.

Bunty started making a stuttering noise, like someone revving a
moped.

'I'd better change her nappy,' said Beth, before I'd had a chance to
get my mitts on her. 'Come and have a coffee and leave this lot to it,'
she said, going back inside.

About to follow, a voice rang out behind me.

'You know that lad who was allergic?' It was Biff, so red his spots
seemed to vanish altogether. 'She paid him to do it,' he blasted, pointing
an accusing finger at Isabel, as if compelled to get it off his chest. 'He's
a mate of mine and his mum's friends wiv her,' another wild arm movement in Isabel's direction, 'and she told my mate he should pretend to be
allergic to peanuts for a laugh so he did, and he probably feels shit now,
cos he's not a bad lad, plus he was jabbed in the leg with that epi-whatsit.'

A pin-drop silence had fallen.

People were exchanging wide-eyed looks of disbelief.

'Did you hear that?'

'Absolutely disgusting.'

'And they were blaming those lovely sweets.'

Biff looked like he wanted to defend himself further, but sensing
the mood change took off down the street like Usain Bolt.

Isabel was parchment-pale beneath her natural tan. She flashed
Chris a look of desperation and he immediately sprang to attention.

'So, about this blog of yours . . .' he began, but I stepped up and
touched his elbow.

'You heard what just happened,' I said, a cocktail of relief and
adrenaline coursing through me. 'You can write a nasty story about

me, and make stuff up, and give her so-called book a massive plug.'
Finally, I had everyone's attention. 'She's clearly offered you some sort
of bribe – an exclusive interview when she's famous, or an introduction to Jamie Oliver, or other promises based on her past career.' I
could tell by the way his ears reddened and by Isabel's fake-shocked
gasp I was on the right track. 'Or you can write the truth,' I said. 'That
I believe in my sweet shop, and no amount of dirty tricks is going to
change that.'

I turned to the crowd. 'And I hope all of you who filmed that boy's
performance earlier have filmed this too,' I said. 'You've no idea what
damage posting something like that on social media can do to someone's livelihood and reputation.'

There was some awkward shuffling, and embarrassed apologies,
then Gerry Sinclair rolled up in his SUV. Looking like a woman given
a reprieve from death row, Isabel flung her placard back in the car,
narrowly missing his head again.

He stuck his face out of the window. 'Sorry about my wife,' he said
to me, with a sympathetic furrow. 'This is what she does.' He sounded
resigned. 'She hasn't really found her feet since giving up modelling,
you know?'

'Not really,' I said coldly.

He heaved a great sigh. 'I was in London this morning and have
been offered a new job, so we'll be going in a few weeks,' he said.
'She'll soon be out of your hair and onto her next project.'

'You can't prove I did anything illegal,' cried Isabel, over the roof
of the car. 'And my book will be in Waterstones soon, you'll see. A
deal is definitely imminent.'

'She's not as connected as she believes,' said Gerry, disloyally, and
pulled his head back in.

I couldn't even manage a pithy riposte. As the car disappeared, and Chris Weatherby headed to the beach with a dejected air, I couldn't help wondering why Donal Kerrigan had come all the way to Shipley to try my sweets. It was hard to believe he'd acted on a throwaway comment.

Then, as the crowd dispersed, I saw Alex.

He was standing on the other side of the road, eating an ice-cream, the sun glancing off his soft, brown hair. And when he smiled, the slow, sexy smile that had melted my heart the day we met on the beach, I knew.

He'd used a connection of his own. For me.

The question was: why?

Chapter 31

'Because he still loves you, you muppet.' Beth rolled her eyes. 'It's obvious.'

'Then why did he walk away?' I said, snuggling Bunty's surprisingly solid body against my shoulder, having finally prised her from Beth.

We were back at Celia's, though Celia had nipped out to see Paddy.

'Because he thinks you're with Josh now?'

'But I'm not with Josh,' I said.

'No, but Alex doesn't know that.'

I'd locked up the shop after seeing Alex, worn out by the day's events, and sent Agnieszka home with the fifty-pound note as a bonus for all her hard work.

'I really thought Josh might come today.' She'd looked rather sad as she took off her apron. 'He missed all the excitements.'

'He'll probably see them on the news,' I said, wondering if I would ever see him again. 'Or, in the paper.'

I wouldn't put it past Chris Weatherby to try to make me look bad, regardless of the facts. Especially on a promise from Isabel.

'Shall I take her back now?' said Beth, holding out her arms.

But I liked the baby-weight, and couldn't stop sniffing her scalp. She had Beth's nose and chin, and a hint of her daddy's copper hair, and her rosebud mouth was making little sucking movements.

'I don't want to put her down either,' Beth said, as I reluctantly handed Bunty over. 'Neither do our parents. She's been passed round like a Christmas present.'

'Is that why you're here?' I said. 'You've had enough of them?'

She nodded and swallowed a yawn. 'Harry's going to make sure our place is ready for this weekend,' she said. 'We want to be on our own with her now.'

'Where is he?' I looked around, aware he hadn't been too keen on coming back with us.

'Your mum said she wanted a word with him.'

My heart bumped. 'Oh?'

'She's looking really well, Marnie.' Beth smiled. 'Is she still with Mario?'

'I honestly don't know.' I felt shifty, remembering Mum's revelation about Steven Fairfax. I'd never had secrets from Beth, but it wasn't mine to tell.

'Do you think it's about his dad and your mum?' she said, rocking back and forth as Bunty began to stir.

'You knew?' I stared.

'Harry came out with it all this morning,' she said, wrinkling her nose. 'But to be honest, I kind of guessed.'

'How?'

'It was the way Steven reacted once, when I happened to mention your mum was home, and Harry went all funny.'

'But you didn't say anything?'

She shrugged. 'I wasn't certain, but it seemed to fit. I know your mum remember, and it explained how Harry was with you, though it doesn't excuse him,' she added sternly. 'I'll be having words.'

'Don't,' I said. 'It's understandable, in a way.' I looked at her. 'He won't want his mum finding out.'

'She won't hear it from me,' Beth promised. 'I honestly don't think she's ever suspected a thing.'

'I think Steven thought I might be his daughter.'

'Do you know, I don't think that even occurred to Harry,' Beth said, brow crinkling. 'He was only being defensive of his mum.' She narrowed her eyes. 'You look nothing like a Fairfax.'

'No, but it explains why Steven always seemed protective of me.'

'I suppose he might have wondered, but not wanted to bring it out into the open.'

'Well, I'm glad he didn't.'

When Harry and Mum came in from the garden, Mum wasn't exactly smiling, but didn't look upset either. As she slipped upstairs, after squeezing my shoulder, Harry came over.

'I'm sorry for being such a twat.' His eyes welled with tears. 'I didn't want to make things awkward between you and Beth, with you being best mates. That's why I never said anything.'

'So you made things awkward by being a twat instead,' I joked, and a tear plopped off his chin.

'It's fine,' I said, leaping up and giving him a hug. Beth looked on, shiny-eyed. 'It's my mum and your dad who've been twats. Your dad especially.'

'Copy that.' He gave a watery grin.

'I'll put the kettle on,' I said, some of the tension easing from my back.

At six, Harry reluctantly departed to do some more work on the house, and although Mum and Beth and I sat in front of the local news, with a plate of stir-fry cooked by Mum, there was no mention of the sweet shop.

'It would have been a great story.' Beth bent to check Bunty in her Moses basket.

'Maybe Kyle forgot to switch on the camera,' I said. 'Still, no news is better than bad news.'

'But it wasn't all bad,' protested Mum. 'The sweets were a hit.'

'That Isabel woman shouldn't be allowed out.'

'Well, hopefully people will spread the word,' Beth said.

'About Isabel?'

'About your homemade sweets.' She smiled at me. 'Word of mouth is always the best endorsement.'

The following morning over breakfast, I had the best endorsement of all.

Donal Kerrigan – standing in for the weekday presenter – popped one of my ginger balls into his mouth, live on *Morning, Sunshine!*, and made an orgasmic face.

'These are absolutely da bomb,' he said, exaggerating his Irish accent for all he was worth. 'I'm telling ya, you should get yourself to The Beachside Sweet Shop in Shipley, like I did yesterday, and try these beauties.' He winked. 'Marnie Appleton, you've made a middle-aged man very happy.'

'See!' cried Mum, putting down her yoghurt to grab my hand. 'There'll be no shortage of customers now, and it means we can put your plan into action.'

'Plan?'

'To refit the kitchen at the shop and make the sweets on the premises,' she said, bright-eyed. 'We should strike while the iron's hot.'

'We?'

She adjusted the fringed scarf draped around her neck.

'I was thinking, Marnie, that if you're really going to Thailand, I could . . . well, I could take over running the shop.'

'You?'

Her eyebrows flew up. 'Is that so hard to imagine?'

Frankly it was impossible, but there was no denying her eagerness.

'What about Mario?' I said, giving up on my cereal.

'He'll be thrilled.' She got up and walked around. 'He's said for a while that I need something to fill my days, and to fulfil *me*,' she said. 'I couldn't see it at the time, but I think he's right.' She looked thoughtful. 'He'd be more than happy to move back here, and even buy a little place.'

'And Steven?'

Her big, grey eyes met mine. 'That's definitely over, Marnie.'

'Well, that's great,' I said, a familiar tightening in the pit of my stomach. It was the perfect solution. It meant I could bring my trip forward, yet something didn't feel right.

Maybe it was because Mum's past job experience would have embarrassed a work-shy trustafarian. She knew nothing about running a business.

'I phoned your Uncle Cliff after you went to bed last night,' she chattered on, resuming eating her yoghurt, 'and he was saying how Phoebe had mentioned moving back this way, and that she'd like to work at the shop.'

'I think she might have changed her mind,' I said, heart dropping another notch.

Mum waved her spoon. 'She could be my assistant.'

'That's . . .' *awful*, 'a good idea, but I'm not sure Pheebs will cope as an assistant, when she's used to being in charge.'

'We could give it a trial run and see how we get on.' Mum had a soft spot for her niece, though they'd rarely seen eye to eye. 'Maybe you could ask her.'

'OK,' I said, but it came out flat. 'Sounds like you've thought it all through.'

'I must admit, I hardly slept all night.' She finished her yoghurt and scooped her hair back over her shoulders. 'I'll ask Mum what she thinks, when she comes back,' she added.

'Back?'

'She and Chester stayed at Paddy's last night.'

'Brilliant.'

I'd wondered where Chester was, but had preferred not to think about his absence. Something to do with Celia's stick and Crocs being missing too.

I collected my bag and keys, and pulled a cardigan over my jeans and top. The air was cool, and the putty-coloured sky outside looked heavy with rain. I wondered bleakly if Alex and Bobbi-Jo were at the airport yet.

'We'll talk later,' I said to Mum.

'Ooh, I'll be down to help in the shop later on,' she said. 'I'm going to make some more sweets and bring them in, because people are bound to want them after that piece on *Morning, Sunshine!* We'll need to settle on a price, and perhaps think about where we can buy the ingredients in bulk.'

I left her rummaging through the dresser drawers for a notepad and pen, and left the house feeling oddly numb.

Across the bay, a stiff breeze had rippled the sea into white-topped peaks, while the beach was empty of the half-term visitors who'd swarmed there the day before.

There was no sign of life at Seaview Cottage, and I wondered if Isabel was lying low. I'd checked her blog the night before, but it hadn't been updated. Remembering Celia's assertion that there'd been no publisher meeting, I almost felt sorry for her.

She was her own worst enemy, I reflected. There'd been nothing wrong with her healthy eating ideals, if only she'd been sincere – and hadn't tried to take me down in the process.

This is what she does, Gerry had said. I felt more sorry for little Fitzgerald, estranged from his grandparents, and with a mummy who clearly missed her old celebrity lifestyle.

Thinking of her, and of Mum and Steven, and Harry, it struck me how dangerously easy it was for adults to get it wrong.

Thank god for Beth, I thought, who was shaping up to be the mother of the century – even if it meant she wouldn't get round to finishing her thesis for a while.

Deep in thought, I let out a yelp of alarm when Doris stepped through her garden gate, dressed head to toe in lilac. 'I've worked it all out,' she said, pulling her notepad from her jacket pocket.

'I can't stop.' I noted with trepidation the dense scribble of words I could see as she flipped the pages open. 'I've got to open the shop.'

'It won't take long,' she said, vibrating with importance.

Resistance was futile. 'Fine.' I braced my shoulders. 'What mysteries have you uncovered?'

She began speaking in a ponderous tone. 'Isabel Sinclair has form for this kind of behaviour.' She checked I was listening. 'It seems she led a smear campaign against a former friend a couple of years ago, when the woman revealed her plan to open a beauty parlour in Wandsworth. Isabel's campaign was centred around the idea that women ought to be natural, and that filling your body with parabens and the like was going against nature, and she was going to write a book that would lift the lid on the beauty industry.' Another sound idea, executed badly. 'Didn't pan out,' Doris confirmed. 'The friend took out a restraining order against her in the end.'

Blimey. Isabel did have form. And Doris *had* been busy.

'How did you find out?'

'I have my sources,' she said, out of the side of her mouth.

'Ellen Partridge, whose daughter runs the yoga class?'

Doris looked up and down the road and behind her lavender bush, as if checking for spies. 'Between you and me, Ellen does a bit of private investigating on the quiet. Errant husbands usually,' she said. 'Not that I really need her, but she's better on the internet than I am.'

'Right.' I was rather impressed. 'Go on.'

Doris licked her thumb and flicked over a page. 'Isabel Sinclair was seen spray-painting your shop window at zero six hundred hours on Sunday morning, by a resident of the adjoining guesthouse, and I have it on good authority that she—'

'Paid and persuaded a boy to act as if he'd been adversely affected by my sweets,' I finished.

Doris's mouth fell open. 'How did you know?'

'You should have been there yesterday,' I said with a smile. 'It all came out.'

'I was visiting Eric and Lance.' Doris snapped her notebook shut. 'They wanted to show me a scan of their baby.'

'That's lovely, Doris,' I said. 'Do you know what it is?'

'A little girl.' Her cheeks bloomed with colour. 'I'm afraid I won't be giving Beth any baby clothes after all.'

'Eric's baby clothes?'

'They're mostly pink,' she said. 'I was convinced he was going to be a girl.'

I tried and failed to compose a suitable reply.

'Will you go to the police?' she said. 'About, you-know-who?'

I thought of Fitzgerald again. 'Probably not,' I said. 'And anyway, they're . . . '

' . . . returning to London any time now,' she finished, clearly not wishing to be outdone on the investigative front. 'Gerry's got a new job, but it's a bit of a comedown from being a publishing CEO. He'll be managing a bookshop near Notting Hill.'

I smiled. 'Well, maybe Isabel will get that elusive book deal one day.'

'Is everything alright after the other night?'

I was touched by the genuine concern in Doris's face. 'I think it's been resolved,' I said. 'Thanks for not . . . you know.'

She touched my hand. 'I do like your mother, but it's a blessing you take after your grandfather,' she said. 'Now I really have to go. I've left some porridge on the stove.'

After letting myself into the shop and turning off the alarm, I stood for a moment and absorbed the peace and quiet. I wondered whether Josh would turn up. Then again, if Mum was determined to come and help out, I wouldn't be needing an assistant.

In the office, I shook off my cardigan and pulled out my phone to text Phoebe. Would you still fancy working at the sweet shop if Mum was in charge? X

It was odd to think of them carrying on without me.

The chimes above the door would wear on Phoebe's nerves, but she'd be great with the money side, and coming up with strategies.

She'd have a new website sorted out in no time. And the male customers would fall in love with Mum, because she was . . . well, she was Mum. And the locals would like that she was an Appleton. Though thinking about her past conduct that might not be a good thing.

I was absently polishing the scales with my apron, trying to empty my mind, when the chimes indicated a customer was entering the shop.

Josh entered, and seeing his face I almost screamed. One of his eyes was swollen shut, the skin around it shiny with purple bruising, while his bottom lip was crusty with dried blood.

'Oh my god, what happened to you?'

He smoothed his dishevelled hair as he approached the counter. 'Let's just say, I went to see my uncle on Sunday night.'

I darted round to him. 'It looks painful,' I said. I lifted a hand to his face but he flinched away.

'I wanted to take his stuff back and tell him I wasn't doing his dirty work any more.'

'And he did this?'

'He . . .' Josh hesitated. 'He said something nasty about you not being able to take a joke, just because he'd . . .' the rest of the sentence seemed to get stuck. He cleared his throat. 'Marnie, was my uncle . . . *inappropriate* with you?'

My silence must have said it all.

Josh pressed his knuckles to his forehead. 'The wanker,' he said. 'I should have guessed when you said you didn't want him here any more.' He sounded close to tears. 'Anyway, I hit him, and he went for me.'

Despite my shock, it wasn't that much of a stretch to imagine.

'Oh, Josh.'

'At least I got the first punch in.' He tried to smile and winced. 'Keep forgetting I've got a split lip.'

'I can't believe he did this to you.'

'Yeah well, when my aunt found out she went ballistic and told him to leave.'

'God, what a mess,' I said. 'Is this why you didn't show up yesterday?'

He nodded. 'I wanted to,' he said, looking at me with his good eye. 'But not like this.'

'Where were you?'

'Stayed in the campervan,' he said, and I noticed it parked outside. 'Kept a low profile, tried to sleep it off.'

'Oh, Josh,' I said again.

'I brought it on myself,' he said, with a self-deprecating shrug. 'If I hadn't been such a tosser, I wouldn't have agreed to his stupid plan in the first place.'

My eyes itched with tears. 'We all make mistakes,' I said. 'You didn't deserve this.'

'And I suppose I wouldn't have met you, otherwise,' he said softly. 'So, no regrets.'

'Oh, Josh.' I was starting to sound like a parrot. 'It sounds like you're saying goodbye.'

'I saw how you were when that bloke turned up the other night.' His eye looked misty. 'Your ex?'

My throat was too full to speak.

'It's obvious you're not over him,' he said. 'And I think maybe I need to get away for a bit.'

'You should do that whole cruise ship thing.' I could barely speak through a golf-ball-sized lump in my throat. It was on the tip of my tongue to tell him I was leaving too, but the words wouldn't make it out.

'Maybe,' he said. 'Or I could take my magic to *Britain's Got Talent.*'

'You'd probably win.' I looked at him, blinking madly. 'I really do like you, Josh.'

'I really like you too.' His voice was thick with emotion. 'And you're going to be fine here now you've made this place your own.'

I couldn't speak.

'You're probably thinking that I need to grow up, and you're right,' he went on. 'I've been arsing around on my skateboard too long.'

I'd actually been thinking how handsome he was, even with a black eye and a fat lip.

'You're man enough,' I said, reaching for his hand. 'And I'm not the only one who thinks so.'

'Oh?'

'If you're ever in this neck of the woods again, I'm sure Agnieszka's got a crush on you.'

He gave a little laugh. 'It's a bit soon to start pairing me off with someone else,' he said, and then I was crushed against his chest, shedding tears on his rumpled T-shirt knowing, deep in my heart, he wasn't the man I longed to spend my life with.

Chapter 32

'All good?' Mum drifted into the shop about two hours after I'd waved Josh off, but not before extracting a promise from him to keep in touch.

'Fine,' I said.

If she noticed my puffy eyes, she didn't comment. I'd closed the shop for ten minutes after Josh left to have a good cry in the toilet, and I still felt a bit wrung-out.

'Not busy?'

I shrugged. 'A few customers, but they mostly wanted to talk about yesterday, and to know where the homemade sweets were after hearing about them on *Morning, Sunshine!*'

'Well, that's good.' Mum came over and gripped my upper arms. 'Have you seen *The Shipley Examiner*?'

'It won't be out yet,' I said, limp as a rag doll between her hands.

'Oh Marnie, no one waits for the paper to come out these days.' She gave an astonished laugh, as though I hadn't heard her ask Beth the day before what 'an Instagram' was.

'I thought it was a new type of stripagram,' she'd hooted, when Beth explained. 'That they whipped their clothes off extra quickly, or something.'

She directed me into the office where the computer now resided, and pressed me down on the swivel chair. 'That reporter's posted an article on the news page,' she said, reaching for the computer keyboard. 'Look.'

'I'll do it,' I said, brushing her hand away. 'It's a bit temperamental.' I really wanted to close the pages I'd been scrolling through before she arrived.

Particularly the Heathrow one, where I'd been checking times of flights to New York, wondering which one Alex would be on, but also Isabel's blog.

Great news peeps, she'd written, as if it was still the nineties. *Darling hubby's been offered a job in London, so we'll be upping sticks and moving very soon. This means, sadly, my book is on hold – not because I've given up on my super healthy recipe ideas –* there was a photo of a cabbage and cucumber smoothie that looked like pondwater – *and I still think sweet shops are a scourge on our society,* but I'm going to be focusing more on interior design, after my publisher, I wondered if she really believed she had one, *pointed out my excellent eye for soft furnishings. I've always been super creative in that area. For instance, I upcycled this lampshade with a pink feather boa last year,* another photo, of what looked like a crushed flamingo, *so WATCH THIS SPACE!!*

At the end of the trickle of 'Good luck, babe' comments, her mother had written *Do you remember that rustic, stripped back, brick and wood look in your first house with Gerry? The walls were running with condensation and I got a splinter in my foot! Now WHEN are you going to pay us a visit? Grandparents have rights you know!*

Isabel had replied, possibly unaware it was visible for anyone who looked, *Had a horrid bank holiday, mummy, me and Fitzy will be coming tomorrow, while Gerry checks out the flat above the bookshop. We'll probably stay until we move in, I hate it round here.*

'What are you doing?' said Mum, craning her neck.

'Just finding *The Examiner* website.'

'There!' she said, as I clicked the link **A Day to Remember**.

'Oh, god.'

'Just read it.'

I skipped through the words through half-shut eyes.

Shipley sweet shop owner, Marnie Appleton (29) – ha! – **held a sweet-tasting session yesterday that went down a storm with locals and visitors, making the most of the unusually bright bank holiday sunshine. Low-sugar versions of favourites, Turkish delight and coconut ice, were an instant hit, while her peanut brittle and ginger balls were declared 'better than the real thing' with one tourist remarking, 'You wouldn't know they were low-sugar.'**

Even *Morning, Sunshine!*'s Donal Kerrigan wasn't immune, putting in a surprise appearance after being tempted by Ms Appleton's delights, 'oo-er' Mum smirked, over my shoulder, **after they were mentioned on his show.**

'But he doesn't say anything about Isabel.' I read it again. 'And there's a really nice photo of us.'

'It's lovely,' agreed Mum, shiny-eyed.

The sweet shop looked like something from a story book, with its twinkly windows and stripy awning, the gold lettering above catching the morning sunlight. Even the letter 'e' I'd sprayed in looked authentic.

We were standing behind the trestle table, Mum smiling as she tonged a Turkish delight cube into the violin prodigy's hand, while I watched a bald-headed man eat a chocolate truffle with a playful grin on my face. My hairband gave me a slightly bohemian air, while Mum looked as winsome as ever.

There was no vomiting woman, no placards, no angry faces, no Isabel, and no Sandi Brent with her glossy hair and jewelled pumps.

'He must have arrived early, before it all kicked off,' I said.

'And had an attack of conscience, after what you said.' Mum's hand curled around my shoulder. 'Isn't it exciting?'

'How come you saw the article?'

'Oh, I often looked on their website for news, when I was in Italy,' she said. 'I Skyped Mario on your laptop after you'd gone this morning and thought I'd take a peek, to see if there was anything horrible we weren't aware of.'

'You've spoken to Mario?'

Her cheeks turned pink. 'I wanted to tell him about this,' she said, sweeping her arm around. 'I feel so . . .' she gazed up, as though trying to find the right word. 'Energised!' Her lips parted in a smile. 'Like I've had a new lease of life.'

'I'm glad,' I said, truthfully. 'What did Mario say?'

'Basically, he's happy if I'm happy.' Her smile broadened. With her milky skin, and hair folded back in a chignon, there was something charmingly old-fashioned about her appearance. 'He's flying over at the weekend, and we might have a look at Seaview Cottage now the Sinclairs are moving out.'

'Oh. Right.' The thought of Mum living so close was strange, but wonderful. It had been so long since she'd stayed in one place, but with Mario at her side, and her issues with Steven Fairfax in the past, maybe it was time.

'What exactly did you say to Harry?'

'That I was sorry for what he'd seen.' She gave me a frank look. 'That it was the reason I went away, and that I didn't want to make trouble.'

'He was OK about it?'

'I think he was.' She thought for a second. 'He actually seemed relieved to let go of whatever he's been carrying around all this time.'

'I think it's having the baby,' I said.

'They have that effect.' Mum's voice was soft. 'New start, and all that.'

'Did you tell him I wasn't Steven's daughter?'

She nodded again. 'It hadn't even occurred to him,' she said, echoing what Beth had said. 'He seemed a bit shocked, but said he'd let his dad know just in case.'

'Blimey.'

'I know.'

We were silent for a moment.

'So. I should go ahead with the homemade sweets then?'

Mum's eyes took on a manic gleam. 'I've already made some and popped them in the fridge out the back,' she said, clasping her hands. 'I had to borrow Mum's car to get them here, and I'm sure I've dislocated my shoulder,' she added. 'We need to decide how we're going to display them. I thought we could take the pick and mix out and put them in those cases, so people can't breathe all over them . . .'

'Actually, I could add a display unit to the counter,' I said, though the thought had just occurred. 'Like they have in that little chocolate shop on Main Street, with nice lighting inside, and everything on silver trays . . .'

'Or we could put them in jars on the shelves over there.' She pointed to the wall, as if I hadn't spoken. 'And maybe have a selection on a plate on the counter, underneath a glass dome.'

'We don't have any glass domes.'

'We'll think of something.'

'I'm looking into other ideas.'

She shifted her eyebrows. 'I thought you were going away soon.'

'I am,' I said, switching the computer off. 'But there are things I want to do first.'

'Such as?'

'Well . . . gift-boxes, for special occasions,' I said, expanding on a germ of an idea that had taken root the night before, standing at my bedroom window, trying not to think about Alex. 'And I could do little party bags of low-sugar sweets for children's parties, instead of the usual sort that probably makes them hyperactive. And think how nice a box of handmade Turkish delight would be as a Christmas gift.'

'Good, good.'

'I don't think people will mind paying that bit more.'

Mum's eyes creased in thought. 'I can just imagine my chocolate truffles in a little gold box, with a matching ribbon, and we could even supply weddings! We need to get this stuff on the website, Marnie.' She refocused. 'You do still have your website?'

'Of course,' I said defensively, remembering I hadn't got round to updating it. 'Actually, I'm going to find someone to design a new one, and set up a Facebook page and a Twitter account.' Excitement unfurled, like an animal waking from hibernation. 'I noticed a table in the shed yesterday that would be perfect in the shop,' I went on. 'I thought I could use it for a weekly display with a theme, or do a "handmade sweet of the day" on one of Gran's tiered cake-stands . . .'

I paused as the door chimed, but before I could move, Mum rushed out with a cheery, 'Hello, how can I help you?'

I sidled into the kitchen, trying to ignore a churlish curl of resentment. The sweets had been my idea – albeit forced by Isabel's hate-campaign – but Mum was taking over.

I couldn't deny hers looked tasty as I took a tray of marzipan crunch from the fridge, but I suddenly felt possessive of the recipes and wanted to make them myself.

There might even be a book in it . . .

My phone buzzed, and I put down the tray to read a text from Phoebe.

> Are we talking about Auntie Laura running the sweet shop??? NO WAY, JOSÉ!! Sorry, but I couldn't work with your mum, hun. I'll think of something else xxx

I knew it. Phoebe and Mum together would be a disaster, even if Mum couldn't see it. Which meant there was no way I could swan off to Thailand and leave her running the shop on her own.

Thinking of Thailand brought Alex to mind. I glanced at my watch, wondering whether he was already back in America. I wanted to text him, and thank him for sending me Donal Kerrigan, but my attempts sounded either sarcastic (thanks for doing me a favour) or over-emotional (what you did for me yesterday meant the world.)

In the end, I messaged Beth.

> How's my soon to be god-daughter? X

> Screamed all night, we're wrecked. Loving every minute xx

A photo of a tired but happy Beth popped up, her glowing face pressed to her daughter's dimpled cheek. Bunty was eyeing the camera like an A-lister suspecting she'd been papped.

Her very first selfie.

'MARNIE!'

Mum's voice made me jump. She sounded panicky.

'Won't be a minute!' I said, pulling out another tray of raisin fudge, and looking around for a jar to put it in.

'Marnie!'

'I'm COMING!'

Grabbing my apron, I pulled it over my head and sprinted through.

'I can't work the till,' she wailed, frantically jabbing at the buttons. It was emitting a series of beeps, like a life-support machine.

I nudged her aside. 'Here, I'll do it.'

'And we've run out of bags, Marnie, where are the bags?'

'In the bottom drawer.' I pointed with my eyes.

She yanked it too hard. It flew out, scattering the contents.

'For the love of Moses,' she muttered, scooping everything back in before attempting to jam it back on its hinges. She stood on a bag she'd missed, leaving a footprint. 'Well, we can't use that.' She sounded close to tears.

'Pass me another.' I exchanged a tense smile with the customer, patiently waiting for her lemon bonbons. 'Hurry up, Mum.'

'Alright, alright.' She slapped one in my hand. 'Here.'

'Thanks.'

Her lips were tight. 'You've got your apron on inside out,' she said, two spots of colour on her cheekbones.

As the customer left, I put my apron on the right way. 'OK, Mum?'

'I'm fine, thank you very much.' Turning, she whipped a jar of chocolate limes off the shelf. It promptly slid through her fingers and smashed on the floor.

'Oh Jesus and Mary Berry!'

'For god's sake, Mum, what's going on?'

'It was an accident, OK?' Her voice shook. 'I'll get the dustpan and brush.'

She dived out, returned seconds later, jaw rigid with tension. 'Where's the dustpan and brush?'

'In the cupboard under the sink in the kitchen.'

'Well, that's just silly.'

As she cleared up the mess she'd made, I served several more customers, blushing as the congratulations kept coming.

'Bit hairy at one point, when the ambulance turned up,' said Ruby, who owned the flower stall in the square at the end of the parade, 'and when I popped in the newsagent's later on he was trying to foist his wholesale peanut brittle on a customer, telling them it was nicer and more brittle than yours.' She shook her stack of straw-blonde hair. 'I reckon he's jealous of you.'

'Who wouldn't be?' Mum said, from where she was crouched at my feet.

Ruby looked startled, as if I'd thrown my voice. 'Just thought you might like to know, the rest of us are rooting for you.'

'Thanks, Ruby.'

Mum hovered anxiously in the office doorway after that, and kept offering to make cups of tea.

'You're not going out are you?' she said, toying with a roll of Parma Violets as I headed out to do the banking.

'You'll be OK for ten minutes, won't you?'

'Of course, of course,' she said, smoothing stray strands of hair back into her chignon. 'Just . . . don't be too long.'

There was a queue snaking out of the door at the bank, and when I returned to the shop, Agnieszka was behind the counter, serving a tired-looking couple with triplet toddlers.

There was no sign of Mum.

Chapter 33

'What's going on?' I said as the couple left, trying to break up a fight between two of their toddlers.

'I came in for gilet I forgot yesterday, under counter,' she said, and she was indeed wearing it again. 'Your mother, she seem distressed.' Her eyebrows arched. 'She mix up order and give man cubes instead of drops, he not very happy and she cry very hard.'

Shit. 'Where is she?'

'Out back.' Agnieszka looked grave. 'You like me to stay, Marnie? I'm not work for pub any more, too many very late night, so am free.'

'Would you mind, Agnieszka?'

'Please, call me Aggie.'

'Oh.' I smiled. 'OK. Thanks, Agnies . . . Aggie. That would be great.'

Mum was outside, in Celia's car, slumped over the steering wheel as though she'd been shot. She jumped when I tugged the door open.

'What are you *doing*?' I said. 'I was only gone twenty minutes.'

'Oh, Marnie, I don't think I'm cut out to be a manager,' she said, her pale cheeks stained with tears. 'I'll just end up giving things away, and I *cannot* get on with that till.'

I tried not to laugh. 'You worked in a supermarket once, Mum.'

'But I was on the *deli*,' she protested. 'Derek wouldn't let me anywhere near the tills.'

'What would you have done if Aggie hadn't turned up?'

She shut her eyes. 'I was going to lock the door until you came back.'

Crouching down, I rested a hand on her knee. 'Maybe you need more time to get used to it.'

She dabbed at her face with her apron. 'Yesterday was *such* fun,' she said. 'But . . .'

' . . . working for a living's a different matter,' I finished. For some reason, I was smiling.

'Something like that.' She gave a watery laugh. 'But I don't want to let you down, yet again,' she said. 'Maybe I could stick to making the sweets, and you can find someone else to be a manager.'

'But *I* want to make them,' I said, not caring if it sounded childish. 'I enjoyed it a lot more than I thought I would.'

The shop was my grandfather's legacy, I realised. The handmade sweets could be mine.

'But your trip . . .'

'Ah yes, my trip.'

And just like that, I knew I'd never intended going all along. I was no traveller. I'd loved being in Peru with Alex, but he'd been right. I had missed home, and I was glad to get back. I'd rejected Shipley because Mum had, not realising then that she'd had her own reasons for wanting to leave.

Looking at her worried face, everything swung into focus.

I loved Shipley, and I loved my sweet shop.

I wasn't Mum. I was me, with several shades of my grandfather. Doris had been right about that.

I'd wasted years planning my escape, instead of running the shop the way it deserved, but it wasn't too late.

'How about I stay?' I said to Mum, and my voice was steady. 'If you really want to, you can be my assistant.' I rejected the idea as I said it, but wanted to give her a chance too.

'Oh, I don't know, darling.' She sniffled a little, and took hold of my hand. 'I don't think I'd be very good at taking orders.'

'What Mario said, about you needing something . . .?'

'He's talked about us opening a wine shop,' she said, perking up. 'It was going to be in Italy, but I kept stalling.' She took a shaky breath. 'I think it's because I wanted to come home.'

'Oh, Mum.'

'I know.' She looked at me sadly. 'I'm an arsehole.'

'Mum!'

A giggle escaped. Mum joined in and we were doubled up, holding our sides, when Agnieszka came out to see what was going on.

'You should offer her a full-time job.' Mum wiped her eyes again. 'She's a little diamond.'

We'd just finished dinner when the doorbell rang.

'I'll get it, you stay where you are,' Celia said to Paddy as he made to get up. 'I'm fully mobile, remember?'

He sat back down, seeming perfectly at home in her kitchen, and the sight of him there, eating her venison casserole while Muttley and Chester eyeballed each other from opposite ends of the room, wasn't as unsettling as I'd imagined.

'It can't be Mario, already,' Mum said, putting her fork down and crossing to the window to look out. 'I know he's dying to see me, but I only called a few hours ago.' Apparently he'd brought his flight forward, keen to discuss their future.

'It's for you,' said Celia, coming back in, her bright eyes resting on me. She looked quietly satisfied, as though something she'd long suspected had been confirmed. She sat beside Paddy, and Chester waddled over to rest his head on her lap. 'You might want to wipe that gravy off your chin.' She winked at me.

Puzzled, I dabbed at my face with my napkin before getting up.

Perhaps Isabel had come to apologise – or say goodbye. On my way home, I'd noticed the SUV had been stuffed with boxes and bin-bags and the life-size picture of her *Vogue* magazine cover.

'It's not Donal Kerrigan is it?' Mum joked, in quite a giddy mood now she knew Mario was on his way, and she didn't have to be a shop manager after all.

'If it is, send him through here when you've finished with him,' called Celia, and there was a comfortable rumble of laughter around the table.

I entered the hallway and saw a figure on the doormat, backlit by the evening sunshine.

'Who is it?' Mum called.

'It's Alex,' I squeaked. It was all I could do not to fling myself into his arms.

'Oh!' I heard Mum say from the kitchen table.

'Hi,' I said, my heart rate tripling.

'Hi yourself.' He glanced through the kitchen door and gave a wave.

When his eyes returned to mine, I knew he was remembering the last time he'd been under the same roof as Mum, after my grandfather's funeral, when she'd asked him if he was castrated.

'Sorry, I meant circumcised,' she'd slurred, and Mario had to explain that she'd taken two Valium for the grief and didn't know what she was saying.

'What are you doing here?'

'I wanted to talk to you.'

'Where's Bobbi-Jo?' I peered out through the front door, in case she was waiting in the car.

'On an aeroplane,' he said.

My legs turned to rubber. 'How come?'

He inclined his head. 'Shall we go for a walk?'

I nodded. 'Just popping out!' I called, grabbing my jacket and following him down the path, loving the sight of his battered old jeans and soft, grey sweater, and the way his hair curled on his neck. The loafers had gone. He was wearing his favourite desert boots, and I wondered what it meant.

We didn't speak as we made our way down the hill, past Doris's house at the bottom. She was polishing her ornaments and her eyes were out on stalks when she spotted Alex.

Wordlessly, we found the spot on the beach where, four years earlier, I'd sat to eat my lunch and watched him walk out of the sea.

When we were sitting on the sand, I scooped up a handful and let it run through my fingers, breathing in his familiar cologne as he shuffled closer to me; the one I'd bought him before he went away.

'I thought you were going back to New York.'

'There was no point.' The intensity in his eyes stopped my breath. 'Not when everything I want is here.'

Exhilaration flooded through me. 'But, you're engaged.'

His brow furrowed. 'What gave you that idea?'

'Er, the giant ring.'

His face cleared. 'That's not an engagement ring,' he said, a smile tilting his mouth. 'Well it is, but it belonged to her grandmother. She wears it when she goes out, that's all.'

'On her wedding finger?'

He shrugged. 'I think that's the only one it fits.'

'Well, that's a bit weird.' My heart started galloping. 'It gives totally the wrong impression.'

'Is *that* why you ran away?'

I studied my feet. 'Maybe.'

'Listen, Marnie.' My head whipped up. 'I tried to move on, because I thought that was what you wanted. Bobbi-Jo's lovely, but it was never going to work.'

My stomach did a cartwheel. 'Oh?'

'It's over between us.'

Joy rushed through me, then I thought of Bobbi-Jo and her little boy. 'Alex, I'm sorry.'

I lifted my head, blinking back tears.

The sky was deepening to orange and purple, the sun a sliver of brightness above the sea. A pair of seagulls wheeled by on the salty air.

'We hadn't been seeing each other that long.' He touched my arm. 'I think she knew I was still in love with you.' His voice was gentle. 'She'll be OK.'

I remembered the way she'd clung to Alex, and wondered. 'I hope so,' I said. *He still loves me.*

'I know you're seeing that other guy, but I wondered . . .'

'I'm not,' I said, brushing away the tears that had started to fall. 'We're friends, that's all, and he's . . . he's gone now.'

Alex's relief was so palpable, I suddenly wanted to laugh.

He shuffled even closer, until our arms were touching. 'So, what do you think?' He looked at me sideways, the last of the sun catching the amber flecks in his irises.

'I think you were right about a lot of things.' I dug my fingers into the sand. 'My mum, my stupid travel plans, all of it, really.' I glanced at him through my hair. 'I think I've been a bit of an idiot, and that I still love you, and that if you want to be my boyfriend again that would make me very happy.'

His eyes were wide with wonder, and I knew it was everything he'd hoped to hear.

'And this?' He dug his hand in his pocket and drew out the ring I'd returned to him a year ago. 'Do you think you might want to wear it again one day?'

Fireworks went off behind my ribcage. 'There's every chance I might,' I said, reaching out to wrap my hand around his. 'Although it might not be appropriate to wear it when I'm working.'

'Oh?' His face drew closer and I saw myself in his pupils. My fringe was already growing back.

'I wouldn't want it to end up in a piece of fudge, or some marzipan crunch,' I murmured, my eyelashes damp with happiness. 'I don't know if you've heard, but I make my own sweets these days.'

'Oh, I know,' he said, his smile slow and broad. 'I heard all about it on *Morning, Sunshine!*'

'You did?'

'Didn't you know?' His eyes danced into mine, and his lips drew closer. 'The Beachside Sweet Shop is famous, Marnie Appleton.'

A Letter from Karen

It's been a privilege to sit down and write about Shipley and its residents, and all the shenanigans there, and I hope you've enjoyed reading Marnie's story as much as I enjoyed telling it.

I grew up in a seaside town, so it wasn't a great stretch to write about one, and although I've never met anyone quite like Doris Day, I'm sure everybody has known a neighbour a little bit like her!

I've lived in a few big towns over the years, but I love the sense of community that comes from settling somewhere like Shipley, where people look out for each other, and wanted to reflect that in my story.

It can be hard to let go of characters once they're written as I've usually fallen in love with them all – even the not-so-nice ones – so I'm looking forward to bringing back a couple in my next book and can't wait to meet them again.

Writers like to know if they're getting it right, so if you enjoyed *The Beachside Sweet Shop* and feel like popping a review online, it would mean a lot. Just a line or two will do.

And if you liked it, you won't have to wait long for *The Beachside Flower Stall*, and I'm currently working on my third book in the series, which has a lovely, Christmassy theme. If you'd like to hear about them when they're released, you can sign up to my email list below.

If you'd like to contact me with thoughts and feedback I'd love to hear from you.

www.bookouture.com/karen-clarke/

www.writewritingwritten.blogspot.com

karen.clarke.5682

karenclarke123

Acknowledgments:

A lot of people are involved in making a book and I would like to thank Kirsty Greenwood for introducing me to the wonderful team at Bookouture who made it happen. Big thanks to Celine, Abi and Emma for making it fabulous, to Kim Nash for getting the word out, and to my fellow Bookouture authors for welcoming me in.

The online writing and blogging community has played a big part in my writing journey and I'm so grateful for their encouragement, in particular Cally Taylor for A Story a Fortnight, which gave me the kick-start I needed, Sherri Turner and Helen Walters for continuing support, and Amanda Brittany for her tireless feedback, and for becoming a good friend in real life.

A great big thank you to family and friends; my mum Anne, sister Julia, Alison, Debbie, Sue Blackburn, and the other Karen Clarke and her daughter Gemma among others, for reading my books and saying lovely things about them.

And last but never least, thank you to my children, Amy, Martin and Liam, for their unwavering support (and for the brilliant throw-away lines I pinched from Amy) and to my husband Tim for making everything possible – I love you.

Made in the USA
Middletown, DE
10 July 2020